THE VERY NEARLY HONORABLE
LEAGUE OF PIRATES

The Terror of the Southlands

CAROLINE CARLSON

THE VERY NEARLY HONORABLE LEAGUE OF PIRATES

The Terror of the Southlands

Illustrations by DAVE PHILLIPS

HARPER

An Imprint of HarperCollinsPublishers

The Very Nearly Honorable League of Pirates #2: The Terror of the Southlands
Text copyright © 2014 by Caroline Carlson
Illustrations copyright © 2014 by Dave Phillips
All rights reserved. Printed in the United States of America.
No part of this book may be used or reproduced in any manner whatsoever without
written permission except in the case of brief quotations embodied in critical articles
and reviews. For information address HarperCollins Children's Books, a division of
HarperCollins Publishers, 195 Broadway, New York, NY 10007.
www.harpercollinschildrens.com

Library of Congress Control Number: 2014937633
ISBN 978-0-06-219436-7 (trade bdg.) — ISBN 978-0-06-236178-3 (int.)

14 15 16 17 18 CG/RRDH 10 9 8 7 6 5 4 3 2 1
❖
First Edition

For Jane, Chris, and Jonathan,
who are all entirely honorable

RULES OF CONDUCT

A pirate must . . .

- Be twice as bold as he is daring,
and twice as daring as he is bold.
- Be handy with a cannon, and handier with a sword.
- Appreciate the finer things in life:
treasure, parrots, and grog.
- Mind his manners only when it suits him.
- Carry his magic piece at all times.
- Be honorable (or very nearly).
- Assist his mates in storms and battles.
- Enjoy a bit of plundering from time to time.
- Be careful with his hook.

A pirate must not . . .

- Mutiny against his captain.
- Attempt to sing if he cannot carry a tune.
- Displease his fellow scallywags.
- Forget to be fearsome.

And most of all . . .

- A pirate must command respect.

Pirate Hilary Westfield, Terror of the Southlands:

Greetings from the VNHLP! I hope this letter finds you with a fair wind in your sails and a pile of magic coins in your treasure chest. I write on behalf of our mutual employer, Captain Rupert Blacktooth, the president of this fine League and (I hope you will agree) the fiercest scallywag on the High Seas.

Captain Blacktooth desires to speak to you as soon as possible about a matter of great importance. You are therefore summoned to a private meeting on the captain's galleon, the Renegade. Do not attempt to seek out Captain Blacktooth: he will find you when he is ready for you. Instead, while you await the Renegade's arrival, please endeavor to polish your boots, sharpen the creases in your pirate hat, and prepare yourself for the profound honor of standing in our captain's presence.

You may not postpone or cancel this meeting, and you may not send another pirate in your place. You may, however, bring your gargoyle, provided he is on his best behavior.

Arr!

Horatio Gull
Private Secretary to the President

CHAPTER ONE

THE *RENEGADE* ARRIVED just after breakfast.

Hilary had been waiting for it, and she spotted it first. From where she stood on the deck of the *Pigeon*, the distant ship resembled nothing more than a small black smudge against the horizon, but when Hilary raised her spyglass to her eye, the smudge resolved itself into the billowing black sails and flaming torches of an impressive pirate galleon. "Isn't the *Renegade* grand?" she said, holding up the spyglass so the gargoyle could peer through it. "Doesn't it make your spine tingle?"

The gargoyle shrugged as well as he could without arms. "I don't know about that," he said, "but it does look a lot like a squashed spider." He drew back from the spy-glass and gave the galleon an approving nod. "Now, back to business. Which do you think sounds better: *courageous* gargoyle or *intrepid* gargoyle?"

Hilary sighed. She was becoming rather used to this sort of question, for a few months ago the gargoyle had decided to write an account of his thrilling adventures on the High Seas. After several ink-splattered attempts to hold a pen in his mouth, however, he had asked for Hilary's assistance, and now she was spending a perfectly good morning taking dictation instead of sailing off on a thrilling adventure of her own. To be fair, it had been quite a while since any sort of adventure had crossed Hilary's path, and the common-place tasks of life on a pirate ship—deck swabbing, sword polishing, and cannon dusting—were starting to make her feet fairly itch in their boots. But now Captain Blacktooth was coming to see her for a most important meeting, and wherever Blacktooth sailed, wasn't adventure sure to follow? Hilary looked out over the sea at the *Renegade* and willed it to hurry along.

The gargoyle nudged her with the end of his tail.

"Sorry!" said Hilary. With a good deal of effort, she turned her attention from the galleon to the parchment in front of her. "*Intrepid* has a nice ring to it, but you've called yourself intrepid five times on this page alone."

"That," said the gargoyle, "is because I am."

Hilary laughed and scribbled a few words on the

parchment. "What do you think Captain Blacktooth wants to discuss?" she said. "He hardly ever pays personal calls." In fact, she had met him only once before, when he had arrived on her doorstep a year earlier to thank her for finding the kingdom's long-lost trove of magical treasure. It had been a most piratical accomplishment indeed, but surely Blacktooth wasn't sailing halfway around Augusta just to congratulate her again. "Do you think he might be planning to promote me? Or to send me on an important mission for the League?"

"Maybe he'll give you a medal for your bravery on the High Seas," said the gargoyle. "And maybe I could share it."

Hour by hour, the *Renegade* drew closer. By eleven o'clock, Hilary could count its sails. By one o'clock, she could smell the smoke from its torches. And at half past three, it sailed into the harbor a few yards away from the spot where the *Pigeon* had dropped anchor. Hilary woke the gargoyle from his nap and hurried to rub an errant scuff from the toe of her boot. "Captain Blacktooth has arrived!" she called, hardly caring that most of her mates weren't close enough to hear. Jasper Fletcher, freelance pirate and captain of the *Pigeon*, was ashore in the village of Otterpool, distributing bits of magical treasure to the townspeople. His first mate, Charlie Dove, was out in the dinghy, rowing piles of magic from the ship's treasure storeroom to the Otterpool shore. And Jasper's wife, Eloise Greyson, was busy at the stern of the ship, where she ran Augusta's only floating bookshop.

It was a shame they wouldn't get a chance to climb aboard the most magnificent pirate galleon in the kingdom, but Hilary was determined to memorize the *Renegade*'s every detail and tell them all about it when she returned from her meeting.

A pirate in a tattered striped shirt lowered a small boat from the *Renegade*'s deck, and he rowed across the harbor until, with an unceremonious jolt, he crashed into the side of the *Pigeon*. "Ahoy!" he cried. "I'm here to pick up Pirate Hilary Westfield. She's to have a word with my captain, and he won't have any arguin'."

Miss Greyson poked her head out of the bookshop. "What in the world was that bump?" she said. "It nearly sent all the detective novels crashing down on me."

"Ahoy!" cried the pirate again. "Are you Pirate Hilary Westfield, ma'am? You're much grumpier than I expected."

Miss Greyson pursed her lips to prevent a scolding from flying out, and Hilary waved her arms in the pirate's direction. "I'm Pirate Westfield," she said. "Are you Captain Blacktooth's mate?"

The pirate gave her a golden-toothed grin. "That's right. The name's Twigget."

"Well, it's lovely to meet you, Mr. Twigget." Hilary tucked the gargoyle into her canvas bag, slung the bag over her shoulder, and hung a rope over the side of the ship. "And I certainly don't intend to argue with you. I know the captain is eager to see me, and I'm rather eager to see him as well."

Miss Greyson looked on with her arms crossed as Hilary lowered herself and the gargoyle into the rowboat. "Be home by suppertime, please," Miss Greyson said, "and remember to mind your manners."

"She used to be my governess," Hilary confided to Mr. Twigget, "and I'm afraid there's still a bit of governess left in her." She waved to Miss Greyson and promised to be home in time for supper—or, at the very least, in time for dessert.

Then Mr. Twigget tugged on the oars, and the rowboat squeaked and groaned its way across the harbor, bumping into the *Renegade* with a crash that nearly sent Hilary toppling overboard. When she had recovered her balance, Mr. Twigget led her up a wobbly rope ladder to the galleon's deck. "If you don't mind takin' your boots off," he said, "the captain likes to keep a tidy ship." He gestured to a large wooden crate, upon which the word *BOOTS* was written in red paint. "And we'll be needin' your sword as well." He pointed to the wooden crate that said *SWORDS.*

Hilary hesitated. She had polished her boots especially for this occasion, after all, and it was thoroughly unpiratical to give up one's sword to another scallywag. Still, this was Captain Blacktooth's ship, and it didn't seem wise to disobey his orders. "I'll get it back, won't I?" she asked as she slid the cutlass off her belt.

"Aye, of course—if you make it back alive." Mr. Twigget chuckled and slapped her on the back. "Just a little pirate humor, Miss Westfield."

"That's Pirate Westfield, thank you," said Hilary. She wasn't sure she cared much for Mr. Twigget's sort of humor, and she stood a little straighter to make up for the lack of boots. "Would you be kind enough to direct me to Captain Blacktooth's quarters?"

"Oh, you won't find the captain in his quarters, matey." Mr. Twigget looked up into the *Renegade*'s billowing sails and pointed. "He's in the crow's nest."

"And he won't come down to speak with me?"

Mr. Twigget shook his head. "He likes a good view, does Captain Blacktooth. You'd better hurry up and get climbin', for he's not too fond of waitin' around."

Hilary supposed there was no use in protesting; she wasn't eager to get into an argument with Mr. Twigget without her cutlass by her side. "Very well, then," she said, giving a brisk nod to Twigget. "If Captain Blacktooth prefers to stay in the crow's nest, that's where my gargoyle and I shall go."

The other pirates on the *Renegade*'s crew, who had been hauling grog barrels up from the galley and polishing the great brass cannons that stood at both port and starboard, stopped their chores and stared at Hilary as she crossed the deck. All of them were barefoot as well, but they had not been asked to relinquish their swords. "That's the pirate who's the Terror of the Southlands," someone in the crowd called to his mates. "I didn't reckon she'd be such a pipsqueak."

Hilary dug her fingernails into her palms but didn't say a word. A true pirate would never let such an ignorant scallywag bother her—though when the gargoyle stuck his head out of his bag and snarled at the *Renegade*'s crew, she didn't bother to scold him. "I would have bitten them, too," the gargoyle said, "if you'd let me get closer."

"That's very kind of you," said Hilary. She stared up into the ship's black sails and swallowed. "The crow's nest is certainly a long way up."

"Do we really have to go up there?" the gargoyle asked. "It seems like an awfully strange way for Blacktooth to give us a medal for our bravery."

"There's something rather strange about this whole meeting," Hilary agreed. But perhaps this was Blacktooth's idea of a test. Well, if that was the case, she had no intention of failing it. Charlie had taught her ages ago how to scramble to the crow's nest on the *Pigeon*, and when her father had been admiral of Augusta's Royal Navy, she'd swung from the ropes of his ships whenever he wasn't paying attention to her, which was often. "You'd better not look down," she said to the gargoyle as she pulled herself up into the rigging. "I know you don't like heights."

"It's not the heights I mind," the gargoyle replied from deep inside the bag. "It's the falling from them."

"In that case, you've got nothing to worry about. I'm going to show Blacktooth and his crew what I'm made of."

"If you splatter all over the deck, they'll see *exactly* what you're made of," said the gargoyle cheerfully. "And it won't be pretty."

Captain Blacktooth's crew had gathered below her by now, and they all stared up, tapping their peg legs impatiently and raising their eye patches to get a better view. Hilary clenched her teeth and climbed until the curious pirates were hardly more than small splotches beneath her feet. She climbed until she could see the *Pigeon* bobbing like a toy in the harbor below her, until the clouds were closer than they had any right to be. Why in the world did the *Renegade* have to be so absurdly tall? And why did her shoulders dare to ache so ferociously? When she reached the crow's nest at last, she hauled herself up and landed on the seat of her breeches, directly in front of a pair of polished black boots.

"Pirate Westfield," said Captain Blacktooth (for he was the owner of the boots). "My goodness. I was beginning to think you'd never arrive."

Hilary scrambled to her feet, set her bag down, and held out a sore hand for Blacktooth to shake. "I'm terribly sorry, sir. I thought most pirates preferred to be fashionably late."

"They do," said Captain Blacktooth, "but it's not a fashion I care for." He took her hand in a hearty grip, and Hilary did her best not to wince. It was peculiar, she thought, that the president of the Very Nearly Honorable League of Pirates didn't look the slightest bit fearsome— at least, not at first. He didn't have an eye patch or a peg leg or a hook, and the wrinkles at the corners of his eyes made Hilary suspect that every so often, when no one was watching, he allowed himself to smile. Still, he managed to seem more thoroughly piratical than all of his crew-mates combined. Perhaps it was because he was the only one allowed to wear boots.

"I see you've brought your gargoyle along." Captain Blacktooth raised an eyebrow at the gargoyle, who had hopped out of Hilary's bag. Then he rubbed his chin and leaned toward Hilary. "Are you sure it's wise to keep a gar-goyle as a pet? Don't you think a parrot would be more suitable?"

The gargoyle gasped in horror.

"He's not a pet, sir," Hilary said. "He's a friend of mine, and a pirate as well."

"That's right," said the gargoyle. "I've got a hat and everything."

"Ah. So you do." Captain Blacktooth pulled a pair of spectacles from his pocket and balanced them on his nose. "But Pirate Westfield and I have more pressing issues to discuss. Do you know why I've called you here?"

"For a medal?" the gargoyle said hopefully.

Captain Blacktooth frowned.

"I've been told that you want to discuss a matter of great importance, sir," said Hilary, "but I'm afraid I don't know what matter you mean."

"What I mean," said Captain Blacktooth, "is this." He reached inside the folds of his pirate coat and retrieved a thin slip of paper, which he passed to Hilary.

✣ Notice of Unpiratical Behavior ✣
This notice certifies that
Pirate Hilary Westfield
stands accused of violating the
Very Nearly Honorable League of Pirates
Rules of Conduct
and of behaving in a most unsuitable fashion.
This is your
[x] first warning [ ] second warning [ ] third warning

Hilary stared at the notice. She read it three times through, and then twice backward, but the words on the paper refused to change. She looked up at Captain Blacktooth to see if he was joking, but his stern expression told her quite clearly that he was not.

The gargoyle nudged her with his snout. "What does it say?" he asked. "Is it something good?"

Hilary folded the paper into a neat square and stuffed it

into the deepest pocket of her breeches. "No," she said, "it's not good at all. I've been accused of unpiratical behavior—though it must be a mistake, for I'm sure I haven't done a thing to deserve it."

"What you haven't done, I fear, is precisely the problem." Captain Blacktooth unfurled a long roll of parchment. "According to my records, you failed to attend this year's League holiday ball, you declined to purchase a ticket for our Buccaneers' Raffle, and you haven't participated in even one of our monthly grog tastings."

Hilary looked down at the parchment, which seemed to be a lengthy list of all the ways in which she had failed to be a good pirate. "I visited my mother over the holidays, sir. And as for the grog, Miss Greyson doesn't quite approve of it, except on special occasions."

"Miss Greyson?" Captain Blacktooth's expression became more serious. "She is the woman who used to be your governess, correct?"

"Well, yes, but she's a bookshop owner now, and—"

"This is grave—quite grave indeed—but it confirms our suspicions." Captain Blacktooth held up the parchment and pointed to an item near the top of the list.

"Consorts with governesses," Hilary read aloud. "Has no parrot."

"You can't be serious," said the gargoyle.

Captain Blacktooth put the roll of parchment aside and looked down at Hilary. "Truthfully," he said, "these small mistakes don't concern me much. Being a true pirate is not simply a matter of purchasing raffle tickets, and piracy often requires a certain disregard for good behavior. But tell me, Pirate Westfield: When was the last time you drew your sword against an enemy? Or stole a stash of loot from a fellow buccaneer?" He paused. "When was the last time you sailed off on a thrilling High Seas adventure?"

The crow's nest swayed as a wave pitched the *Renegade* forward, and Hilary fought to keep her balance. "I suppose it has been a while."

"It has indeed," said Captain Blacktooth. "I hope you can understand that all of this puts me in a rather difficult position. When you found the treasure the Enchantress of the Northlands had hidden away, the VNHLP was thoroughly impressed—and of course we are still grateful to you for bringing such vast quantities of magic back to the kingdom. It's made pilfering and pillaging a good deal easier for all of us." He lowered his voice. "Then, of course, there was the matter of your father. You know as well as I do that he would have locked up all the scallywags in the kingdom if you hadn't prevented him from getting his hands on that magic. Only the most cold-blooded of pirates could have sent her own father to the Dungeons."

Hilary hesitated. "Thank you," she said at last, for she supposed Captain Blacktooth had meant to compliment her. She rather wished, however, that he hadn't mentioned her father. Admiral Westfield had nearly seized the Enchantress's treasure for himself, but Hilary had stopped him, and he'd been trapped in a gloomy prison cell ever since. Hilary was sure her father would never forgive her for betraying him. Still, he was nothing more than a villain, and Hilary was the Terror of the Southlands now. She couldn't allow herself to feel the slightest bit sorry about the whole affair, for sorriness was a thoroughly unpiratical emotion.

"When I admitted you to the League," Captain Blacktooth continued, "I put my own reputation on the line. More than a few scourges and scallywags felt that League membership shouldn't be open to girls—and certainly not to High Society schoolgirls," he added apologetically.

"But I'm not a schoolgirl!" Hilary said. "I'm a pirate!"

"And that's precisely what I said to the League. I told them not to worry and that you'd soon prove yourself to be the most fearsome pirate on the High Seas, but I'm afraid that over the past few months, you haven't done much to impress your fellow scallywags. There have even been rumors that your recovery of the Enchantress's treasure was a fluke—or that you wouldn't have been able to manage it without Jasper Fletcher's help."

Hilary drew in her breath. "That's completely absurd."

"Absurd or not, if you don't do something to prove those rumors wrong, you'll make both of us the laughingstock of the High Seas." Captain Blacktooth peered at Hilary over the rims of his spectacles. "And I don't enjoy being a laughingstock. Do you?"

The wind whipped Hilary's braid into her face, and she pushed it aside. She was having a perfectly pleasant time sailing around the kingdom and helping Jasper distribute treasure, but perhaps it wasn't quite the swashbuckling voyage she'd dreamed of during all those years of endless lessons and tedious parties at Westfield House. She'd longed to swap her utterly proper, utterly dull life for High Seas adventures like the ones her father had always boasted about. If you didn't count helping Jasper retrieve his pirate hat from the harbor, however—and Hilary didn't—this meeting with Captain Blacktooth was the closest she'd come to adventure in months. If adventure refused to find her, why shouldn't she set off to find it instead? She couldn't let Blacktooth and his mates believe that she was a poor excuse for a pirate—and she certainly couldn't risk allowing such a rumor to make its way to her father's ears. "No," said Hilary, "I don't believe I'd care to be a laughingstock either."

"I hoped as much." Captain Blacktooth nodded and adjusted his spectacles. "Still, I must take measures to ensure that you don't disappoint me, and that is why I am setting you a challenge. Instead of spending your days helping the softhearted Mr. Fletcher with his thoroughly unpiratical work, I want you to complete a bold and daring task—a task that will prove to me and my fellow scally-wags that you deserve to be a member of this League. A task," said Captain Blacktooth, "that only a true pirate could perform."

The gargoyle's ears perked up. "Do you mean an adventure?" he asked.

"Of course I mean an adventure!" Captain Blacktooth bellowed with such force that the gargoyle's ears quivered. "It's difficult to be bold and daring when one is sitting at home on one's pirate ship, darning one's socks. Far better to embark on a journey to the far north to slay the sea monster that's been terrorizing the city of Summerstead for months! Or," he said, "if such a voyage doesn't tempt you, Pirate Westfield, I hear there's a pirate king in the southern kingdoms who claims he can defeat any swash-buckler on the High Seas in a sword fight. Perhaps you shall be the one to prove him wrong."

Hilary had never even seen a sea monster, let alone slain one, and her sword-fighting skills were not entirely up to VNHLP standards, but she had no intention of shar-ing either of these facts with Captain Blacktooth. If he wanted her to perform one of these tasks, she would sim-ply have to find a way to do it. "Of course I can slay a sea monster," she said, "or defeat a pirate in a duel. It shouldn't be any trouble at all."

"I'm glad to hear that." Captain Blacktooth placed a hand on Hilary's shoulder. "But I must warn you that if you fail to impress me, your membership card will be burned and your cutlass sacrificed. No pirate loyal to the League will be permitted to associate with you, and I will be required to send you off the *Renegade*'s plank as though you were nothing more than a common sea scamp. Many scallywags survive the plunge"—Captain Blacktooth lowered his voice—"but many do not. Do you understand?"

"Perfectly," said Hilary. She was fearsome enough to endure a walk off the plank—or at least she hoped she was—but after all the work she had done to earn a place in the League, being dismissed from its ranks would be too humiliating to bear. "You have nothing to worry about, sir. I'll be bolder and more daring than any other pirate on the High Seas."

"That's right, Captain Blacktooth," the gargoyle said. "Hilary is the finest pirate in the kingdom, and I am *definitely* the finest gargoyle. Prepare to be impressed!"

"I shall do exactly that," said Captain Blacktooth. "For now, however, I must say good-bye to you both, for I've made arrangements to visit my niece." He took Hilary's hand and gave it another hearty shake. "Hurry home, Pirate Westfield, decide upon your task, and for heaven's sake, do your best to be bold and daring."

Hilary tucked the gargoyle away, said her farewells to Captain Blacktooth, and clambered down from the crow's nest as quickly as she could manage. When the Jolly Roger that flew above them looked as small as Hilary's thumbnail, the gargoyle peered over the edge of her bag. "That didn't go *too* badly," he said, though he didn't sound entirely certain. "At least Blacktooth didn't make us walk the plank."

"And he never will, if I have a thing to say about it." Hilary swung herself down from the ropes and landed hard on the deck. "Don't worry, gargoyle; the next time we see Captain Blacktooth, he'll be awarding us our medal at last." She gave her most fearsome look to the pirates who had crowded around her, sending them scurrying back to their posts. Good, she thought; perhaps that would prevent them from spreading any more absurd rumors about her behavior.

Twigget was waiting for Hilary near the crate marked *BOOTS*, filing his fingernails with the side of his knife, and she marched up to him in what she hoped was a thoroughly piratical fashion. "Mr. Twigget," she said, "you'd better fetch my things at once. I'm off to do something bold and daring, and I simply can't begin until I have my cutlass."

an extract *From*

The Gargoyle: History of a Hero
BY THE GARGOYLE
AS TOLD TO H. WESTFIELD

You might be wondering, "How did the gargoyle rise from his position as a humble stone sculpture to become the bravest and best-loved hero in the kingdom?" Well, dear reader, I am more than happy to tell you.

In my early years, I was employed as the magical protector of Westfield House. But a life cemented above a doorway is no life for a gargoyle of spirit, so I resigned from my position and (with the help of my trusty assistant, Hilary) set off in search of fame and fortune. After taking an accidental trip to finishing school in my assistant's luggage, I introduced myself to the well-known pirate Jasper Fletcher, who agreed to take me on board his ship as a figurehead. (You may not know this, dear reader, but the figurehead is one of the most important sailors on a pirate ship, second only to the captain himself.) Jasper was also kind enough to employ my assistant when he realized how lonely she would be without me.

Soon enough, we were off on a thrilling voyage to find the greatest prize in the land. Our beloved kingdom of Augusta had mined all the magic ore from its hills, and hardly any magic was left—except, that is, for a large collection of treasure hidden away long ago by the Enchantress of the Northlands. Naturally, your intrepid hero volunteered to find this lost magic and return it to the people of Augusta.

But I was not the only one seeking treasure! You will never believe this, dear reader, but my trusty assistant's father, Admiral Westfield, wanted the magic for himself. He and his High Society friends had been stealing magic from the noble households of Augusta for months, and they planned to use the treasure to banish the queen and rule the kingdom in her place. I knew that if Admiral Westfield reached that treasure before I did, I would never be famous.

Using my sharp wit and my even sharper

teeth, I deciphered the Enchantress's treasure map, fought off an entire fleet of naval officers, won legions of adoring admirers, and guided my trusty assistant to the treasure's location. (My assistant says this is not precisely how she remembers the course of events, but this is not her memoir, is it?)

In any case, the treasure was nearly ours when disaster struck: Admiral Westfield had found us! He soon learned, however, that he was no match for a gargoyle. With some help from my assistant, I defeated the villain and sent him off to the Royal Dungeons. I received a fashionable pirate hat as a reward for my efforts, and Jasper generously gave my assistant the title of Terror of the Southlands. We can't all be the most heroic gargoyle in the kingdom, but my assistant seems pleased with her title nonetheless.

INTRUDER REPORTED NEAR ENCHANTRESS'S RESIDENCE

PEMBERTON, AUGUSTA—The queen's inspectors were called to Miss Pimm's Finishing School for Delicate Ladies last week to investigate a report of one or more suspicious persons trespassing on school grounds. Miss Eugenia Pimm, who divides her time between her leadership of the finishing school and her position as Enchantress, summoned the authorities late at night after hearing footsteps outside her window.

Inspector John Hastings states that no intruder was found anywhere near the school building. "Frankly," Mr. Hastings told the Gazette, "I don't believe there's a crime to investigate. If you ask me, it's nothing more than a handful of schoolgirls playing a prank on their headmistress."

Miss Pimm herself, however, was adamant that no pupil of hers would ever dream of prowling around the school grounds after dark. "If only I'd had my magic crochet hook nearer at hand," she said, "I would have apprehended the intruder myself. As it was, I could do no more than light a candle and run to the window before he slipped away."

In her role as Enchantress, Miss Pimm keeps new magic users in line and attempts to prevent the kingdom's rogues and villains from using magic for their own nefarious purposes. Therefore, she claims, it is quite natural for her to have enemies. "Half the kingdom is furious at me for scolding them when they use their magic improperly," she said, "and the other half of the kingdom is furious because they haven't yet received their magic pieces from Jasper Fletcher. The entire business gives me a splitting headache. My greatest desire is to find the next Enchantress and retire to my family home in the Northlands, but my search for a talented young lady of quality to take my place has been rather a disaster so far. I'm beginning to doubt whether anyone in the kingdom is up to the task—but you mustn't report all this in the Gazette. What are you scribbling, young man?"

At this point in our conversation with the Enchantress, the Gazette reporter was promptly kicked out.

CHAPTER TWO

BY THE TIME Hilary returned to the *Pigeon*, she was already late for supper. She slipped into the captain's cabin, took her seat at the end of the long wooden table, and cast a skeptical glance at the charred remnants of what had probably been a fish. Then she drew her cutlass and helped herself to two enormous slices of apple pie, one of which she set down on the bench so the gargoyle could reach it.

Around the table, the others were discussing the news of the day. Jasper was preparing to leave the next morning for a freelance pirates' convention a few days south of the kingdom, and he wondered whether anyone had seen his seventh-best hat feather. Miss Greyson had sold three cookbooks that afternoon to an elderly pirate who'd grown tired of hardtack. Fitzwilliam, Jasper's budgerigar, had learned to whistle several notes from a sea chantey, and Charlie had been chased down the streets of Otterpool by a rather aggressive enchanted harpsichord. (Flying instruments had become a frequent hazard in the past few days since the members of the Otterpool Royal Orchestra had received their new magic pieces.) "And of course," said Jasper, "our Terror must have some news to share with us." He turned to Hilary. "How was your meeting with Captain Blacktooth?"

Hilary took a large bite of pie to give herself a few moments to think. She wasn't particularly eager to admit that she'd been found unpiratical. If Jasper found out about it, he'd most likely insist on giving Captain Blacktooth a piece of his mind, and Hilary couldn't imagine anything more humiliating than that. Why, the crew of the *Renegade* would spread word around the League that the Terror of the Southlands wasn't even brave enough to fight her own battles! And there would be plenty of time to tell everyone the truth later, after she had slain a sea monster or defeated a pirate king. She swallowed the pie and set down her fork. "The meeting was perfectly fine."

The gargoyle stared up at her. "It was?"

"Yes," she said firmly, giving the gargoyle a look. "Blacktooth only stopped by to say how disappointed he was that I didn't attend the League holiday ball."

Charlie raised his eyebrows. "He sailed all the way to Otterpool for that?"

"That's right," said the gargoyle, nodding his head with vigor. "Definitely."

Charlie frowned at Hilary, the way he often did when she broke a rule during a swordplay lesson. Then he shrugged and turned back to his supper.

"The League holiday ball!" Jasper put his feet up on the table. "Are all pirates required to attend it now? That sort of nonsense is exactly why I left the VNHLP."

Miss Greyson smiled and swatted Jasper with her handkerchief. "I thought you were forced to leave when Blacktooth overheard you calling him— What was it? A sea cucumber?"

"The details," said Jasper, "are hardly important. But I'm glad to hear the meeting went well, Hilary." He smiled at her. "I can't say I care much for Blacktooth, but he's a valuable friend to have. When you're friendly with the League, you've got access to the best treasure maps, the best cannons, and the finest magic pieces this side of High Society. You've got a fleet of fellow scallywags who are obliged to help you out of a tight spot, and you don't have to sail nearly all the way to the southern kingdoms to find an island that's willing to host your gatherings." Jasper pushed his chair back and stood up. "At any rate, my advice to all of you is to stay on Blacktooth's good side—and to keep track of your seventh-best hat feather, for you never know when you may need it."

"I'll certainly try," said Hilary. She knew for a fact that her own hat feathers were stowed safely in her cabin, and as for Captain Blacktooth—well, with any luck at all, she'd be back in his good graces soon enough.

EARLY THE NEXT morning, Hilary stood watch while Jasper departed for his freelance pirates' convention in a rather pungent fishing boat he'd borrowed from a gentleman in the next village over. She waved good-bye and promised quite sincerely not to do anything that Jasper himself wouldn't do. Then, once the fishing boat had disappeared behind the waves, she stepped out of her boots and slipped down to the treasure storeroom, taking great care not to wake Charlie and Miss Greyson as she passed their cabins.

Although a good deal of the Enchantress's treasure had already made its way into the cupboards and pockets of the kingdom's citizens, the storeroom was still filled with piles of golden coins, crochet hooks, and other magical odds and ends that glinted in the morning light. Hilary plucked something that looked like a golden porridge bowl from the top of the nearest pile and scooped up a few handfuls of coins for good measure. Then she gathered them all in her pirate coat and clutched the bundle to her chest as she hurried back up to the deck. Miss Greyson would be awake soon, and she certainly wouldn't approve of Hilary's plan.

The gargoyle had been keeping a lookout for villains and scoundrels from his Nest, but he turned around and stared at Hilary as she unrolled her bundle on the deck. "What are you doing with all that magic?" he cried. "Just looking at it is enough to make my ears twitch!"

"There's no need to shout," Hilary whispered. "This is going to help me with Blacktooth's bold and daring task. I've got to slay a sea monster or defeat a pirate king before I get another one of those blasted warnings, so I thought I'd better get started."

The gargoyle wrinkled his snout. "You're going to whack the sea monster over the head with a magical porridge bowl?"

"Not exactly." Hilary sat back on her heels. Truthfully, she wasn't quite sure how to accomplish either of Captain Blacktooth's tasks on her own—but that, of course, was why magic was so useful. She placed the coins inside the porridge bowl, where they began to jitter and twitch.

"Um, Hilary?" The gargoyle peered into the bowl. "Are you sure you're strong enough to use all that?"

"Of course," said Hilary. "At least, I'm *nearly* sure." She'd never used more than one magic coin before, and even that could be difficult to control, but a single coin was nowhere near powerful enough to accomplish what she had in mind. And anyway, hadn't Captain Blacktooth told her to be bold and daring? She picked up the porridge bowl in both hands and tried to ignore the gargoyle, who was covering his eyes with his tail. "Magic," she said, addressing the bowl, "I wish for the fastest pirate ship you can manage, and a crew of scallywags to help me sail it. Please," she added, because the magic seemed to appreciate good manners. "Oh, and could you arrange for the scallywags to be excellent sword fighters?"

As Hilary spoke, the familiar thrill of magic tugged at her lungs and tingled along her arms. She held the golden porridge bowl as tightly as she could. For a moment she thought the enchantment had worked, and the gargoyle peeked out from under his tail. Then, too soon, the tug of magic stopped, the tingling ceased, and the coins flew out of the bowl and clattered to the deck.

"Oh, blast!" Hilary rubbed her sore arms and scanned the harbor, but no pirate ship had appeared. "I didn't even conjure up a single scallywag."

The gargoyle lowered his tail and looked around. "Cheer up," he said; "it could have been worse. You could have turned yourself into a wheel of cheese."

Hilary blinked. "Did someone *do* that?"

"A week ago, in Pemberton. I heard Jasper say so. Besides, if you'd *really* made a mess of things, you would have gotten a scolding from the Enchant—"

But the gargoyle was interrupted by a prim and proper voice that rang out from the air directly above Hilary's head:

To use your magic, you must be stronger!
Don't attempt it any longer.

Hilary groaned and covered her ears, but there was no use in trying to shut out the Enchantress's reprimands, for the less eager one was to hear them, the louder they became. The gargoyle tilted his head to one side. "I don't think I've ever heard that one before," he said when the Enchantress's voice had faded away at last. "She must be trying out a new batch of rhymes."

"Yes," said Hilary, "and she's probably woken half of Otterpool in the process." She started to gather the spilled coins together. "Blasted magic."

The prim and proper voice cleared its throat.

Be polite, and pleasant too,
or you can bid your coins adieu!

Hilary and the gargoyle exchanged a look. "Sorry, Miss Pimm," Hilary said into the air.

The voice seemed satisfied with this, for it didn't return again. At the stern of the ship, however, a cabin door squeaked open, and Charlie stumbled out in his nightclothes.

Hilary scrambled to bundle up the magic in her pirate coat, but she could tell from the way Charlie rolled his eyes that he had already spotted it. "I thought I heard the

Enchantress out here," he said. He nudged the bundle of magic with his foot. "You're lucky you didn't wake Miss Greyson as well. What have you two been up to?"

"I," said the gargoyle, "have been sitting quietly in my Nest."

"And what has the Terror been doing?"

"It's a long story," said Hilary. A magic coin still glinted on the deck, and she stepped on it. "Long and terribly boring. You wouldn't like it one bit."

"Let me guess." Charlie leaned against the *Pigeon*'s starboard rail. "This has something to do with Blacktooth."

The gargoyle coughed, and Hilary did her best to count the stripes on Charlie's nightclothes.

Charlie laughed. "You both look so guilty that I know I'm right," he said. "I didn't attend the League holiday ball either, and no one's sailed halfway around the kingdom to chide me for it. What really happened? Was Blacktooth cross with you?"

"I suppose 'cross' is one way of putting it," said Hilary. "He says it's been far too long since I've done anything to impress the League. I've been given a warning, and Blacktooth's ordered me to perform a bold and daring task to prove that I'm a good pirate."

"But of course you're a good pirate! In a year or two, if you set your mind to it, you might even be as good as me." Charlie grinned and dodged the glare that Hilary aimed in his direction. "Anyway, I like the bit about the bold and daring task. It's been ages since we've had an adventure."

"Exactly," said Hilary. "I'd hoped to set off this morning to slay a sea monster or defeat a pirate king in battle, but since I couldn't manage to magic up a ship or a crew—"

"Wait a moment," said Charlie. "You can't truly mean to suggest that you were about to sail off on a voyage without your first mate." He crossed his arms. "That's me, by the way."

"I'm sorry. I thought you'd be busy. And I know you don't care for magic."

Charlie's parents had died when their pirate ship was sunk and their magic treasure stolen, and ever since, he'd wanted very little to do with magic of any sort, though at least he seemed to enjoy the gargoyle's company. "That's true enough," he said, "which is why going on an adventure sounds heaps better than helping Jasper cart wagonloads of magic all over the kingdom for the rest of the year." He shoved the bundle of magic off to one side. "We'll get the ship and crew sorted out later, but for now it seems to me that you'd better decide which of Blacktooth's tasks is less likely to send you to the bottom of the sea. How's your swordplay coming along?"

All through the morning and into the afternoon, Hilary and Charlie practiced every dueling drill they knew. Hilary's swordplay had improved quite a bit since her first days on the *Pigeon*, but Charlie still bested her in more than half their matches, and she suspected that the undefeated pirate king from the southern kingdoms was a good deal more talented than Charlie was. "I suppose it'll have to be the sea monster, then," she said, fanning herself with her hat.

"Are you sure?" the gargoyle asked. His Nest was stacked high with reference volumes about sea monsters that Hilary had borrowed from the bookshop when Miss Greyson wasn't looking. "Half these books say that sea monsters don't even exist, and the other half say that the monster who lives near Summerstead is particularly nasty. His teeth are as sharp as a thousand cutlasses, and he can destroy an entire village with one swish of his tail." The gargoyle used his snout to turn a page. "It says here that he likes to eat pirates as snacks."

"That doesn't sound pleasant," said Hilary. "Do you think all piratical adventures are required to end in being run through or eaten?"

The gargoyle began to say that he certainly hoped not, but he was interrupted by a series of loud, impatient knocks on the *Pigeon*'s hull. Hilary leaned over the rail to see the postal courier's boat bobbing on the waves, while the postal courier himself rapped a stick against the ship. "Urgent delivery for the *Pigeon*!" he called.

"Just a moment!" Miss Greyson hurried up the deck. "Welcome to the floating bookshop and magic dispensary! Would you care for some hot chocolate?"

"No time for that, ma'am," said the postal courier. He pocketed his stick, handed a cream-colored envelope up to Miss Greyson, and sailed away as rapidly as he'd arrived.

Miss Greyson frowned down at the envelope. "Oh dear," she said, "it's addressed to Jasper. Shall I call the postal courier back?"

"He said it was urgent." Hilary looked over Miss Greyson's shoulder. "Perhaps you'd better open it and see what it's about."

"I suppose that wouldn't be too improper under the circumstances," said Miss Greyson. She turned the envelope over and slid her finger under the blob of purple sealing wax that had been stamped quite clearly with a figure eight.

Hilary drew in her breath. "It's from Miss Pimm."

❀ • • • • ❀ • • • • ❀ ❀ ❀ • • • • ❀ • • • • ❀

Dear Mr. Fletcher (Miss Greyson read aloud),

I hope that this note finds you well and that your distribution of my treasure is proceeding smoothly. I was pleased to receive last month's update on your progress, but I shall take this opportunity to remind you that eating jam while addressing one's correspondence is not entirely proper. (Perhaps you thought I would not notice the sticky smudge that adorned your envelope, but I assure you: I notice everything.)

I am writing not to scold you, however, but to ask for your assistance. Mr. Fletcher, I have reason to believe that

*our beloved kingdom is under threat—and that I myself
may be in peril. As the queen and her royal inspectors have
shrugged off my suspicions, and I am not certain which
of my friends can be trusted, I find myself with no other
choice: I shall need the services of the most fearsome pirate
in Augusta to help me address the matter.*

*I dare not say more in this letter, but I hope you will
travel to my school in Pemberton immediately so we may
talk further. Since I know your crew is occupied with
treasure distribution and bookselling, I shall arrange
for my private carriage to meet you in Otterpool on the
morning after you receive this letter. Do not be late, and
bring your sharpest sword.*

> *Yours in haste,*
> *Eugenia Pimm*
> Enchantress of the Northlands

❋ • • • • ❋ • • • • ❋ ❀ ❋ • • • • ❋ • • • • ❋

By the time she finished reading, Miss Greyson had
gone very pale indeed. "Jasper will be leagues away by
now," she said. "Do you suppose I should send the letter
along to him?"

"It won't reach him for days," Charlie pointed out.
"And Miss Pimm says she needs to see him immediately."

"Oh dear, you're quite right." Miss Greyson rubbed her

forehead and frowned. "Shall I write to Miss Pimm? Whatever shall I say?" She stared at the letter and began to read it again.

Hilary took Charlie by the elbow and tugged him over to the Gargoyle's Nest. "We've got to do something!" she whispered. "Miss Greyson is very sweet, but writing Miss Pimm a letter won't save the kingdom from peril. She says she needs help from the most fearsome pirate in Augusta, and aren't I the Terror of the Southlands? If Jasper can't help her, I've got to go instead."

Charlie looked worried. "But what about Blacktooth's tasks? We're supposed to stay on his good side, remember? If he finds out you've been helping the Enchantress instead of doing something piratical, he's sure to kick you out of the League for good. I don't think it says anything about helping Enchantresses in the VNHLP handbook."

Hilary's spirits sank, for Charlie was almost certainly right. A dutiful pirate would follow Blacktooth's orders, choose one of his bold and daring tasks, and do her best to forget about Miss Pimm's letter altogether. Then again, hadn't Blacktooth himself said that piracy often required a certain disregard for good behavior? And what if Miss Pimm was really in danger? She could be terribly bossy and more than a bit stubborn, and Hilary couldn't honestly say she cared for her rhymes. Still, she had always treated Hilary kindly, not even raising a finger in protest when Hilary withdrew from finishing school to sail the High Seas. In fact, she had been a great deal more understanding than Hilary's own mother had been. She never disapproved of Hilary's breeches or tried to send her off to High Society balls, and whenever the *Pigeon* docked in Pemberton, Miss Pimm invited Hilary and the gargoyle over for tea and spiders.

"Oh, blast the handbook!" Hilary said. "Perhaps helping Enchantresses isn't a traditional pirate activity, but Miss Pimm is my friend, and a true pirate assists her mates in storms and battles. It says so right in the VNHLP Rules of Conduct. Helping a friend in peril is far more piratical than getting sliced to bits by a scallywag or eaten as a snack, and I'm sure Captain Blacktooth knows that as well as anyone." She crossed her arms. "So should you, Pirate Dove."

Charlie looked down at his boots. "You're right," he said at last. "And I suppose saving the kingdom will be loads more interesting than sitting around Otterpool Harbor."

"We'll be bold and daring!" the gargoyle cried. "Just like Captain Blacktooth wanted us to be."

Hilary grinned. "Then it's settled. We'll help Miss Pimm, we'll have a grand adventure, and we'll make Blacktooth impressed in spite of himself."

VNHLP MIDSUMMER'S EVE PICNIC. All pirates are reminded that the annual League picnic on Gunpowder Island is only a few days away. Spots are still available in the hardtack-eatin' contest, the swimmin' relay, and the one-legged race (peg-legged pirates only, please). Come sing sea chanteys round the bonfire, blast cannons over the bay, and catch up with your mates.

෨

TERROR IN TROUBLE. Miss Hilary Westfield, former High Society girl and current Terror of the Southlands, has earned her first reprimand for unpiratical behavior. This news is sure to be received with pleasure by those scallywags who have protested Pirate Westfield's membership in the League. VNHLP president Rupert Blacktooth assures us, however, that she is willing and eager to mend her ways. We at the Picaroon wish Pirate Westfield the best of luck during this difficult time.

෨

SCANDAL IN THE RANKS? An anonymous source tells the Picaroon that a pirate of some repute has been seen in the company of a certain government official, one Miss E— P—. Rumor has it that the two dine together often and once spent an afternoon playing croquet. The pirate in question is warned that befriending members of the government is frowned upon, and that sharing League secrets outside the pirate community is strictly forbidden.

୬୭

MISSING. One eye patch, best quality, with green silk ribbon ties. Believed to be lost near Pemberton. If found, please return to Cannonball Jack on his houseboat, the *Blunderbuss*, in Pemberton Bay.

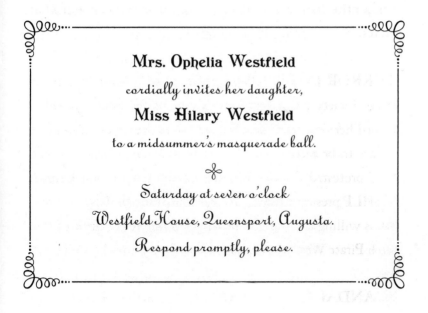

Mrs. Ophelia Westfield
cordially invites her daughter,
Miss Hilary Westfield
to a midsummer's masquerade ball.

❖

Saturday at seven o'clock
Westfield House, Queensport, Augusta.
Respond promptly, please.

Hilary,

I do hope you will attend my masquerade. Are you still flitting about on that pirate ship? I shall remind you once again of the damage you continue to inflict on the Westfield name. Due to your reputation for piracy and your father's reputation for villainy, I must work twice as hard to convince the finest High Society families to set foot on the grounds of Westfield House. I fear, however, that my plight will not convince you to change your ways. If you will not attend my ball, please pay me the courtesy of visiting me in Queensport. We shall have lunch! I shall ask my dressmaker to fit you for a new gown! What do you think of that?

And dear, wouldn't it be nice for you to visit your father? My High Society friends have persuaded me that even the most notorious villain in Augusta might be reformed through the attentions of a loving wife, so I have begun to travel to the Dungeons every fourth Tuesday. Despite my efforts to make polite conversation, your father remains rather cheerless, but I am sure a pleasant smile from his daughter would help to mend the rift between you.

Your loving
Mother

PIRATE HILARY WESTFIELD
TERROR OF THE SOUTHLANDS

◇ ◇ ◇ ◇ ◇

Dear Mother,

I am sorry to say that I cannot attend your masquerade ball. I've told you a thousand times that I don't care for dancing or for gowns, and on top of it all, I have to admit that I find the idea of High Society guests clad in masks to be slightly alarming. If I must be in the company of dull and self-absorbed young lords and ladies, I prefer to know exactly who is boring me to tears.

In any case, I hope you will not send me any more invitations, for I am about to set off on a piratical adventure, and I expect that I shall be rather busy in the future. I am sorry to upset you, Mother—for I know you are upset—but you mustn't overreact and lock yourself in your wardrobe again. You know how it distresses the maids.

I shall come to see you in Queensport as soon

as I'm able. Please do not ask your dressmaker to measure me for anything at all; she always sticks me full of pins, and my seafaring clothes are perfectly serviceable. I have never attempted to climb ship's rigging in a ball gown, but I feel sure that such an attempt would put both the gown and my neck in an unnecessary amount of peril.

You know perfectly well that Father wants nothing to do with me. If he wants me to visit him in the Royal Dungeons, it is surely only to scold me for putting him there in the first place. I am sorry he is lonely, and I am glad that you are visiting him, but I doubt that even your dressmaker could sew up the rift between us. And don't you dare ask me to apologize, Mother. Pirates don't apologize—especially not to villains.

I hope your masquerade ball is a smashing success.

Arr! and love from
Hilary

CHAPTER THREE

"**Y**OU MUST PROMISE to write," Miss Greyson said as she rowed the dinghy up to the weatherworn Otterpool docks, "and please give my best to Miss Pimm. I do hope you all won't put yourselves in too much danger."

Hilary loved Miss Greyson dearly, but it was occasionally quite difficult to sail the High Seas with one's former governess. "Danger," she said, "is what being a pirate is all about. But we'll write as often as we can. Are you sure you'll be all right on the *Pigeon*?"

Miss Greyson gave a brisk nod and set down her oars. "I shall be more than capable of keeping the treasure out of unscrupulous hands, but I believe I'll write to ask a few of Jasper's former crewmates for assistance with the ship's work until Jasper returns. I'd hate for the bookshop to be neglected."

When Hilary, Charlie, and the gargoyle had all said their good-byes to Miss Greyson, they climbed out of the dinghy and walked down the small dirt road to the center of the village, where a fine black coach drawn by four chestnut horses stood waiting for them. Most carriages in the kingdom were adorned with large family crests, or with a row of stars indicating a carriage for hire, but this one was painted with a golden figure eight—the mark of the Enchantress. When the driver caught sight of the pirates, he tipped his hat and stepped down from his box. "Is one of you Jasper Fletcher, then?" he asked.

"I'm Pirate Hilary Westfield." Hilary tipped her own hat to the driver, who was looking rather confused at the sight of her braid. "I'm afraid Jasper Fletcher isn't available at the moment, so my mates and I will be visiting Miss Pimm in his place."

"I've been told to bring a pirate back to Pemberton with me," the driver said, "so as long as I've got my pirate, I'm not much bothered about which one it is. I'd advise you to get yourselves settled comfortably, for it's four days' journey to Miss Pimm's." Then he helped them into the coach, and the chestnut horses led them east out of Otterpool, away from the sea.

The road to Pemberton was poor, and they had to stop often to give the horses water and rest. Charlie didn't enjoy traveling more than a few miles from the sea, and he fiddled with the buttons on his pirate coat as the coach rolled through the gray and green Southlands Hills. "It's a bit like looking at the world inside out," he said. "There's supposed to be land on the horizon and sea under your boots, not the other way around."

To distract them all from the dry ground that bumped beneath the carriage wheels, Hilary read aloud from the books Miss Greyson had let the gargoyle borrow for the journey—stories of quick-witted heroes, treacherous villains, and (Charlie groaned) true love. Apart from the occasional moments when a story ended sadly and Hilary had to console the gargoyle, the trip passed without incident, and as the sun set behind them on the third day, the driver turned the coach toward the south, where he knew of a fine place to spend the night.

They had just turned onto the Pemberton road when the air around them filled with the shrill squeal of metal and the sound of galloping hoofbeats. The coach began to tremble as the noise grew louder, and the driver cursed. Then, quite without warning, the four chestnut horses reared up and dragged the coach off the road, sending them bumping and swaying into a ditch. Hilary put a hand on her cutlass, Charlie bumped his head on the top of the coach, and the gargoyle pressed his snout against the window. "Look!" he cried as they shuddered to a rather tilted halt. "Here come some scallywags!"

Hilary wrapped the gargoyle in her arms and watched as a carriage charged past them in a flurry of dust. It was painted all in black and drawn by a fleet of jet-black horses. Dark curtains masked its windows, and the coachman's hat sat so low on his head that Hilary wondered how he could see anything at all. The ground shook beneath them as the black horses passed. Within moments, the mysterious carriage disappeared over the crest of the hill, and the road was empty once more.

Hilary had only just recovered her breath when Miss Pimm's driver pulled the carriage door open. "There's no serious damage done," he said, dabbing at his forehead with the sleeve of his jacket, "though the horses are pretty well spooked. Are you pirates all right?"

"Some of us are a bit shaken," Hilary admitted. She looked down at the gargoyle, who was still quivering slightly in her arms. "Whoever do you think was driving that carriage? I couldn't make out any markings on the doors."

"A coach without markings?" Charlie rubbed the top of his head and winced. "That's awfully strange, isn't it?"

"Strange indeed," the driver said, "but hardly stranger than driving two pirates and a gargoyle to finishing school."

When the horses were calmed at last, the driver guided the carriage out of the ditch and down the road to an inn owned by a gentleman who turned out to be a retired pirate. He had abandoned the seafaring life for a large, shingled hilltop house with nautical prints on the walls, where he plied Hilary and Charlie with homemade biscuits and showed them to their cots in the snug attic. If the day was fine, the pirate gentleman claimed, you could catch a glimpse of the sea through the uppermost window. A warm biscuit before bed and a hopeful glance toward the sea were enough to dismiss all thoughts of the mysterious carriage from Hilary's mind, and she woke the next morning feeling bolder and more daring than ever.

As THE CARRIAGE rumbled southward, the dirt road widened, and cobblestones began to sprout from its edges. Just before lunchtime on the fourth day, the stone spires of Pemberton rose into view, and bells rang out on the breeze as the clock in the market square chimed the hour.

"When we get to Miss Pimm's," said the gargoyle, "will there be fanfare? Will there be crowds? Will they announce us as the fearsome pirates who've come to save the kingdom?" He hopped up and down on the carriage seat. "Oh, I can't wait!"

"I can," said Charlie. He was fiddling with his buttons again. "That place is absolutely crawling with High Society girls."

Hilary rolled her eyes. "Charlie Dove, your father was the Scourge of the Northlands. If you have any intention of filling his boots, you'll simply have to face your fears. The High Society girls won't eat you—or at least I'm fairly sure they won't."

The carriage turned down the shady avenue toward Miss Pimm's Finishing School for Delicate Ladies, and the driver slowed the horses. "I'm afraid I'll have to let you out here," he said. "I'd take you to the front gate, but there's a whole knot of people standing about in the lane."

The gargoyle's ears perked up. "I *knew* there would be crowds!" he cried.

But the people gathered in the lane didn't seem to be there to greet the pirates, and there wasn't the slightest bit of fanfare when Hilary stepped out of the carriage. Outside Miss Pimm's front gate stood a cluster of gentlemen in red jackets and gray trousers. Some of the gentlemen were using exquisitely small brushes to dust the gate with chalky powder, while others bent down to examine the front path through round glass lenses. Several of the gentlemen seemed to be arguing with one another, and all of them looked quite solemn indeed. A long row of carriages painted with the queen's emblem lined the lane behind them. Every so often, another carriage would pull up and another red-and-gray gentleman would emerge from it, looking just as grave as his fellows.

The gargoyle poked his head out of Hilary's bag and

squinted at the red-and-gray gentlemen. "Are these the adoring masses?" he asked, looking up at Hilary. "I thought there would be trumpets."

"These," said Hilary, "are the queen's inspectors—nearly all of them, from the looks of it." She tilted her pirate hat at a jaunty angle, smoothed the wrinkles from her good coat, patted her cutlass, and marched down the lane toward Miss Pimm's. "Come along, Pirate Dove," she called over her shoulder to Charlie. "Something very odd is happening, and I intend to find out what it is."

As Hilary approached, the inspectors with brushes stopped dusting, and the inspectors with magnifying glasses stopped examining. They all turned to stare at her, just as Captain Blacktooth's crew had done on the *Renegade*. Hilary stared right back and kept marching, though she felt a bit as though she were marching directly off a plank. The gargoyle had apparently decided that the masses were not so adoring after all, for he ducked back into Hilary's bag, leaving only his pirate hat visible over the clasp.

At the tall, spiked front gate, Hilary stopped. The gate usually stood open, but today it was shut, and a particularly stern-looking inspector stood in front of it. "Please step aside, sir," Hilary said as loudly as she could manage. "I am Pirate Hilary Westfield, Terror of the Southlands. I've come for an urgent meeting with Miss Pimm."

The stern inspector's brow wrinkled, and he studied Hilary through his magnifying glass. "Pirates, eh?" he said at last. "I thought as much. So you're the ones responsible, are you? It's awfully bold of you to return to the scene of the crime. But then I suppose you pirates are known for your boldness."

Hilary drew herself up as though Miss Greyson had poked her in the ribs. "You're right to think that I'm bold, Inspector," she said, "but I don't know anything about any sort of crime, and I certainly haven't committed one."

"Ah!" said the inspector, looking quite pleased with himself. "That's precisely what a criminal would say, isn't it?"

"Listen here," said Charlie. "We're pirates, not criminals, and we've got to see Miss Pimm at once. If you won't be good enough to tell us what's going on here, perhaps she will."

"My lad," said the inspector, "if Miss Pimm could explain what has happened, I wouldn't need to be here at all, and I could return to my newspaper and my fine woolen slippers. But alas, I can't." The inspector leaned forward. "And if you don't provide some proof that you aren't rogues and rapscallions, I'll have to take you both to the Dungeons for questioning."

Hilary dug in her bag and pulled out Miss Pimm's letter. "This should be proof enough," she said. "Miss Pimm sent this letter to our captain, Jasper Fletcher, requesting his presence especially. But Mr. Fletcher is traveling at the moment, so we've come in his place."

The inspector held Miss Pimm's letter very close to his nose. He squinted at it through his magnifying glass. He ran a gloved finger along its border. Finally, he shook his head and thrust the paper back into Hilary's hand. "It looks genuine enough, I suppose," he said, "though what Miss Pimm would want with all you pirate folk, I can't imagine. But no matter—you can't come in, and that's that."

"Whyever not?" said Hilary. She was beginning to grow rather tired of this inspector. "I'm sure Miss Pimm won't be pleased to hear that you've inconvenienced her companions."

"She'll hear no such—" The inspector broke off as a door slammed behind him. "Good gracious, is it that pesky schoolgirl again? Didn't I tell you to stay inside?"

"Oh, thank goodness," Hilary murmured as Claire Dupree scurried down the path in a whirl of petticoats. Claire had stayed on at Miss Pimm's after Hilary had left to become a pirate, but a year of finishing school had done very little to calm her exuberance, and she waved at them wildly.

"Hilary!" she cried as she opened the gate. "I hoped you'd come! And Charlie, hello, it's ever so wonderful to see you again." She pushed past the inspector to wrap Hilary in a fierce hug, and then, ignoring the look of terror on Charlie's face, she hugged him as well. "But there's no time for pleasantries. Quick, both of you, come inside before that horrid inspector bores you half to death." She tugged them through the gate and latched it behind her before the inspector could do more than fumble his magnifying glass in alarm. "Now that you've arrived, I'm sure you'll know what to do. Those inspectors have been here for *hours* already, but they haven't discovered a thing and I'm quite sure they never will. Inspectors are so useless, don't you think? Always sniffing about and dusting—but I simply can't see how dusting will improve the matter at all!"

"Just a moment," said Hilary. "You'd better tell us exactly what's happened. We've come to see Miss Pimm, but she didn't warn us that the place would be swarming with queen's inspectors."

Claire blinked. "You haven't heard? Oh, how foolish of me; I should have told you right away, but I thought— well, it's absolutely *tragic*. You see," said Claire, taking an enormous breath, "Miss Pimm has vanished!"

Magic users, take note! The Scuttlebutt has discovered this morning that the Enchantress of the Northlands, Miss Eugenia Pimm, has gone missing from her home in Pemberton, where she oversees Miss Pimm's Finishing School for Delicate Ladies. The captain of the queen's inspectors, a Mr. Hastings, confirms that the Enchantress's whereabouts are unknown but will not tell our reporters whether she has vanished of her own accord. The inspector claims it is possible that the Enchantress has merely taken a well-deserved vacation, but we at the Scuttlebutt fervently hope that the case proves to be far more scandalous. Could the Enchantress have been kidnapped, captured, pursued, or purloined? Will nefarious scoundrels use her absence as an opportunity to wreak magical havoc across Augusta? Without an Enchantress to watch over us, will the kingdom erupt in an explosion of battles, thefts, and ill-conceived enchantments—or will everyone remember to mind their manners? (We suspect that the first possibility is far more likely than the second.)

We shall report more details as we manage to pry them from the remarkably tight fists of Inspector Hastings.

WE ASKED, YOU ANSWERED:
What has happened to the Enchantress of the Northlands?

"She's always vanishing, isn't she? The last time she disappeared, she didn't return for nearly two hundred years, and we simply can't afford to wait that long for her to return again. It's quite rude to go off on one's own for hundreds of years at a time without even leaving a note."
—L. Devereaux, Nordholm

"I read in the *Gazette* that Miss Pimm longed to return to the Northlands. Perhaps she's given up on her search for the new Enchantress and gone home at last."—N. Feathering, Queensport

"The Enchantress must have a lot of enemies, mustn't she? She's very strict about magic, and no one seems to care much for her rhymes. Do you think someone got fed up with her and did her in? Oh dear, that would be dreadful."—P. Scattergood, Otterpool

"I have no idea where Eugenia Pimm has gone, but I think it's disgraceful of her to abandon her students—not to mention her kingdom! What are we to do without an Enchantress? Why, people will run absolutely wild with magic! I hope Miss Pimm will return at once, but if she does not, I trust the queen will hurry to fill the vacant position Miss Pimm has left behind."—G. Tilbury, Nordholm

"Perhaps she turned herself invisible with all that magic she's got. I should very much like to be invisible. When Mr. Fletcher arrives with my magic piece, I'll try it at once."—O. Cheresky, Little Shearwater

an extract From

The Gargoyle: History of a Hero
BY THE GARGOYLE
AS TOLD TO H. WESTFIELD

I was born in a lovely little quarry in the
Southlands Hills, but I was nothing more
than a chunk of granite until I met the
Enchantress. Eugenia Pimm selected me herself
and carved me into the handsome gargoyle
you admire so much today. (It's true that
Miss Pimm and I don't look quite as elegant
as we did back then, but if you'd been around
for two hundred years, dear reader, you
wouldn't be looking so great either.) She made
my heart from a powerful lump of magic,
and when I was finished, she enchanted me
to move and talk just as humans do. After
I introduced myself, Miss Pimm explained
that she had created me to protect her friends
in Westfield House from villainy. "You are
full of strong magic," she told me, "but I
have placed an enchantment on your heart to
ensure that your magic may only be used for
protection."

I was proud to have such an important job to do, but I wasn't very happy about being stuck on the wall of Westfield House. Being a gargoyle isn't easy at the best of times, and it became even more difficult when Miss Pimm ran away from her life as an Enchantress and took most of the kingdom's magic with her. I had no idea what had happened to her—no one ever remembers to tell the gargoyle what's going on—so I sat above my doorway and gave protection to anyone who bothered to ask for it. If you're not a magical creature, dear reader, you probably don't understand how unpleasant this is. Your heart feels funny, like it might explode without any warning, and your whole body starts to shake. Even worse, you're forced to protect rude, selfish people who don't seem to notice that your arms are crumbling to bits. It was a huge relief when my trusty assistant, Hilary, came along to dust the cobwebs from my snout, although I wish she'd shown up at least half a century earlier.

As for Miss Pimm, it turned out that after she'd run away all those years ago, she'd opened a finishing school for young ladies. When my assistant and I discovered where she'd hidden all the magic she took with her, we convinced her to return to her job as Enchantress. Miss Pimm and I are still very good friends, for without Miss Pimm, there would be no gargoyle, and without the gargoyle, what would happen to the kingdom? Honestly, dear reader, I can't bear to think about it.

CHAPTER FOUR

IN THE FEW minutes since Hilary had arrived at Miss Pimm's, the queen's inspectors seemed to have multiplied several times over. The school's main hall was packed practically from floor to ceiling with curious red-jacketed gentlemen who chewed on their pipe stems and waved their magnifying glasses about, while clusters of schoolgirls clutched one another and spoke in small, nervous voices. Although it was well after midday, some of the girls were still dressed in their nightclothes and wrapped in blankets. Hilary felt sure that Miss Pimm would have disapproved severely of the entire spectacle. "And you're sure she hasn't simply enchanted herself away?" Hilary asked Claire as they wove through the crowd.

Claire tugged at the sleeves of her green cardigan, which was unraveling at the wrists. Even the dancing sheep embroidered in golden thread was starting to come unpicked. "To be honest," she said, "I'm not terribly sure of anything. The inspectors refuse to tell us what's happened, but no one seems to have seen Miss Pimm since yesterday afternoon, and it's been absolutely *hours* since she's scolded anyone in rhyme."

This was very grave news indeed. "I can't imagine Miss Pimm missing an opportunity to deliver a good reprimand," Hilary said. A few months earlier, Miss Pimm had told her in confidence that scolding was the only one of the Enchantress's duties that she really enjoyed.

"Exactly," said Claire. "And I don't think there would be so many inspectors underfoot if Miss Pimm had simply decided to take a holiday." She brushed past an inspector who was peering at Charlie's dirt-scuffed boot through his magnifying glass. "What if she's been stolen away by scoundrels? Or worse?"

"Worse?" The gargoyle's ears drooped considerably. "I don't like thinking about *worse*."

"I don't like it either," Hilary said. They had reached a clearing in the crowd, and she stopped for a moment to gather her thoughts. "Especially not after what Miss Pimm said about peril."

Claire frowned. "Whatever do you mean?"

Hilary unfolded Miss Pimm's letter and passed it to her. "She wrote to Jasper that she believed she might be in peril, and she wasn't sure who could be trusted. What if the peril has come along and snatched her up?" She sighed and wished the journey from Otterpool had not been quite so lengthy. "If only we'd gotten here sooner, we might have been able to protect her."

"Or we might have vanished right alongside her," said Charlie. He looked rather uncomfortable at the thought of it.

"Well, at least we're here now." There was no point in having regrets, Hilary reminded herself, for regrets were thoroughly unpiratical, and they wouldn't do Miss Pimm a smidgen of good in any case. "We came here to help our friend, and that's exactly what we'll do."

Claire clapped her hands together. "You will?"

"Of course!" said Hilary. "Unless you think it's wise to leave the search in the hands of these ridiculous inspectors." She glared at a gentleman who was attempting to dust her elbow for fingerprints, and he scurried away. "If Miss Pimm is truly in danger, she'll need the Terror of the Southlands to rescue her."

"And the Terror's first mate," Charlie put in.

The gargoyle's ears still hadn't perked up, and Hilary put a hand on his head to comfort him. "What do you think, gargoyle?" she asked. "Can you be bold and daring enough to help the Enchantress?"

The gargoyle thought for a moment. Then he twitched his ears so forcefully that his pirate hat nearly flew off his head. "If I couldn't," he said, "I'd hardly be the finest gargoyle on the High Seas. We'll save Miss Pimm and bring her home, and then there will be trumpets!"

THE FIRST THING to do, Hilary decided, was to confront the queen's inspectors. After their encounter outside the school gate, she didn't relish the idea of talking to any more red-jacketed gentlemen, but it was possible that the inspectors knew more than they were letting on about Miss Pimm's whereabouts. "And if they do," said Hilary, "we've got to pry that information out of them—at swordpoint, if necessary."

The gentleman in charge, Inspector Hastings, had established his headquarters in Miss Pimm's private office. "I think that's awfully rude of him, don't you?" Claire said as she rapped her fist against the door. "Poor Miss Pimm. Disappearing is enough of an insult to one's pride without losing one's office as well."

The door squeaked open just enough to allow a gentleman's round, bespectacled head to poke through. "Who's there?" the gentleman asked. Then he blinked and adjusted his spectacles. "Pirates? My goodness! I'm afraid I don't allow pirates in my office."

The gentleman attempted to close the door, but Hilary pushed past him and settled herself in a chair. "I'm the

Terror of the Southlands," she said, "and I need to speak to Inspector Hastings at once."

Charlie and Claire hurried into the room as the gentleman took off his spectacles, rubbed at them with a handkerchief, and replaced them on his nose. He seemed on the verge of saying a number of cross things, but when Hilary moved her hand ever so slightly toward her cutlass, he resorted to giving an irritated sniff. Hilary was rather pleased to see that at least someone in the kingdom had the good sense to be impressed with her.

"I am Inspector Hastings," the gentleman said—rather too grandly, in Hilary's opinion—"and since I have done you the favor of welcoming you into my office, pirates, I hope you will do me the favor of keeping your weapons to yourselves." He sat down behind Miss Pimm's desk, which was stacked high with all manner of notebooks and papers, though the inspector had cleared out a small area amid the stacks to make room for his tea service. He took a sip of tea and surveyed the row of pirates in front of him, wrinkling his brow at Claire and wrinkling it further still at the gargoyle. "Have you come to confess to the crime, then?" he asked. "Or to deliver a ransom note, perhaps?"

"Neither, I'm afraid," said Hilary. "Miss Pimm happens to be a friend of ours, and we're here to find her. Would you be kind enough to tell us what you know about her disappearance?"

Perhaps Mr. Hastings was not quite as impressed

with Hilary as she had hoped, for he nearly spit out his tea. "Reveal the results of our investigation?" he said. "To a band of pirates? Why, it's out of the question! If I broke protocol in such a fashion, the queen herself would throw me in the Dungeons—and rightly so." He put down his teacup and folded his hands. "If you are truly the Enchantress's friends, you may rest assured that my men and I have the matter of her disappearance well in hand. We hardly need assistance from a group of scallywags without a magnifying glass or a dusting brush to their name." He glanced sideways at Hilary. "You don't have a dusting brush, do you?"

"No," said Hilary, "but I really don't see—"

Mr. Hastings nodded. "I thought as much."

"You know, Terror," Charlie said slowly, "it's possible that the inspectors haven't learned a thing. Perhaps Mr. Hastings won't share his information because he hasn't got any information to share."

Hilary grinned at him. "I do believe you're right, Pirate Dove."

"He's not right at all!" cried Mr. Hastings. "I'll have you know that we've received some valuable evidence from the young lady who witnessed the crime. She observed a most unscrupulous individual lurking near this very room!"

"A witness?" Claire leaned forward. "And who might that be?"

Mr. Hastings raised his chin and looked down his nose

at each of them in turn. "That information," he said, "is confidential. It is certainly *not* to be shared with pirates—or with schoolgirls, for that matter." He laid a protective hand over a sheet of paper on the desk. "And don't imagine for one moment that I'll be willing to share my list of suspects, either. My men had to sort through the Enchantress's appointment book for nearly an hour to compile it, and they are already searching for the villains in question."

"When they find the villains," the gargoyle remarked to Hilary, "they'll probably dust them."

Hilary eyed the steaming teapot that stood at Mr. Hastings's elbow. Then she gathered her courage and gave the inspector her most charming High Society smile. "I understand your predicament, sir," she said. "We wouldn't dream of asking you to share your list of suspects."

Charlie narrowed his eyes. "We wouldn't?"

"Absolutely not." The charming smile was beginning to hurt Hilary's cheeks; however did High Society ladies sustain it? "I see you've finished your tea, Mr. Hastings. May I pour you another cup?"

"By all means." Mr. Hastings leaned back in his chair. "Thank you, pirate. I knew I could make you see reason. You're not much of a Terror after all, are you?"

Hilary aimed her charming smile directly at Mr. Hastings, picked up the teapot, and dumped its contents onto the desk.

A great river of tea streamed over Mr. Hastings's papers

and cascaded onto Mr. Hastings himself. "You clumsy scallywag!" he cried, leaping up and overturning Miss Pimm's chair in the process. "Look what you've done! That's my evidence!"

Hilary hurried around to the other side of the desk and began to pat the papers dry with a tea towel. "I'm terribly sorry!" she said, taking great care to knock over a pile of notebooks with her elbow. "I never should have offered to pour your tea. Pirates are notoriously bad at it."

"It's true," said Charlie, reaching across the desk and scattering a sheaf of papers to the floor. "As a general rule, pirates are quite untidy."

"I can see that!" Mr. Hastings snapped. He bent to retrieve his documents, but Claire sprang up from her chair and crashed into him at high speed, sending the papers flying in every direction. Hilary had to bite her lip to keep from laughing out loud as she wiped the pool of tea from the inspectors' list of suspects.

"Get out!" cried Mr. Hastings, who was now thoroughly steeped in tea. "For goodness' sake, wreak your piratical havoc somewhere else! And tell my lieutenant that my shirt needs cleaning."

The pirates nodded gravely and marched out of the office, through the main hall, and out the front door. When they had reached the safety of the school's front steps, however, they collapsed into laughter. "That poor inspector," said Claire. "He thrashed about so much that I was quite tempted to wrap him in newspaper and sell him at the fishmonger's."

Charlie looked around and lowered his voice. "Did you get a good look at his notes, Hilary?"

"Only the list of suspects," Hilary said, "and I'm afraid it's awfully peculiar. It's only got one name."

The gargoyle hopped up and down in her bag. "Who's the villain, then?" he asked. "Is it a fearsome brute? A heartless rogue? A sea monster?"

The gargoyle looked so eager that Hilary was reluctant to dampen his mood. "Actually," she said, "it's a pirate. The inspectors think Miss Pimm has been kidnapped by Cannonball Jack."

"I don't believe it," said Charlie at once.

Hilary couldn't believe it either. "He's a friend of mine," she explained to Claire, who was looking puzzled. "We met when I became Jasper's apprentice. Oh, you must remember him; he was at the wedding. He's got a hook, a peg leg, and an eye patch, and he spent half the night dancing reels with Miss Pimm."

"Oh, yes." Claire nodded. "*That* pirate. He didn't seem like the kidnapping sort."

"He's not!" said Hilary. "I suppose he can be fearsome from time to time, but that's his profession."

"Still, he ended up on the inspectors' list somehow." Charlie looked concerned. "I don't suppose they'll tell us why they suspect him."

"Then we'll have to find out for ourselves." Hilary settled her pirate hat more firmly on her head. On the *Pigeon*, she had become used to listening to Jasper make plans and give orders, but it was rather refreshing to give those orders herself, even if she didn't sound nearly as confident as Jasper did. "Cannonball Jack usually anchors the *Blunderbuss* in Pemberton Bay. If he's really got Miss Pimm aboard his ship, then we'll know where she's gone, and if he hasn't, he might have some idea of what's happened to her—but either way, we'd better reach him before the inspectors do, or they're likely to make a complete hash of things."

Charlie considered this. "It's a good plan," he said, much to Hilary's relief.

"Nearly as good as one a gargoyle might make," the gargoyle agreed.

For a moment, Claire was quiet. "Hilary," she said at last, "I was wondering . . . Well, without Miss Pimm here, the entire school is a bit of a mess, and I overheard the games mistress talking about canceling the whole summer term." She tugged at her sleeves so sharply that an entire row of stitches squirmed free from her cardigan. "I'm not sure I can bear to go home and work at the fish market until she's found. I know I'm not a pirate, not really, and I'm sure you don't need a schoolgirl to help you—though I *am* quite good at embroidery, and I can play a bit on the tin whistle—but anyway, oh, do you think I might come with you?"

Hilary laughed. "Of course!" she said. "I'd be honored if you'd come along as pirate's assistant."

Charlie's eyes went wide, and he suddenly became very busy examining the buttons on his coat.

"Really?" Claire flung her arms around Hilary. "Oh, thank you, Hilary—I mean, Pirate Westfield. I won't let you down, I promise. And thank you too, Pirate Dove. I'll just take a moment to gather my things, and then we'll all be off to rescue Miss Pimm!" Claire hurried up the steps. "I believe this is the most thrilling thing that's happened to me in months."

When Claire had pulled the door shut behind her, Charlie took off his hat and scratched his head, making his hair stick out in several directions at once. "Are you sure we should let her come with us?" he asked. "I mean, she's a High Society girl—or at least she will be when finishing school is done with her." Charlie shivered. "And she doesn't even seem to mind it."

Hilary grinned at him. "You don't mean to tell me that you're scared of *Claire*."

"Of course I'm not!" said Charlie—rather hastily, Hilary thought. "A pirate is never scared. But Claire likes ball gowns, and embroidery, and manners . . ."

"And she's perfectly capable of being a good pirate," Hilary said firmly. "She helped us find treasure last year, didn't she? And she did a lovely job of crashing into Mr. Hastings."

"Besides," said the gargoyle, "she's very good at scratching me behind the ears."

Charlie shrugged. "All right. If you think she'll be a good pirate's assistant, I suppose I can give her a chance."

"Thank you." Hilary picked up Charlie's hat and handed it back to him. "Now, if you're done being entirely silly, I believe we've got an Enchantress to find."

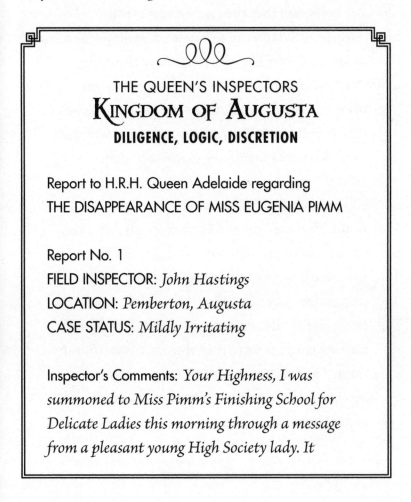

THE QUEEN'S INSPECTORS
KINGDOM OF AUGUSTA
DILIGENCE, LOGIC, DISCRETION

Report to H.R.H. Queen Adelaide regarding
THE DISAPPEARANCE OF MISS EUGENIA PIMM

Report No. 1
FIELD INSPECTOR: *John Hastings*
LOCATION: *Pemberton, Augusta*
CASE STATUS: *Mildly Irritating*

Inspector's Comments: *Your Highness, I was summoned to Miss Pimm's Finishing School for Delicate Ladies this morning through a message from a pleasant young High Society lady. It* appears that Miss Eugenia Pimm, Enchantress of the Northlands, has either misplaced herself or been misplaced by an unknown villain. We believe she left her home yesterday evening for a dinner appointment with an acquaintance and never returned.

It appears that the Enchantress is now too far away from Pemberton to be traced by magic, and in any case, very few of my men have the strength or talent to track down missing persons in this manner. We are forced, therefore, to rely on more traditional forms of detection. Inspectors have been outfitted with magnifying glasses and fingerprint kits.

Every inch of Miss Pimm's office is perfectly neat and proper, suggesting that she departed the school calmly and without a struggle. She seems to have left several of her magic pieces behind unguarded, suggesting that she planned to return to the school in short order. However, Miss Pimm's favorite magic piece (a golden crochet hook that she carried everywhere, according to her students) is nowhere to be found. We can only assume it is still in her possession.

Thanks to evidence supplied by the pleasant young lady I mentioned earlier, we have identified a nefarious-sounding gentleman named Cannonball Jack as our prime suspect in Miss Pimm's disappearance. I have sent my best inspectors to interview this individual and detain him if necessary. I must admit, however, that I am concerned about a number of points:

First, who is most likely to have captured the Enchantress? I would list the Enchantress's enemies here, but such a list would fill the streets of Pemberton, for many people from High Society to the High Seas wish her ill.

Second, who is capable of capturing the Enchantress? She is a powerful woman and would be difficult to overtake by magical means. Our villain must therefore be remarkably strong—or perhaps he is an even stronger magic user than the Enchantress herself. If my men are forced to confront such a powerful individual, they will surely require assistance; therefore, I am requesting that thirty additional inspectors be dispatched to Pemberton at once. I would, of course, humbly accept any token of aid that Your Highness might be willing to supply to our cause.

Finally, why in the world is this case so alarmingly full of pirates? A small and clumsy scallywag called the Terror of Something-or-Other has taken an interest in our investigation, and she severely disrupted my afternoon tea. Perhaps I shall order a few of my men to track her movements.

Signed
John Hastings
Captain, Queen's Inspectors

TERROR OF THE SOUTHLANDS BAFFLES SCALLYWAGS. In a curious turn of events, Pirate Hilary Westfield and her mates were spotted leaving a finishing school in Pemberton this afternoon, accompanied by a High Society schoolgirl. As Pirate Westfield is supposed to be restoring her good name in the League, we cannot understand why she would be engaged in such strange activities. Our sources suggest that Pirate Westfield is attempting to find the missing Enchantress of the Northlands. This strikes us as a noble quest, to be sure, but perhaps Pirate Westfield has forgotten that pirates are not supposed to be noble. Will the Terror mend her ways, or will she become an embarrassment to the League? The Picaroon is eager to find out.

ꙮ

PIRATE INVOLVED IN ENCHANTRESS MYSTERY? According to gossip in Pemberton Bay, a pirate was seen leaving the Enchantress's private quarters around the time of her disappearance. Could one of the League's own be responsible for this shocking turn of events? We asked VNHLP president Captain Rupert Blacktooth to comment on the matter. "If a villainous scheme has been carried out against the Enchantress, I sincerely hope that no League members were involved," Captain

Blacktooth said this morning in Pemberton Bay. "I know that not all pirates are fond of the Enchantress, and her rules make plundering treasure rather difficult, but the VNHLP believes that disagreements are best resolved through duels, battles, or discussions over grog. Causing someone to disappear is not endorsed by the League's official handbook." Any pirates with information about the Enchantress's whereabouts are advised to contact Captain Blacktooth immediately.

∾

COMPETITION RESULTS. Our Midsummer's Eve picnic last night was a swashbuckling success! We are pleased to report that Burly Bruce McCorkle won the hardtack-eatin' contest, eating thirty-three squares of hardtack in ten minutes. The crew of the dread ship *Matilda* won the swimmin' relay, and the VNHLP's membership coordinator, One-Legged Jones, emerged victorious in the one-legged race.

CHAPTER FIVE

THE ROAD TO Pemberton Bay stretched wide enough for Hilary, Charlie, and Claire to walk side by side. Hilary's cutlass bounced against her leg in time to the notes from Claire's tin whistle, and the gargoyle sang along with gusto in his bag. As they walked, Pemberton's grand shops and stately homes gave way to hillocks and pine groves, and the pirates soon found themselves on a lonely little bend of road where the trees stood in clusters like gossiping schoolgirls.

It seemed to Hilary that a good pirate captain should take care of her mates, so she pulled a corked glass bottle of water from her bag and passed it around as they walked.

"Much appreciated," said the gargoyle, who had managed to take a few sips of water before it began to dribble down his snout. "My voice was starting to go all gravelly."

"I'm sorry I don't have anything to eat," said Hilary. It had been far too many hours since breakfast, and although Miss Greyson had given them a few squares of hardtack wrapped in a handkerchief, Hilary had split the last piece with the gargoyle the day before. "I suppose I could magic something up," she said, "though it would have to be small." After the incident with the porridge bowl, she had no intention of asking her magic coin for anything larger than a lump of cheese—and perhaps some bread to go with it.

"Oh!" said Claire. "Would you mind terribly if I tried? I've finally got a magic piece of my own!" She set down her traveling case and pulled out a gleaming golden crochet hook, which she held in the air like a trophy. "Truthfully," she said, "I haven't been allowed to use it yet. Our magic lessons at school just began last week, you see, and it's been nothing but dry old theory so far. But how difficult can it possibly be to conjure up a luncheon?"

Before Hilary could get a word in edgewise, Claire pointed her crochet hook toward the sky. "Magic," she said, "please bring me a tray of egg sandwiches"—she looked down at the gargoyle—"and a small bowl of spiders."

As Hilary watched, the crochet hook quivered in Claire's hand. It twitched to the right and to the left. "Is it working?" the gargoyle asked. "I don't see any spiders."

He'd hardly finished speaking when a ball of light—or was it something even brighter and fiercer than light?—flared up around Claire's crochet hook so furiously that Hilary could hardly look at it. Then a tremendous bang shook the trees to their very roots, and the hook exploded.

Hilary dove to the ground and covered the gargoyle's head with her hands as bits of crochet hook clattered down on the cobblestones. Claire yelped, Charlie cursed very loudly indeed, and the air around them took on a damp, singed smell, like bonfire smoke after rain. When Hilary felt sure she was no longer being peppered by stray bits of magic, she looked up at Claire, who was still standing upright, staring at her hand and wobbling slowly from side to side.

"Are you all right?" Hilary scrambled to her feet. "Charlie, help me steady her." Hilary held one of Claire's elbows, and Charlie held the other, and together they guided her to the side of the road, where she sat down on a pine-tree stump and blinked several times in a row.

"I'm fine," she said at last. "I believe I've burned my hand—but not too badly." The fingers that she'd used to hold the crochet hook were red; Hilary dug a handkerchief from her bag and wrapped it around Claire's hand. "That's not what's supposed to happen," Claire said shakily. "Is it?"

"No," said Hilary, "it's certainly not. I've never heard of a magic piece exploding before." She looked over at

Charlie. "Has this happened to anyone who's gotten magic from Jasper?"

"I don't think so." Charlie must have been badly shaken, for he looked as serious as Hilary had ever seen him. "I didn't even know it was possible."

The gargoyle shuddered. "I don't like it one bit."

"Well, I suppose that's just perfect," said Claire. "I'm the only girl in Augusta who can't use magic properly, my crochet hook is blown to bits, and I don't believe I'll ever have a hope of entering High Society." She buried her head in her hands. "And to top it off, we still don't have our sandwiches."

That, at least, was something Hilary could fix. She pulled out her magic coin and asked as politely as she could for a tray of sandwiches, which appeared promptly and without any fuss. With their crustless edges and dainty fillings, the sandwiches were hardly suitable for a group of bold and daring pirates, but Hilary was too hungry to care, and by the time she'd eaten three, her mood had improved considerably. "If you're feeling all right, Claire," she said, "we'd better hurry along. I'd prefer not to run into any queen's inspectors on Cannonball Jack's doorstep."

CONJURING UP THE plate of sandwiches had taken more of Hilary's strength than she'd realized, and to make matters worse, she could feel her feet beginning to blister in her boots as she marched along. Hilary reminded herself quite sternly that a true pirate wasn't bothered by such small inconveniences; she sincerely doubted that Captain Black-tooth had ever allowed a mere blister to slow him down. Still, she was nearly ready to abandon her boots altogether by the time they reached a wooden signpost that read, in carefully painted blue letters:

Pemberton Bay
1 MILE

DANGER!
HIGH TIDES AND SCALLYWAGS AHEAD
NO MISS PIMM'S GIRLS BEYOND THIS POINT

Claire studied the sign and frowned. Then she turned her cardigan inside out and scrunched her hair into knots. "That's better," she said. "No one shall know I'm a Miss Pimm's girl now."

Just past the signpost, the road rushed downhill toward the stretched and rumpled sea. Dozens of boats in every size and color bobbed on the waves, and even more were tied up along the docks, where they rocked back and forth like a small floating village. The gargoyle peered out from his bag and sniffed the air. "That," he said happily, "is the smell of adventure!" He thought for a moment. "And fish."

With the spare spyglass she'd swiped from Jasper's quarters, Hilary scanned the bay for a glimpse of Cannonball

Jack's houseboat. She had visited the *Blunderbuss* several months earlier, when Miss Greyson had insisted on delivering holiday cakes to all their friends and relations, but she would have recognized the gleaming black ship at the far end of the docks even if she'd never seen it before in her life: its skull-and-crossbones flags were wreathed in smoke, and a cascade of cannonballs flew from its deck, nearly scraping the underbellies of passing seagulls before splashing into the sea. Charlie raised his eyebrows, and Claire clasped her hands to her chest.

"Oh, good," said Hilary. "Cannonball Jack must be at home."

Half a dozen more cannonballs burst forth from the *Blunderbuss* as the pirates hurried down the hill. The gargoyle said he hoped that no one would mistake *him* for a cannonball, for he didn't think he'd enjoy plummeting into the sea. "Cannonball Jack wouldn't do any such thing," Hilary reassured him. "I feel almost sure he's not a villain, and even if he is— Oh, *drat*."

There, directly in front of her, was a red-jacketed queen's inspector. He was crouched on his knees in the middle of the road—a ridiculous place to crouch, in Hilary's opinion—and he seemed to be studying the cobblestones through his magnifying glass.

"There are loads more of them," said Claire. "Look." She pointed down to the shoreline, where five more gentlemen in red jackets were crawling about.

Hilary glanced over at the *Blunderbuss*, but the inspectors clearly hadn't discovered it yet. Then she marched up to the closest inspector, whose nose was nearly touching the cobblestones by now. "Whatever are you doing?" she asked.

The inspector jumped and dropped his magnifying glass to the ground, where it shattered. "Stay back, scallywag!" he said. "You've broken my glass, but you won't break my bones!"

"Of course I won't," said Hilary. "What would be the point of that?"

"You are a pirate, aren't you?" The inspector frowned and studied Hilary through a shard of magnifying glass. "Are you by any chance Cannonball Jack?"

The gargoyle buried himself in Hilary's bag, but even the canvas couldn't muffle his snorts of laughter.

"No," said Hilary, "I'm afraid I'm not Cannonball Jack, and neither are my mates."

"Are you sure?" the inspector asked. "We're supposed to find a fearsome pirate by that name and bring him back to Pemberton for questioning, but I haven't seen any sign of him at all."

"How silly!" said Claire. "Staring at the road isn't likely to do you a bit of good. Why aren't you looking in pirate ships?"

The inspector closed his eyes as though Claire were an irritation to be borne with as much patience as possible.

"Little girl," he said, "it's clear that you don't possess the powers of deduction. I assure you that our methods are both modern and effective."

Hilary rolled her eyes. If all the queen's inspectors were this foolish, they wouldn't be able to find the Enchantress unless she placed herself directly under their magnifying glasses. All they seemed to be good for, in fact, was getting in Hilary's way. "I'd be happy to direct you to Cannonball Jack's ship, sir," she said, "but I'm afraid it's not in this bay. It's a good walk from here, just south of the fish market." She pointed back up the hill, well away from the *Blunderbuss*. "You'd better let the other inspectors know. Perhaps one of them will let you borrow his glass."

Without so much as a nod of thanks, the inspector leaped up and went to gather his companions. A few moments later, all six inspectors hurried by them, waving their dusting brushes and looking very confident indeed.

"Well done, Terror," said Charlie. "That should keep them occupied for a few hours at least."

Hilary gave her mates a little bow. "It's a shame," she said, "that no one seems to have warned the inspectors that pirates lie."

ONCE THE INSPECTORS had disappeared over the hill, the pirates made their way down the docks to the *Blunderbuss*. Smoke still billowed from the deck, making it rather difficult to see the ship's cheerful checked curtains and the window boxes planted with wildflowers. A large copper bell hung next to the door, and under it was a neatly printed sign that said PLEASE RING AN' ANNOUNCE YERSELF.

"Well," said Charlie, "that's surprisingly civilized."

"We'd better do as he asks," said Claire. "He seems to have a great many cannons."

Hilary rang the bell. Then she cleared her throat and cupped her hands around her mouth. "Ahoy!" she called over the din of the cannons. "The Terror of the Southlands has come for a visit!"

The gargoyle poked her with his tail. "Ahem," he said.

"Sorry," said Hilary. "I mean, the Terror of the Southlands and her gargoyle."

"And her mates," Charlie pointed out.

"Oh, very well," said Hilary. "And her mates!" She dearly hoped Cannonball Jack would answer his doorbell before someone else came along and demanded to be announced.

The cannon blasts stopped, and there was a good deal of stomping. Then the houseboat door flew open. Hilary felt her boots leave the deck as Cannonball Jack wrapped her in a hearty and gunpowder-scented embrace.

"Well, blast me buckles," he bellowed, setting Hilary back down with a solid thump. "If it isn't the Terror." He stepped back and tugged his eye patch up to his forehead. "Ye be a finer sight to see than a parrot on a bowsprit. And

I see ye brought yer mates along. Any friend o' the Terror is a friend o' mine." He bowed to Claire, tipped his hat to the gargoyle, and extended his hook to Charlie, who shook it gingerly.

Cannonball Jack looked every inch a pirate, from the broad plume of his hat feather to the toes of his boots, but there were shadows under his eyes, as though he hadn't slept soundly, and his fine ruffled shirt was wrinkled and worn. He brushed himself off with his hook and rolled up his sleeves. "I've been doin' a bit of blastin'," he said by way of explanation. "Would ye care to come with me? 'Twould be helpful to have more scallywags to man the cannons."

Cannonball Jack led them around to the gun deck, where he began to stuff the nearest cannon with bits of paper and quite a lot of gunpowder. As he worked, Hilary did her best to look through the *Blunderbuss*'s portholes. She couldn't see any sign of Miss Pimm, but the air was so thick with smoke that it was hard to be certain.

"Are you sure this is entirely safe?" Claire whispered as Cannonball Jack struck a match on the sole of his boot and lit the cannon's fuse. "What if he truly did kidnap Miss Pimm? What if he's already blasted her to bits?"

Cannonball Jack spun around. "Did ye say Miss Pimm?"

At that moment, the cannon went off with a bang. A great cloud of gunpowder filled the air, and the cannonball sailed into the harbor, where it splashed down near a young couple in a flimsy green rowboat. The drenched young woman shook her parasol in the *Blunderbuss's* direction, but Cannonball Jack didn't seem to notice; instead he stared at Claire.

"I asked ye a question, me hearty," he said, and his eyes narrowed. "Did ye utter the name of Miss Eugenia Pimm?"

Claire looked far too terrified to speak another word, so Hilary stepped forward. "Miss Pimm's gone missing," she said, "and we're trying to find her. If she's here, you'd better let us know at once."

Cannonball Jack turned his stare toward Hilary. "So that's why ye've come," he said. "I wondered." He put his good hand on Hilary's shoulder. "I'm sorry, Terror. Eugenia's not here. I wish she were—but perhaps ye'd better come inside."

INSIDE THE *BLUNDERBUSS'S* buttercup-yellow cabin, Cannonball Jack settled himself in a comfortable armchair and put his peg leg up on the footrest. Hilary, Charlie, and Claire balanced on overturned grog barrels, and the gargoyle nestled on a pillow that Cannonball Jack had set down for him. Every so often, feathers floated out of it from the places where Cannonball Jack had pierced it with his hook.

Cannonball Jack himself seemed distressed indeed, and Hilary was not sure how to comfort a pirate without insulting his fearsomeness. "Would you like another piece of shortbread?" she asked, passing the platter of cookies that Cannonball Jack had set out for them.

"Aye," he said miserably. He munched on the shortbread. "Eugenia's very fond of sweets, ye know. We get together once a month fer dinner, an' she always has at least two bowls o' chocolate mousse. 'Tis me own recipe," he added, "with a pinch o' sea salt an' just a hint o' gunpowder."

Hilary could hardly imagine the prim and proper Enchantress sitting down to dine with a pirate, let alone accepting extra helpings of the pirate's dessert. "I had no idea you and Miss Pimm were such close acquaintances," she said.

"Aye, we've been good friends since we met at Jasper's weddin'. I like the chance to cook more than the usual hardtack an' jam, an' Eugenia wanted to know more about pirates. She was concerned, ye see. She knew well enough that plenty o' scallywags didn't care fer her, an' she asked me to tell her what they were sayin' about her on the High Seas." Cannonball Jack looked fairly abashed at this. "I know it's not piratical to share what yer mates tell ye in confidence, but none o' them is as loyal a friend as Eugenia—and none o' them has ever complimented me chocolate mousse."

Hilary tipped her grog barrel forward. "What were the scallywags saying about Miss Pimm?"

"'Twas nothin' out o' the ordinary, fer the most part.

Pirates don't much like Enchantresses, ye know. Havin' a High Society lady in charge of yer treasure can be hard on a buccaneer's pride." Cannonball Jack shrugged. "But I think Eugenia was more worried about the High Society folk. That blasted Admiral Westfield——" Cannonball Jack stopped abruptly and bit down on his shortbread. "Apologies, Hilary; I know he be yer father."

Hilary looked fiercely at her knees. "It's all right."

"In any case," said Cannonball Jack, "no one's ever found a good bit o' the magic he stole. They won't let him out o' the Dungeons, o' course, but Miss Pimm thought he might have accomplices. Other High Society folk, I mean, who still want lots o' magic fer themselves. Those folk don't care fer her either, an' they'd prefer to go without an Enchantress altogether."

Charlie nodded. "I'll bet they're the ones who've made her disappear," he said.

"Aye, perhaps." Cannonball Jack brushed the shortbread crumbs from his beard. "All I can say fer sure is that Eugenia never showed up fer dinner last night. I'd made me best butterscotch puddin' an' everything. After a while, I went out to the road to look fer her—she usually walked here, ye see. 'Twas awfully chilly last night, though, an' a carriage nearly ran me over, so I came back aboard the *Blunderbuss* soon enough. This mornin' I walked up to Pemberton an' searched her rooms, but I couldn't find her anywhere." He cleared his throat. "An' that's not the worst part. The postal courier delivered this note a few hours ago. It put me in such a damp mood that I had to do some blastin' to distract meself." He reached into the pocket of his breeches and pulled out a folded piece of heavy notepaper, which he handed to Hilary. "Ye'd better read it, Terror. I can't look at the thing."

Hilary took the notepaper from him and unfolded it. The message inside was quite short, and written in an elegant hand:

❂❂❂❂❂❂❂❂❂❂❂❂❂❂❂❂❂❂❂❂❂❂❂❂❂❂❂❂❂

Dear Cannonball Jack,

By now, you will have discovered that Miss Eugenia Pimm has disappeared. Did she lose her way on the road, perhaps? Did she set off for a relaxing week at the seashore? No! She was kidnapped—and we are the kidnappers.

You do not seem to be an entirely foolish pirate, so we feel confident that you will follow our instructions. If you want your friend to remain unharmed, you must not tell anyone what you saw last night. Perhaps you saw nothing. That would please us immensely. If you spied anything unusual, however, we are sure you will be wise enough to stay quiet. You don't wish to cause

Miss Pimm any discomfort, do you?

Now that we have introduced ourselves, you may be planning to show this note to the authorities, or to go in search of Miss Pimm yourself. If you attempt any such thing, however, you shall soon become the main course in a sea monster's luncheon. You may find it difficult to hold your tongue, but rest assured that we shall make ourselves known to all of Augusta when the time is ripe.

With regrets for spoiling your dinner plans,
The Mutineers

❖❖❖❖❖❖❖❖❖❖❖❖❖❖❖❖❖❖❖❖❖❖❖❖❖❖

By the time Hilary finished reading the letter aloud, the *Blunderbuss* had gone as still and silent as the air after a cannonball blast. Charlie twisted his hat in his hands, Claire swayed back and forth on her grog barrel, the gargoyle blinked furiously, and Cannonball Jack's lower lip was quivering. "The scallywags must think I saw 'em take Eugenia," he said, "but I didn't see a thing, I swear!"

Hilary felt as though a piece of shortbread had gotten lodged in her throat and no amount of coughing would loosen it. She examined the letter once more, trying to find the faintest glimmer of hope in the villains' note.

"At least now we're certain that Miss Pimm has been kidnapped," she said, "and what's more, we know who the villains are—or we've got their name, at least. They can't be too difficult to track down, can they?"

But Cannonball Jack shook his head. "I be sorry to say I've never heard o' them. I've met many a rogue on the High Seas, but none o' them be named the Mutineers." He thought for a moment. "Then again, none o' them left me their callin' cards, so I can't say fer sure what their names were."

"I haven't heard of them either," said Charlie. "Jasper's never mentioned them, and you know how he's always going on about all the villains he'd like to defeat in battle."

Hilary frowned. "Well, in that case—"

"In that case," the gargoyle cried, "we'll never find Miss Pimm! Oh, I can't bear to think about it." He buried his head in his pillow.

"Don't ye be worryin', little beast." Cannonball Jack bent down to stroke the gargoyle's wings. "The Terror will rescue Eugenia an' make those scallywags walk the plank. Be that right, Terror?"

Hilary wished she felt as confident as Cannonball Jack did. Miss Pimm seemed to be caught up in even more peril than Hilary had expected—but the more perilous Miss Pimm's situation was, the more she needed Hilary's help. And despite what Captain Blacktooth and his mates might think, Hilary was not the sort of pirate who backed away from a challenge. "Of course I'll rescue her," she said. "Perhaps these Mutineers won't be so easy to find, but we'll find them anyway—and we'll defeat them, too. A soggy band of Mutineers is no match for the most fearsome pirates on the High Seas." She nodded firmly at Charlie and Claire, and they nodded back, though neither of them looked entirely convinced of their own fearsomeness.

"There, gargoyle. Did ye hear that?" Cannonball Jack gave Hilary a golden-toothed grin. "I know the Terror won't let us down."

--------------------- ◇ ◇ ◇ ◇ ◇ ---------------------

PIRATE HILARY WESTFIELD
TERROR OF THE SOUTHLANDS
◇ ◇ ◇ ◇ ◇

Dear Miss Greyson,

We have arrived in Pemberton at last, and I have finally grabbed a spare moment to write. I fear, however, that we have not been able to help Miss Pimm overcome any sort of peril, for she has been kidnapped! I suppose you have read all about the crime in the papers by now, but you may not yet know that Miss Pimm has been whisked away by a group of villains calling themselves the Mutineers.

As mutiny usually involves stranding one's captain on a deserted island and commandeering his ship, and as it does not usually involve capturing an Enchantress in the process, I can't imagine who these villains might be or what they might be planning. I must admit, however, that they have chosen a sufficiently chilling name for their organization. It sends a thrill down my spine just to write it.

Since I can't assist Miss Pimm, I have decided to rescue her instead. I don't intend to let a band of Mutineers roam freely across the kingdom snatching up my acquaintances, and I am hoping the VNHLP will be impressed with me when I succeed. You must be fretting at this news, but I assure you we are safe, for Cannonball Jack has let us spend the night on his houseboat. From here we shall go in search of the Mutineers. Do you have any idea where Mutineers might lurk?

I hope you will not be too cross with me, but I have a favor to ask. Could you order your golden crochet hook to point you in Miss Pimm's direction, and could you let me know the results? I know you are very good at using magic to find people, since you persist in finding me even when I don't care to be found. I would use my own magic piece to do this if I could, but I don't have the strength for such a large enchantment, and you have the strongest magical talent of anyone I know—aside from Miss Pimm, of course—so I believe you have the best chance of discovering something useful.

(While we are on the subject of magic, do you know what might cause a magic piece to explode in one's hand? Please don't worry; I am inquiring for a friend.)

Charlie has made us a hearty dinner of fish stew, Claire has tucked Cannonball Jack into bed, and the gargoyle is impatient for me to help him write his memoirs, so I must dash. I shall be hot on the trail of the Mutineers by the time you receive this letter, but I hope you will write back to me soon. With any luck, the postal courier will be able to find me.

Arr!, and lots of love from
Hilary

◇ ◇ ◇ ◇ ◇

THE VERY NEARLY HONORABLE LEAGUE OF PIRATES
Servin' the High Seas for 153 Years
THE RENEGADE
CABIN OF THE PRESIDENT

✦ ✦ ✦ ✦ ✦

NOTICE OF UNPIRATICAL BEHAVIOR

Pirate Westfield:

When you left my ship last week, I believed we had reached an understanding regarding your behavior. You had agreed to regain your good standing in the League by performing one of the bold and daring tasks I had personally selected for you. Perhaps you can imagine my concern, then, when I read in the most recent Picaroon that you and your questionably fearsome crew are not setting out to slay the Summerstead sea monster or defeat a pirate king in battle. Instead, you have chosen to prove your worth by rescuing the missing Enchantress.

Pirate Westfield, let me be frank. While the Enchantress's disappearance is most alarming, it is not a matter fit to be handled by pirates. What can a buccaneer like you possibly know about rescuing missing Enchantresses? (As I hope you are already aware, pirates are not traditionally known for their rescuing skills, nor do they go out of their way to assist government officials.) I understand that you care for Miss Pimm, but for the sake of your reputation as well as my own, I must recommend

that you abandon this adventure. Perform one of the tasks
I assigned you, and leave the Enchantress's recovery in the
capable hands of the queen's inspectors.

Then there is the matter of your crew. I am pleased
to hear that at least one of your companions is a pirate
of the League, though I am sorry to say his name does not
strike much fear in the hearts of scallywags across the High
Seas. Your other companions, a schoolgirl and a gargoyle,
are not included on the VNHLP's list of approved crew
members. (Might I suggest a rough-voiced ship's cook and
a bedraggled cabin boy as suitable replacements?) To make
matters worse, you have been traveling by foot and by
carriage rather than by ship, and you have not yet obtained
a parrot. I hope you will scrounge up a seaworthy vessel as
soon as possible—and do you think you could convince your
gargoyle to perch on your shoulder and answer to the name
of Polly?

I look forward to the moment when you deliver a sea
monster's head to my desk, Pirate Westfield, but since that
moment has not yet arrived, I must give you your

[ ] first warning [x] second warning [ ] third warning

Arr!
Captain Rupert Blacktooth
President, VNHLP

CHAPTER SIX

"**B**LAST!" SAID HILARY. She folded up Captain Blacktooth's letter and slammed her fist down on
Cannonball Jack's dining table, sending soggy lumps of
porridge sailing across the cabin. "I believe I'd like to sink
the *Renegade* straight into a sea monster's gullet."

The gargoyle looked up from his plate of silk moths.
"What's the matter?" he asked. "What did Captain Blacktooth say? And can someone get this porridge off my
snout?"

"I'm sorry, gargoyle." Hilary wiped his snout clean with
a bit of rag that Cannonball Jack had passed to her. "It's just
that Captain Blacktooth doesn't seem to be impressed by

our boldness and daring. He says that rescuing Enchant-resses simply isn't done in the pirate community. And he wants me to hire a bedraggled cabin boy instead of Claire!" The gargoyle looked so horrified at this news that Hilary decided not to mention what Captain Blacktooth had said about obtaining a parrot.

Across the table, Claire stuck her spoon straight up in her porridge. "Well, I never!" she said. "I'm perfectly capable of being bedraggled, if that's what this Blacktooth person prefers. And I should like to see a cabin boy faint on command or jab his enemies with an embroidery needle."

"Don't worry," said Hilary; "I don't intend to replace you. And I won't give up searching for Miss Pimm just because some overstuffed pirate gentleman thinks I won't succeed." Hilary scowled at a grayish lump of porridge that was beginning to harden on the table. "I hoped Captain Blacktooth would see that rescuing a friend is a perfectly piratical thing to do, but now I suppose I'll have to write to him to explain."

Charlie had taken the letter from Hilary's hand, and his face turned as hard as the porridge as he read it. "So he thinks my name doesn't strike fear in the hearts of scallywags, does he? He'd better think again." Charlie brandished his spoon like a sword. "Do you think I could beat old Blacktooth in a duel? I could, couldn't I?"

"Aye, maybe so," said Cannonball Jack, "but not with that contraption." He plucked the spoon from Charlie's hand and began to scrape porridge lumps off the table. "Don't ye be mindin' Captain Blacktooth, Terror. He may be a bit overstuffed, as ye say, but he be a good captain all the same. Why, I had him on the *Blunderbuss* for dinner just a few weeks ago, an' he was tellin' me how much he admired yer guts. He said he felt awfully bad about callin' ye in for a scoldin'."

Hilary crossed her arms. "Then it's a shame he felt obliged to scold me anyway."

"'Tisn't easy bein' president of a league of rogues and rapscallions," said Cannonball Jack. "But I think he made a mistake askin' you to give up on findin' Miss Pimm. Ye go ahead an' show him what ye can do, an' I'll stick up for ye if ye get in trouble."

Cannonball Jack was clearing the breakfast dishes from the table when a familiar shade of red caught Hilary's eye. She pushed aside the checked curtains and pressed her nose to the porthole window. Even without her spyglass, she could see the queen's inspectors marching down the hill toward the harbor. There were only two of them this morning, but they traveled quickly, not stopping once to wave their magnifying glasses or flick their dusting brushes. Hilary sighed. "The queen's inspectors are heading this way," she said when Cannonball Jack came back from the galley. "I suppose they were bound to find you eventually."

Cannonball Jack sat down heavily on a grog barrel.

"An' what would the inspectors want with me?"

"They think you kidnapped Miss Pimm," said Hilary. "You're the only suspect on their list, and they want to bring you in for questioning."

"Let 'em ask me whatever they'd like," said Cannonball Jack. "I'll answer 'em with cannons."

Claire had been watching the inspectors' progress through her own porthole, and now she frowned. "I can't believe they still don't know where the *Blunderbuss* is. They've just gone into that tall blue building at the edge of the bay."

"The Eaglet?" Cannonball Jack looked where Claire was pointing. "Aye, that be our local guesthouse. Maybe yer inspectors have found themselves a new scallywag to bother."

Hilary kept watch for a good ten minutes, but the inspectors didn't emerge from the Eaglet. "Do you think they've truly found something in there?"

Charlie shrugged. "They're probably dusting every inch of the place."

"Or taking a nap," the gargoyle suggested.

"Perhaps," said Hilary, "but I'd still like to know what's going on. I believe I'd be mortified if Mr. Hastings's men managed to track down the Mutineers before I did." She stood up and cleared the porridge bowls from the table. "Shall we pay the inspectors a visit, then?"

Charlie and Claire agreed that a trip to the Eaglet

couldn't do any harm, so they gathered their things and thanked Cannonball Jack for his hospitality. "Are ye sure ye don't want me to come along?" he asked as he walked them down the gangplank. "I'd like to ask those inspectors why they're callin' me a suspicious person. Don't they know I'd never hurt a hair on Eugenia's head?"

"I don't think they care much for pirates," Hilary said. "And I wish you could come with us, but it's far too dangerous. If the inspectors discover who you are, they're sure to toss you in the Dungeons—and if the Mutineers hear you've been poking about in their business, they might carry out their threats." The very thought made Hilary's stomach squirm.

"All right, Terror," said Cannonball Jack. "I'll take the *Blunderbuss* out to sea fer a few days, then, till this storm blows over. But if I can't come with ye, let me give ye this." He pressed a small leather pouch into her hand. "Ye might be needin' these fer rescuin' Eugenia."

Hilary untied the pouch's strings and looked inside. A small pile of golden coins shone up at her, and the gargoyle's ears twitched the way they always did when he came close to bits of magic. "But this is your treasure," Hilary said. "Won't you need it yourself?"

"I've got plenty more where that came from, though I can't be tellin' ye where I've buried it, o' course." Cannonball Jack raised his eye patch and winked. "I've put some o' me shortbread in the pouch, too, in case ye be needin' a snack."

Cannonball Jack put out his hand for Hilary to shake, but Hilary ignored it and gave him a thoroughly unpiratical hug instead. "Thank you," she said. "You're a kind pirate—though I'd never smudge your reputation by letting anyone know it. I'll write to you if we have any news, and if those Mutineers give you trouble, I hope you blast them to smithereens."

THE PIRATES ARRIVED at the Eaglet just as the queen's inspectors were coming out the door. When the inspectors spotted Hilary and her crew, their faces grew tense. Hilary recognized one of the gentlemen as the inspector she'd talked to on the Pemberton road the day before, for his magnifying glass had been hastily mended, and his expression was particularly furious.

"Go away, pirates!" he said. "If you've come to threaten our witness, you're too late. Mr. Sturgeon and I have already conducted our final interview."

"Your witness?" Hilary raised her eyebrows at Charlie and Claire. "Do you mean that the person who saw Miss Pimm disappear is here at the Eaglet?"

The inspector named Sturgeon scowled. "Certainly not," he said.

"And she'll be leaving soon," his partner added.

Hilary grinned. "I'd be interested in speaking to your witness," she said, "so if you'd please step aside—"

But Mr. Sturgeon blocked her way. "You're not allowed

in, pirate," he said. "Neither are those other children." He waved his hand at Charlie and Claire, who looked quite murderous. "And if that vicious stone creature doesn't stop trying to bite my fingers, I'll have the lot of you thrown in the Dungeons."

The gargoyle bared his teeth. "Fine," he said as he retreated into Hilary's bag, "but you won't like what I have to say about you in my memoirs."

Claire grabbed Hilary's shoulder. "We can't just leave, can we? When the witness might be able to tell us what happened to Miss Pimm?"

"Of course not," said Hilary. "Surrendering is hardly piratical. But let me think for a moment." She pulled Cannonball Jack's pouch of coins from her bag and weighed it in her hand.

Charlie tugged at the collar of his pirate coat. "What are you thinking of, Terror?"

"There's no need to worry, Pirate Dove," Hilary said. "I'm almost sure this plan will work."

"Almost?" said Charlie.

Hilary steadied herself, shook a magic coin into her palm, and whispered a few words so the queen's inspectors couldn't overhear. The inspectors fumbled for their own magic pieces, but they were too late: to Hilary's delight, her cutlass floated out of its sheath and hovered in front of the inspectors, directing its point at their chests when they attempted to move. Claire clapped her hands, and even Charlie looked very nearly impressed.

Hilary's arms felt weak from the magic, and her breath was strained, but she had more than enough strength left to grin. "If you move an inch from this spot," she told the inspectors, "or if you try to stop us in any way, my cutlass will run you through, so I suggest you stay put until I come back to collect it." The inspectors began to nod, but they stopped at once when the cutlass moved closer to their heads. "I'll give the witness your best regards."

ONCE THE PIRATES were safely inside the Eaglet, Hilary leaned against the wall to catch her breath. "That was brilliant!" Claire cried. "And you didn't make anything explode! I'm simply seething with jealousy."

"I'm impressed you had enough strength to manage it," said Charlie. "I'd think running someone through would take an awful lot of magic."

"I may have exaggerated a bit," Hilary admitted. "All I asked the cutlass to do was hover in front of the inspectors in a menacing sort of way—but I hope they'll be too nervous to test its limits." She stood up straight and tucked her magic coins away. "Now, do you see anyone here who looks like a witness?"

The small downstairs room was empty except for the harried-looking landlady, who made no secret of sighing as the pirates approached. "First queen's inspectors," she said, "and now pirates. I do hope you're not here to do any pillaging. I won't allow the Eaglet to gain a reputation for pirate attacks; it would attract quite the wrong sort of crowd."

Hilary assured the landlady that her pirate crew wasn't the pillaging sort. "Actually," she said, "we're here to see the same young lady the inspectors just visited. Can you tell us where she is?"

The landlady looked through a window. "Miss Tilbury is about to depart," she said, "but if you hurry, I believe you'll be able to catch her in the back drive."

Claire stared at her. "Did you say Miss Tilbury?"

"That's correct," said the landlady. "Miss Philomena Tilbury."

The color drained from Claire's face, and Hilary could hardly blame her. Philomena Tilbury may have been from one of the noblest families in Augusta, but she had been the least pleasant student at Miss Pimm's, and she'd particularly enjoyed threatening the other girls with her magic crochet hook. She had taken an immediate dislike to Claire, who was attending Miss Pimm's on scholarship, and she wasn't much fonder of Hilary.

"*Philomena* is the witness?" Claire cried as the pirates hurried around to the back of the Eaglet. "We'd just gotten rid of her at last! She turned seventeen in the spring and left school to enter High Society. Whatever is she doing back in Pemberton?"

"I don't know," said Hilary, "but I'd very much like to

find out." She rounded the corner, where a black carriage gilded with the Tilbury crest stood waiting in the lane. Four elegant, cream-colored horses chewed politely on carrots as a coachman in peacock-blue livery struggled to lift half a dozen trunks, carpetbags, and packages into the carriage. When Hilary cleared her throat, the coachman jumped, and a jumble of hatboxes crashed to the ground around him.

The carriage door swung open, and Philomena stepped out from behind it. "I've told you a hundred times, Lewis, that you must be more careful with my hats! If you insist upon tossing them to the ground, I shall have to tell Mama all about it, and the news will undoubtedly send her into a rage. But then I suppose one must not expect too much when one is traveling with one's second-best coachman."

"I'm ever so sorry, miss," said Lewis, who looked as if he would prefer to climb into one of Philomena's hatboxes and stay there until the danger had passed. "It's just— well, the pirates, miss, they startled me."

"Pirates?" Philomena turned to stare at Hilary. Her hair was drawn into a tight little bun, and her mouth was drawn into a tight little frown that only grew firmer as she took in the crowd in front of her.

"I'm afraid Lewis is right." Hilary set the gargoyle down on the ground, and the four pirates gathered around Philomena and the trembling Lewis. "It's been ages since we've seen each other, hasn't it? I'm so glad we were able to catch you before you left the Southlands."

"Miss Hilary Westfield," said Philomena. "Whatever do you think you're doing here?"

Hilary stepped forward, keeping one hand on her magic coins, for she had learned from her dueling lessons with Charlie that with certain opponents, it was best to be cautious. "We're searching for Miss Pimm," she said, "and we believe you know something about what's happened to her."

Philomena shot her a look of pure exasperation. "That's true," she said, "but I've already told the queen's inspectors everything I know, and I don't see why I should have to say a single word to pirates. Or to fishmongers' daughters," she added, aiming a sharp look at Claire. "Lewis, please send these intruders away at once."

Lewis shifted his weight from one foot to the other. "Er, miss," he said, "I believe one of them's got a sword. And I don't like the look of that little one with the wings."

"That's all right, Philomena," said Hilary. "Lewis doesn't have to send us away. If he does, I'll tell those queen's inspectors about how little you care for Miss Pimm. The last time we met, I believe you were furious at her for taking your magic crochet hook away. You flew into a rage and stomped out."

"And now," said Claire, "you turn up at the scene of poor Miss Pimm's disappearance. Don't you think the inspectors would find that suspicious?"

The gargoyle looked up at Philomena. "If she doesn't say anything," he said, "can I bite her? Oh, Hilary, *please*?"

Philomena squirmed and stepped away from the gargoyle's teeth. "Very well," she said. "I'll tell you exactly what I told the inspectors, if you pirates will promise to leave me alone after that. I've got to get back to Tilbury Park, and I've been delayed enough as it is."

Hilary nodded. "All right, then. What's happened to Miss Pimm?"

Philomena sat down on a hatbox. "I'd arranged to meet her yesterday morning at ten o'clock precisely. She was going to return my magic crochet hook to me. She'd kept it locked away all year—no thanks to the lot of you—but she'd finally agreed that I should be allowed to have a magic piece again. And I should be!" Philomena looked up from the hatbox. "I've put childish games aside now that I'm entering High Society, and why shouldn't I have a golden crochet hook just like any other Miss Pimm's girl?"

Claire tucked her burned hand into the pocket of her dress.

"In any case," said Philomena, "Lewis and I traveled down from Tilbury Park and arrived in Pemberton yesterday morning just before ten. I was relieved not to be late, for you know how much Miss Pimm values promptness. I waited outside her office, but she never appeared. At first I thought she'd been caught up in some bit of Enchantressing business, but then I saw a horrid, villainous pirate leaving her office. When he opened the door, I saw that Miss Pimm wasn't at her desk, and I knew at once that something simply terrible had happened, so I sent a message to the queen's inspectors immediately." She glared up at Hilary. "I swear to you, that's all I know. I haven't got a clue how that wretched pirate made Miss Pimm disappear, but I'm sure he's responsible."

"That wretched pirate," said Hilary, "happens to be a friend of ours—and a friend of Miss Pimm's as well. He's perfectly innocent. And in any case, Miss Pimm went missing on Friday night, not Saturday morning. Why would a villain return to the scene of the crime?"

Philomena frowned. Then she crossed her arms. "To hide the evidence, of course."

Hilary decided that leaving school had not done much to make Philomena less infuriating. On top of that, her story didn't seem to be the slightest bit helpful. She hadn't even been in Pemberton when Miss Pimm had disappeared! No wonder the inspectors' investigation was going so poorly. "Have you ever heard of a group of villains called the Mutineers?" Hilary asked.

Philomena wrinkled her nose. "I suppose that's one of your nasty pirate terms. Honestly, Miss Westfield, I'm shocked by your crude seafaring language. I can't imagine how disappointed your father would be if he heard you speaking in such a manner."

Hilary's fine pirate coat suddenly felt far too tight and

unbearably warm. Philomena was hardly kind at the best of times, but mentioning Admiral Westfield was heartless even for her. Hilary rolled up the sleeves of her coat and wished she hadn't left her cutlass floating in the air on the other side of the Eaglet. If she gave Philomena a hearty punch instead, would that be unpiratical?

"I've got a question," Charlie said. "If you only came to Pemberton for one day, why do you have so much luggage?" He poked at a parcel with the tip of his sword.

Philomena laughed and snatched the parcel away. "I'm sure a boy of your upbringing can't possibly imagine the amount of clothing one has to travel with if one doesn't want to look like a grubby commoner."

Charlie flinched.

"Ignore her, Pirate Dove," said Hilary. "You're perfectly right; even my dratted mama doesn't bring her entire wardrobe with her when she visits her friends for a few days." She looked back toward the Eaglet. "If I asked the landlady how long you've been staying here, Miss Tilbury, what would she tell me?"

Without a word, Philomena stood up from her hatbox. Lewis coughed as though he wished to say something, but Philomena glared at him and he looked down at his peacock-blue knees.

Hilary studied the pile of luggage. "I suspect that you've been here for at least a week. That means you were here in Pemberton on the very evening Miss Pimm disappeared."

Philomena looked furious, but she didn't deny it, and Hilary nearly broke into a jig right there in the lane. "You lied to us," she said, "and I'm sure you lied to the inspectors as well. Is that because you kidnapped Miss Pimm yourself?" Hilary took another step toward Philomena. "Are you a Mutineer?"

Charlie raised his sword, and the gargoyle bared his teeth. "Oh my," said Claire, tugging another row of stitches out of her cardigan.

"Stop!" cried Philomena. She looked around the lane and lowered her voice. "All right, you horrid pirates. It's true that I've been in Pemberton for days—but I swear I didn't kidnap Miss Pimm."

"Prove it," the gargoyle growled.

This seemed to be enough to terrify Lewis. "Perhaps you'd better tell them, miss?" he said. "About young Sir Feathering?"

Philomena looked as though she would like to step hard on Lewis's foot.

"Who's young Sir Feathering?" the gargoyle asked. "He's not a bird, is he?" The gargoyle was not at all fond of birds, for they had a tendency to perch on his head.

Claire clasped her hands together. "Surely you can't mean Sir *Nicholas* Feathering! The most eligible young gentleman in Augusta?" Her eyes went wide. "They say he's terribly rich and handsome."

"I don't care one bit about that," said Hilary. "What

does he have to do with the Mutineers?"

Philomena rolled her eyes. "Not a thing," she said, "but now that you pirates have stuck your noses into my business, I suppose I must make my confession." She straightened her spine and raised her chin to its best advantage. "I've been in Pemberton this week to prepare for my debut ball."

"Really?" said Hilary. "*That's* your confession?"

"Why, it's hardly news at all!" Claire said. "High Society has been buzzing about your debut for weeks."

"How kind of you to say so, Miss Dupree," said Philomena, looking anything but pleased. "What you must swear not to tell, however, is that during the ball, I shall announce my betrothal. I am marrying Sir Nicholas Feathering in a year's time."

Claire gaped at her. "The most eligible gentleman in Augusta is going to marry *you*?"

"An open mouth, Miss Dupree, is more suitable for herrings than for young ladies. My mama is simply dying to announce the news of our marriage in the grandest possible fashion, and if anyone discovers our plans before the ball, she'll most likely send me to the Dungeons herself." Philomena pressed her gloved fingers to her temples, as though the mere thought of her mama had summoned up a headache. "I've been spending the past week shopping for my trousseau; you must know how superior the Pemberton shops are to anything we've got in the Northlands."

Hilary and Claire both grudgingly admitted that this was the case, but Charlie looked skeptical. "I can't believe," he said to Hilary, "that she expects us to think she couldn't have kidnapped Miss Pimm because she was too busy shopping."

"I don't expect you to think any such thing," Philomena said. "But you said Miss Pimm disappeared on Friday evening. Well, I was dining with Sir Nicholas Feathering at the time, here at the Eaglet." She flushed, and for a moment she looked like nothing more than a nervous schoolgirl. "It was all perfectly proper, of course, but we had to slip past the landlady. If anyone had seen us dining unchaperoned, Mama would have had my head—just as I'll have all your heads if you tell a soul."

Hilary took a few steps back. Could Philomena be telling the truth? She did seem genuinely flustered, but if Hilary had learned one thing on the High Seas, it was the danger of taking a person at her word. "Perhaps," she said, "I'll pay Sir Nicholas a visit myself. If you're telling us a pack of lies, he should be able to clear up the matter in no time at all."

Philomena blanched. "Hilary Westfield, you'll do no such thing!"

"Really?" Hilary gave Philomena her most piratical stare. "Why not?"

"Because . . ." Philomena hesitated. "Because the Featherings are one of the finest families in Augusta, and I won't allow you to poke about in their affairs."

"A pirate," said Hilary, "may poke about wherever she wants to. And that's exactly what I intend to do, no matter if you care for it or not."

Philomena produced a hairpin from her reticule and jabbed at her bun so ferociously that the gargoyle hopped behind Hilary's legs. "Don't you dare say a word to Nicholas Feathering," she snapped. "It won't do you a bit of good. If there's anyone you ought to be suspicious of, it's that horrid old pirate friend of yours. I expect he wrote that threatening note from the Mutineers himself."

Philomena gave Hilary a triumphant little smile, but Hilary simply stared at her. "How did you know about the Mutineers' note?" she said. "I never mentioned it to you."

"She's a villain!" cried the gargoyle. "I knew it!"

"For heaven's sake, I'm no such thing." The smile had slipped off Philomena's face. "Everyone knows villains are always sending threatening notes to people, and I'm sure these Mutineers are no different." She climbed up into her carriage. "Now, I'd thank you all to hurry off to some leaky rowboat and leave me alone—forever, if you can manage it."

"What makes you think we'll do any such thing?" Hilary asked.

"If you don't," Philomena said, "I shall drive directly to Miss Pimm's and ask Inspector Hastings to arrest the lot of you. He's a terribly obliging gentleman." She slammed the carriage door shut. "Hurry up with my things, Lewis. We've wasted enough time already, and Mama will be furious if we're late."

Lewis nodded and stammered his apologies, and a few moments later the Tilbury carriage stormed away, leaving the pirates in an elegant and imposing cloud of dust.

"I do *not* like her," the gargoyle said.

Hilary scuffed at the dirt with her boot, kicking up a far less elegant dust cloud than the one the carriage had produced. "She seemed awfully suspicious," Hilary said, "but even if she *is* a Mutineer, we can't prove it, and we still haven't got any idea where Miss Pimm might be."

"Perhaps the landlady can help us," Claire said. But when they piled back into the Eaglet, the landlady proved to be no help at all. She hadn't noticed Miss Tilbury engaging in any sort of suspicious behavior, nor had she seen the Enchantress pass through the guesthouse. When Hilary asked if Miss Tilbury had gone out on Friday evening, the landlady stiffened and said quite firmly that she would not engage in conversation about her guests with a band of pirates, no matter how honorable those pirates might be.

"What now, Terror?" Charlie asked as the landlady shooed them out the front door. "Is there anyone else who might know what Philomena's been up to?"

Hilary was pleased to see that her cutlass was still hovering in front of the inspectors; she retrieved it from the air and waved it in the inspectors' direction a few times as they ran away down the lane. "I suppose we could speak to Sir Nicholas Feathering," she said at last. "Philomena looked absolutely terrified when I suggested it. If he was with her on the night Miss Pimm disappeared, perhaps he knows something useful."

Charlie nodded. "If Philomena doesn't want us to talk to this Feathering person, then it seems to me that he's exactly the right person to talk to." He sighed and dusted off his pirate hat. "Even if he *is* terribly rich and handsome."

"They say he lives in Feathering Keep," said Claire, blushing a bit. "I believe it's close to Queensport."

"Then we'll track him down at once," said Hilary. "And we'd better find a suitable pirate vessel for our journey. If we're not on board a magnificent ship when we rescue Miss Pimm, I'm sure Captain Blacktooth will still be disappointed."

Charlie grinned. "That won't be any trouble, Terror. If you're in need of a first-class galleon, I know exactly where to find one."

PIRATE HILARY WESTFIELD
TERROR OF THE SOUTHLANDS

◇ ◇ ◇ ◇ ◇

Dear Captain Blacktooth,

I understand that you are not the sort of pirate who often makes mistakes. When you accused me of unpiratical behavior in your most recent letter, however, I believe you were very much mistaken. I have been a model pirate ever since our meeting on the Renegade, and I hope that by the time you finish this letter, you will agree to take back your warning.

You are quite right that pirates are not traditionally known for rescuing Enchantresses, and I suppose I'm not exactly a traditional pirate. I have, however, been trying my best to follow the VNHLP Rules of Conduct. That's why I feel sure that assisting one's friends when they are in trouble is entirely appropriate behavior for any scallywag. Wouldn't you do anything you could to keep your own mates out of danger? And wouldn't you want to do battle against any villains who threatened them? Of course you would—you are a pirate! Though Miss Pimm is not strictly one of my mates, she is a good friend, so rescuing her is a very piratical thing to do.

As for your suggestion that I leave the search in the capable hands of the queen's inspectors, all I can say is that I have seen the hands of several inspectors, and none of them looked very capable to me.

You should be pleased to hear that I've followed your orders to find a seaworthy vessel. My mates and I have traveled to Wimbly-on-the-Marsh, where we have located a most impressive ship; we shall be setting sail as soon as we make a few small repairs. I hope this will help you to see that I am every inch a pirate.

Arr!
Pirate Hilary Westfield, Terror of the Southlands

P.S. I'm sorry, sir, but the gargoyle would like me to tell you that anyone who tries to call him Polly will be lucky to escape alive.

———————— ◇ ◇ ◇ ◇ ◇ ————————

MISUSE OF MAGIC
ALARMINGLY ON THE RISE

QUEENSPORT, AUGUSTA—It has been less than a week since Miss Eugenia Pimm, Enchantress of the Northlands, disappeared from her Pemberton home without a trace, but the use of magic by the kingdom's citizens has already begun to get rather out of hand. Without the Enchantress's commanding voice pealing out across Augusta, all manner of magical pranks, crimes, and uproars have occurred. Two short days before the Little Shearwater Cabbage Festival, a person or persons unknown used magic to turn Lord Otto Braithwaite's most impressive cabbage a shocking shade of pink and shrink it down to the size of a pea. "That cabbage was sure to win the grand prize," Lord Otto lamented, "and now I can hardly see it! I'm afraid I'm not clever enough with magic to restore it to its proper size and color, but I believe I may still earn a ribbon for Most Unusual Cabbage. Still, I wish the Enchantress hadn't chosen such an inconvenient moment to disappear. She would have given the scoundrel a stern talking-to, I'm sure."

Lord Otto's tale may have a fortunate ending, but that is not the case for the sad story of Miss Elsie Carter, who attended a masquerade ball last Saturday at Westfield House. Miss Carter engaged the attentions of a certain young High Society gentleman for the evening's first three dances, prompting a jealous guest to transform Miss Carter's turkey-feather headpiece into an actual turkey, which began pecking at Miss Carter's elaborate hairstyle without an ounce of concern for propriety or fashion. The High Society gentleman fled Miss Carter's company at once, and Miss Carter herself is suffering from a nasty headache. The young lady responsible for the vicious prank has not been identified, however, and the turkey managed to escape into the halls of Westfield House.

"My nerves are simply shattered," said Mrs. Ophelia Westfield, who climbed into her wardrobe after the incident of the turkey and spoke to our reporter from the other side of the door. "I never cared terribly much for that Enchantress, but I do wish she could help me capture the vicious beast that's been set loose in my house! I believe I hear it clucking at this very moment."

Mrs. Westfield may have reason to hope that the Enchantress will soon be recovered, for the Gazette has learned that her daughter, the pirate Hilary Westfield, has embarked upon a search for Miss Pimm. As the queen's inspectors have not yet located the Enchantress, all the kingdom's hopes for a return to polite society may hinge on Pirate Westfield's ability to rescue her as quickly as possible. Some citizens have even reported that they are beginning to miss the sound of the Enchantress's rhymes ringing out across the hills and valleys of Augusta. We wish Pirate Westfield well and look forward to celebrating her success—or mourning her failure, as the case may be.

ᘓᘓᘐᘐ ᘓᘓᘐᘐ *From the Humble Pen of* ᘓᘓᘐᘐ ᘓᘓᘐᘐ
ELOISE GREYSON

Dear Hilary,

Thank you for your letter. I must admit that I have had a few sleepless nights since I learned of your plan to rescue Miss Pimm. I know, however, that I am no longer your governess, so although I would dearly love to remind you to be careful, sharpen your sword, and eat a hearty breakfast before going into battle, I shall hold my tongue.

I am sorry to say that I can't be of much help to you regarding the identity of the Mutineers. I have never heard of them before, and all the reference books I consulted on the subject were entirely unhelpful. These Mutineers must be a rather new band of villains, for even the most recent edition of The Who's Who of Augustan Scoundrels *makes no mention of them.*

As you requested, I attempted to use my magic piece to search for Miss Pimm, but I'm afraid I had no luck with that task either. The crochet hook can only point me toward people who are close by, you see, and Miss Pimm must be quite far from Otterpool Harbor. For that, I rather envy her—it seems as though I have been moored here for ages! In the days since you left, three of Jasper's old crewmates have arrived to help me take care of the Pigeon. They make for entertaining company, but I am still quite cross because Jasper has not yet replied to any of my letters. (I have sent six.) He is a dear pirate, but an infuriating correspondent.

I look forward to hearing more news of your journey, Hilary, and I have every confidence that you shall bring Miss Pimm safely home. Please give my best wishes to your crew.

With love,
Miss Greyson

CHAPTER SEVEN

THE SHIP WAS called the *Squeaker,* and it was moored in the shallow cove behind Jasper's back garden. Charlie had certainly been joking when he'd called it a first-class galleon: it wasn't much larger than the *Pigeon*'s dinghy, its sails were torn and moth-eaten, and its hull badly needed painting. It was hardly the grand pirate ship Hilary had imagined, but she supposed that with a little work, it would do perfectly well for the voyage to Queensport.

For the next few days, Charlie painted and hammered. Hilary sanded and mended. Claire tried to use Cannonball Jack's magic coins to help them along, but she only succeeded in exploding four coins in a row. After that, she disappeared into Jasper's bungalow and, in a fit of sewing, produced an entirely new set of sails, though she still looked rather frustrated.

At last, though the *Squeaker* creaked and groaned at the slightest provocation, Hilary decided it was seaworthy enough. When the pirates set off from Little Herring Cove, the ship's fine new sails caught the breeze, and its Jolly Roger flapped so ominously that Hilary was quite sure no one on the High Seas would know it had once spent its life as Jasper's flowered dishcloth.

"Arr!" cried the gargoyle from his perch inside the fruit crate that Hilary had fashioned into a makeshift Gargoyle's Nest. "All fear the *Squeaker* and its daring pirate crew! All fear their sharp swords—and their even sharper teeth!" The gargoyle looked over his shoulder at Hilary. "Did that sound all right? Do you think it's impressive enough?"

"I think it's absolutely perfect. You'll have all the villains in Augusta diving under their bedclothes to hide from us." Hilary leaned forward to give the gargoyle a quick scratch behind the ears. The *Squeaker* was not exactly the most spacious pirate ship on the High Seas, and the Gargoyle's Nest was only an arm's length from the helm. There wasn't any room for a cabin, so they would have to sleep on the deck under the stars, and although there was a plank for villains to walk, it was a rather short one. Jasper hadn't had any spare cannons lying about, but Hilary had piled several armloads of cooking pots onto the *Squeaker* in the hopes that attacking ships would flee from the sight of a saucepan flying through the air in their direction. And Charlie had found a few pounds of hardtack, which were supposed to be used for breakfasts and suppers but could also serve as small, dense weapons in a pinch.

Although the *Squeaker* was nowhere near as grand as the *Renegade*—or even the *Pigeon*—Hilary was happy to be back on a pirate ship at last. The sea breeze freckled her nose with salt and tugged her hair out of its braid as she sailed through Pemberton Bay. Hilary couldn't think of a single thing she liked more, and for a moment she forgot all about Philomena and the Mutineers and Captain Blacktooth. She even nearly forgot about trying to find Miss Pimm. She was a pirate, the captain of her very own ship, and nothing in all of Augusta could be finer than that.

A small bang echoed from the *Squeaker*'s stern. "That'll be Claire again," Hilary said to the gargoyle. "I knew I shouldn't have given her that spare coin."

The gargoyle shook his head. "Poor Claire. I just hope she never wishes for something while she's scratching my head. I don't think I'd enjoy exploding into bits."

"Oh, drat!" said Claire as she walked a bit unsteadily toward the front of the ship. She had taken to wearing one of Jasper's thick gardening gloves on her right hand to keep the magic coins from injuring her, but the palm of the glove was smoking a bit. "I was hoping to use some magic to improve my sea legs—it's been ages since I've been on a boat this small, and I think the sea is remarkably wobbly, don't you? But I believe I've been too hopeful once again." She looked down at her smoking glove and sighed. "I just wish I weren't quite so horrid at magic. Or at standing up," she added, clutching the rim of the Gargoyle's Nest as the *Squeaker* bounced over a wave.

"The wobbling gets better after a while," the gargoyle said, "but what you really have to watch out for is the moss. It's very tickly when it grows behind your ears."

Claire looked up into the rigging, where Charlie was whistling a sea chantey. Then she took a few steps closer to Hilary. "I've been meaning to ask," she whispered, "if you think Charlie isn't terribly fond of me. I should like to be his friend, but he looks dreadfully nervous whenever I talk to him, and I don't think he liked it at all when I exploded those magic pieces." She wrinkled her brow. "I'm not very good at making friends, but I believe I'm quite good at *being* one."

Hilary took one hand off the ship's wheel and put her arm around Claire's shoulders. "You are a wonderful friend," she said. "Please don't worry about Charlie. He's a good friend, too, but I believe he'd be much more comfortable at the sharp end of a sword than he is around High Society girls. And you mustn't blame him for being squeamish about magic—his parents were sunk for their magic treasure, you know." Hilary decided not to add that it had been Admiral Westfield who'd sent their ship to the bottom of the High Seas. Perhaps if she didn't say it, it wouldn't be so terribly true.

Claire squeezed her eyes shut. "Oh, I didn't know that at all!" she whispered. "How awful!" Then she opened her eyes and nodded. "By the end of this voyage," she said firmly, "Charlie and I shall be the best of friends. If we're not, you may make me walk the plank."

The very thought made Hilary tighten her grip on the wheel. "I'll do no such thing!" she said.

"You won't?" Claire looked distinctly relieved. "But I thought that was the usual punishment for scallywags who break their oaths. Don't you think your Captain Blacktooth has some sort of rule about it?"

The *Squeaker* groaned as it tilted toward starboard. "He probably does," Hilary admitted, "but I simply can't be the sort of pirate who sends her dearest friends splashing into the High Seas, no matter what the VNHLP has to say about it." Perhaps the Terror of the Southlands was heartless enough to send her father to the Royal Dungeons, but she would never, ever abandon her mates.

THE HIGH SEAS seemed much larger than Hilary remembered, but then again, the *Squeaker* was very small. Even with the kingdom's finest wind in its sails, it moved over the waves more slowly than Hilary would have liked, and using Cannonball Jack's coins to nudge the *Squeaker* toward Queensport was out of the question if she wanted to have any strength at all left over for captaining. Larger ships passed them by at twice their speed, and once Hilary swore she saw a ship that looked very much like the *Pigeon* speeding along the horizon in the opposite direction. But it couldn't be the *Pigeon*—it was anchored on the other side of the kingdom—and by the time Hilary had managed to dig her spyglass out of her bag, the ship had passed out of sight. Several hours later, she thought she saw a small boat full of red-jacketed gentlemen in the *Squeaker*'s wake, but when she looked again, the boat had faded into the coastline.

They had been at sea for a few days when a small boat flying a white flag with the queen's golden emblem scurried toward them. "Arr!" cried the gargoyle. "I think there's a scallywag coming our way!" He leaned over the edge of the Gargoyle's Nest and studied the boat. "Is the postal courier a scallywag?"

"Probably not," said Hilary. "Anyway, you'd better try not to bite him. Perhaps he's got a letter of apology from Captain Blacktooth."

The postal courier's boat was piled high with canvas bags and brown paper parcels, and the postal courier himself waved urgently when he caught sight of Hilary. "Ahoy, Pirate Westfield!" he called. "If you'd be kind enough to drop your anchor, I've got a few letters to deliver."

Hilary lowered the *Squeaker*'s anchor, and the postal courier burrowed into one of the immense canvas bags, emerging triumphantly after a few moments with two thick envelopes in his hand. Charlie leaned over the side of the *Squeaker*, causing it to wobble alarmingly, and the postal courier passed him the letters.

Charlie studied the envelopes. "Both for you, Terror," he said, handing them to Hilary, "but I don't think they're from Blacktooth."

Both letters were printed on fine, thick paper, but only one was addressed to the Terror of the Southlands. The other was addressed to the Esteemed Miss Hilary Westfield, Formerly of Westfield House, Currently of the High Seas, and Hilary sighed heartily as soon as she saw it. "It's from Mother," she said, tearing the envelope open with her cutlass and glancing at the enclosure. "Another invitation to another tiresome ball. She says if I can spare a few moments from swashbuckling, I'm sure to make a splash in High Society."

"She's probably right, you know," said Charlie. "You'd definitely be the first High Society girl to strap a sword over her ball gown."

"That does sound tempting," said Hilary, "but I'm not going. Poor Mother; I believe she would have been much happier with a daughter who could actually stand to wear a dress for more than half a minute." She tucked the card away and turned her attention to the other envelope, which was addressed in an elegant hand and secured with blue sealing wax. "If this is another ball invitation," she said, "I may scream."

Dear Hilary,

We have learned that you and your pirate crew have set out on a voyage with the intent of rescuing Miss Eugenia Pimm. As you might imagine, we are extremely displeased. We have put a great deal of effort into capturing Miss Pimm, and we are simply not prepared to give her up—especially not to a silly young girl who calls herself the Terror of the Southlands. You have been a dreadful nuisance to us for quite some time now, and we will not allow you to ruin our plans again. Therefore, we hope you will pay us a simple courtesy and abandon your quest for Miss Pimm at once.

If you are foolish enough to ignore our request, we will be forced to take action, and we are not well known for our kindness. (Actually, we are not well known for anything at all at the moment, but please believe us when we say that that will soon change.) You would not want any of your friends to find themselves on the wrong side of our swords, would you, Pirate Westfield? We would so regret having to run them through.

Menacingly,
The Mutineers

"What does it say?" The gargoyle hopped up and down in his Nest. "It looks very official. Is it good news? Has the queen declared a National Day of the Gargoyle at last?"

"I'm afraid it's not anything nearly as wonderful as that," Hilary said. As she read the letter aloud, Charlie's face grew stormy, Claire's jaw grew tense, and the gargoyle's stony wings beat more and more indignantly.

"They think you're a nuisance?" the gargoyle cried. "You're *much* worse than a nuisance, Hilary. And they don't even mention me! Those Mutineers have a lot of nerve."

"It's quite unfair," said Hilary, "that they should know all about me when I don't know a thing about them." She turned to ask the postal courier if he could remember what the person who posted the letter had looked like, but he had already scurried away.

"They can't know you *that* well," Claire said in a comforting sort of way. "They call you a silly young girl, after all, and you're not anything of the sort!"

"That's true enough," said Charlie. "I don't suppose the Mutineers specialize in being kind. But you know, the fact that they bothered to send a letter at all is awfully flattering. It means we've ruffled them somehow; they're frightened we'll find them out, and they want to give us a good fright in return." He leaned down to study Hilary's face. "What's got you worried, Terror? You can't be taking these villains seriously."

If the Mutineers were only trying to frighten them,

Hilary didn't care to give them the satisfaction of succeeding. She could feel the gargoyle's heart thrumming fast in his little stone chest, however, and she realized with a start that her own heart was matching it beat for beat. "I'm not terribly fond of the way they talk about my friends," Hilary said; "that's all. I don't want any of you to be hurt on my account."

"Don't talk nonsense," said Charlie. "Isn't danger what being a pirate is all about?"

"Yes," said Hilary, "of course it is, but—"

"Well, then, if we're in danger, it means we're better pirates than ever." Charlie looked rather proud of himself for coming up with this argument. "Besides, we can take care of ourselves."

"If any Mutineer comes along and waves his sword at me," said Claire, "I shall send him to the bottom of the sea." She nodded vigorously. "I'm not quite sure *how* I shall do it, but I shall. Charlie is quite right; you don't need to worry about us."

The gargoyle looked up at Hilary. "You can worry about *me* if you want," he said. "I don't think danger is what being a gargoyle is all about."

Hilary gave the gargoyle a squeeze. "I promise," she said, "that whatever else may happen, I'll keep you far away from the Mutineers' blades."

The mood on the *Squeaker* soon turned cheerful as Charlie and Claire traded stories of what they would do to defeat the villains when they found them at last, but Hilary didn't join in, for she was still thinking about the Mutineers' letter. She hadn't enjoyed the threat against her friends, of course, but she had no intention of telling Claire or Charlie about the bit that bothered her most of all. "We will not allow you to ruin our plans again," the Mutineers had written in their elegant way. This meant that Hilary had ruined their plans at least once before, but how could she have done any such thing? The only villain she'd ever truly managed to thwart was her own father.

Could Admiral Westfield be a Mutineer? It was unlikely that he'd be able to capture Miss Pimm from behind the bars and padlocks of Queensport's Royal Dungeons, and it was even more unlikely that he'd bother to write a letter to Hilary afterward. Besides, the Admiral's handwriting was hardly elegant; it hopped across his papers like a disgruntled toad, and Hilary felt sure the Mutineers' letter hadn't come from him. Still, she didn't like the situation one bit. She knew she ought to hurry to the Dungeons and ask Admiral Westfield what he knew about the Mutineers—but perhaps the Terror of the Southlands wasn't quite as daring or quite as bold as she'd hoped to be. She could fend off a whole galleon full of Mutineers if that was what it took to rescue Miss Pimm, but coming face-to-face with her father was a very different sort of battle, and Hilary wasn't sure it was the sort she knew how to win.

THE QUEEN'S INSPECTORS
KINGDOM OF AUGUSTA
DILIGENCE, LOGIC, DISCRETION

Report to H.R.H. Queen Adelaide regarding
THE DISAPPEARANCE OF MISS EUGENIA PIMM

Report No. 2
FIELD INSPECTOR: *John Hastings*
LOCATION: *Pemberton, Augusta*
CASE STATUS: *Rather Confounding*

Inspector's Comments: *Your Highness, I am sorry to report that the Enchantress of the Northlands still eludes us. I believe, however, that we have made some progress toward locating her, and I am proud to present to you the following theory:*

Miss Eugenia Pimm has been captured by pirates.

We have a number of reasons to suspect that this theory is accurate. First, pirates are notoriously ill-mannered. It is extremely impolite to capture a person—especially a person who is both a High Society lady and a government official—but I am told that pirates do not care a bit for politeness.

Second, when my inspectors conducted a thorough search of the Pemberton road, they found two items of interest approximately one mile from Pemberton Bay. The items were lying by the side of the road directly next to each other, as though they had been dropped (or perhaps tossed from a fast-moving carriage—there are deep wheel ruts in the road nearby). One of the items is a golden pin in the shape of a dancing sheep; we believe this piece of jewelry belongs to the Enchantress herself. The other item is a handsome black eye patch with ties of green silk. Its owner is currently unknown, but we believe this eye patch most certainly belongs to a pirate. I suspect that when this pirate attempted to capture the Enchantress, she put up a bit of a fight and tore off the pirate's eye patch. In the struggle, however, her pin came loose, and the pirate overtook her and smuggled her into his carriage. (I have heard, Your Highness, that pirates usually travel by ship and not by carriage, but I have asked my men to investigate this point further.)

Finally, my men tell me that the pirate Cannonball Jack—our prime suspect in this investigation—has disappeared from his usual waters in Pemberton Bay. I have sent several

inspectors to search the High Seas for this scoundrel.
Additional inspectors are still on the trail of the
Terror of Something-or-Other, who is believed to
be an acquaintance of Cannonball Jack. After
creating a ruckus here in my office, she proceeded to
mislead my men and threaten them with magical
weaponry, so there is no doubt in my mind that she
is both a scoundrel and a villain. She is currently
traveling toward Queensport in a very curious ship.

I believe, Your Highness, that we shall shortly
crack this case.

Signed
John Hastings
Captain, Queen's Inspectors

CITIZENS OF AUGUSTA!

❖

Are you
TIRED OF WAITING
for the Enchantress to reappear?

❖

Do you desire
A RETURN TO ORDER AND PROPRIETY
in the kingdom?

❖

Would you like to prevent
FURTHER MAGICAL SHENANIGANS
from taking place?

❖

Then join us as we ask the queen to

APPOINT A NEW ENCHANTRESS WITHOUT DELAY!

SAFEGUARD OUR KINGDOM'S MAGIC!

SAFEGUARD OUR KINGDOM'S FUTURE!

❖

THIS PAMPHLET HAS BEEN PRODUCED BY
CITIZENS FOR MAGICAL OVERSIGHT,
A DIVISION OF THE
COALITION OF OVERPROTECTIVE MOTHERS.

Chapter Eight

ROM A DISTANCE, Feathering Keep seemed to rise up from the sea itself. Hilary supposed it had once been a grand building, guarding the cliff's edge against storms and scallywags, but now its stone walls slumped toward the waves, as though they had determined that being swallowed up by the sea was a far more dignified fate than crumbling to dust. It didn't seem possible that anyone could truly live in such a damp and ancient place, but the Featherings seemed to be in residence, for atop each of the keep's four turrets, a purple pennant flapped in the wind.

As they drew closer to the keep, Hilary pulled out her spyglass and studied the cliff face. The rocks had been polished by waves, and there didn't seem to be any footholds nearly large enough for a pirate's boot. "I don't know how we're going to get up there," she said. "Perhaps if we sail around the cliff . . ."

Then a tremendous splash drenched her from her hat feather to her boot buckles, and the *Squeaker* rocked perilously from side to side. "Horsefeathers!" cried Claire as her feet flew out from under her. "What in the world was that?"

Hilary blinked the seawater from her eyes and reached for her cutlass. Tendrils of smoke rose up from behind the cliff, and the air smelled strongly of gunpowder. "I might be mistaken," she said, "but I'm almost sure that was a cannonball."

"Shiver me timbers!" said the gargoyle as he shook himself off. "Oh, Hilary, I think I've gotten some sea up my snout."

Charlie had already drawn his sword and was looking about for someone to duel, while Claire grabbed the heavy skillet that Jasper often used to prepare his morning flapjacks. "But who would want to blast us?" she asked. "Do you think it's the Mutineers?"

If the Mutineers had progressed from menacing notes to cannonball blasts in a matter of days, they were even more dangerous than Hilary had thought. "I can't see who's firing on us," she called back, "but I think they're behind the cliff. Oh, for goodness' sake, *duck*!"

Another cannonball splashed down in front of the

ship, nearly grazing the Gargoyle's Nest on the way down. The gargoyle yelped and buried himself as well as he could under his hat.

Then a small, fierce voice rang out through the smoke. "Ahoy!" it called. "Who dares to approach Feathering Keep?"

"Don't answer the scallywag," Hilary said to her mates. When both she and the *Squeaker* had stopped trembling, she took hold of the ship's wheel and sailed directly toward the cliff face. Perhaps she didn't have a cannon, but she could do a fair bit of damage with a well-aimed piece of hardtack if only she could get close enough.

The small, fierce voice returned. "Drop your weapons," it ordered, "or prepare to suffer a pirate's wrath!" It paused. "And could you please drop your cooking pan as well?"

Claire flushed and lowered her skillet, but neither Charlie nor Hilary put down their swords. Instead they stared at the elegant ship that was speeding toward them from the far side of the cliff. Its hull gleamed as white as the wave caps, and its spotless sails looked as though they'd never been sullied by a breeze. But atop its mast flew an imposing Jolly Roger, and along its deck stood a line of small iron cannons. Two of the cannons were still smoking from the blasts that had rocked the *Squeaker*.

"They're pirates?" Charlie frowned. "That's the strangest pirate ship I've ever seen."

Stranger still, Hilary thought, was the girl perched

on its bowsprit. She was small and sturdy, and she wore a ruffled white dress that made her look rather like an iced pastry from one of Queensport's fine bakeries. But her feet swung back and forth in shiny pirate boots, and her red hair tangled cheerfully beneath her pirate hat. She certainly didn't look much like a villain, but she'd nearly turned the *Squeaker* into a heap of rubble, and that was not a mistake Hilary intended to let her make again.

"You must be a very bold pirate indeed," Hilary called, "to fire your cannons at the Terror of the Southlands and her crew. But we're twice as bold, and we won't drop our weapons, so you'd better surrender at once."

The girl reached under the satin sash around her waist, pulled out a spyglass, and peered through it at the *Squeaker*. Then she gave a little gasp that nearly toppled her off the bowsprit. When she had recovered her balance, the girl pulled herself back onto her ship and hurried over to the other sailor on board, a tall, red-haired young man who was standing behind the row of cannons. She waved her arms ferociously for a few moments, and the young man laughed and nodded. Then the small white ship sailed directly toward the *Squeaker*.

Hilary tightened her grip on her cutlass. "It doesn't look like they're surrendering," she said. "They must be awfully foolish pirates if they think they can face the Terror of the Southlands in battle."

"You don't think they'll sink us, do you?" said Claire.

"It would be terribly embarrassing to be shipwrecked by a girl in a party dress." She squeezed water from her damp skirts, leaving them even more wrinkled and worn than usual. "I believe perishing at sea is dreadful enough without being mortified in the process."

"They wouldn't dare sink us," said Charlie, "and if they try, we'll just have to sink them first." He looked worried, though, and he kept shifting his sword from one hand to the other as the pirate ship drew nearer.

It pulled alongside the *Squeaker* with a scrape of wood and a squeak of metal as the red-haired young man lowered the anchor. "You really can put down your swords," the girl in the white dress said, "if you'd like. But you don't have to, of course. Oh, I can't believe I fired on Hilary Westfield! How awful!" She grimaced. "You *are* Pirate Hilary Westfield, aren't you?"

Hilary hesitated for a moment before lowering her cutlass. "Yes," she said, "I am."

"I *told* you it was really the Terror!" The girl spun around, and her billowing skirts spun with her.

"So you did," said the young man with a smile. "But perhaps you'd better introduce yourself. I'm ever so sorry," he said, turning to Hilary. "My little sister doesn't always remember her manners."

The girl rolled her eyes. "I've told you a thousand times," she said, "that pirates mind their manners only when it suits them. But very well." She leaned over the side of her ship and stuck out her hand for Hilary to shake. "I'm Alice Feathering, and this is my ship, the *Calamity*." She patted the *Calamity*'s shiny white hull. "And this is my brother, Nicholas, but he's old and dull. He thinks he's supposed to look after me, even though everyone knows pirates don't need looking after. I should have made him walk the plank ages ago."

"It's an honor to meet you, Pirate Westfield," said Nicholas Feathering. "Alice has told me you're the finest buccaneer on the High Seas."

Hilary was so surprised that she nearly forgot to shake Nicholas's hand. She had not quite expected to find the most eligible gentleman in Augusta floating about on a pirate ship, and she had certainly not expected him to be kind. Sir Nicholas Feathering looked, however, like a perfectly normal and rather friendly young man. He was paler than his sister, but he had the same cluster of freckles scattered along the bridge of his nose. His clothes were nearly as fancy as Alice's, but without quite so many ruffles, and he had tied a handkerchief around his head in a dashing sort of way. "Are you a buccaneer yourself?" Hilary asked him.

Nicholas laughed and patted his handkerchief. "Alas, I'm not," he said, "but Alice won't allow me on her ship unless I look the part. This is my father's best pocket square—I'm hoping to replace it before he finds out, but I'm dreading ironing the thing."

Hilary nodded. "No good pirate enjoys ironing," she said. "And it's nice to meet you as well. This is my first mate, Pirate Charlie Dove. He's hoping to be the Scourge of the Northlands soon. And this is Claire Dupree, pirate's assistant." Charlie raised his sword in greeting, and Claire curtsied. "And this—"

But Alice Feathering interrupted her. "Oh, this must be your gargoyle!" she said. "Hello, gargoyle. I've heard lots about you. They say you're the most fearsome beast in the kingdom."

"They do? Really?" The gargoyle leaned forward in his Nest. "Do they mention my hat?"

Alice gave Hilary a shy smile. "I can't believe you've come to Feathering Keep," she said. "I've always wanted to be a pirate, but my parents said it simply wasn't *done*. And then you became a pirate, so I told them it was absolutely *done*, and by High Society girls, too! I can't wait to join the VNHLP, but I'm not nearly old enough yet." She gave the *Calamity* another fond pat. "So until then, I'm practicing."

"You're certainly good with a cannon already," said Charlie. He wiped away the water that was dripping off his hat brim and onto his nose.

Alice's face turned nearly as red as her hair. "I'm awfully sorry about that," she said. "We don't get many visitors poking around Feathering Keep, and I hoped you might be scoundrels." She sighed. "I've spent ages waiting for a scoundrel to sail past us. It's difficult to practice having a pirate battle when you've got no one to do battle with, and Nicholas isn't fond of dueling with me."

"Alice is a much better pirate than I'll ever be, I'm afraid," said Nicholas, "but I'm a better host. Why don't you all come inside and dry yourselves off? I'm almost certain the chimney in the great hall won't collapse if we light a fire."

THE FEATHERINGS GUIDED the pirates around the cliff to a little dock, where they moored the *Squeaker* next to the *Calamity*. Someone had once carved a set of steps into the rock face, but they were badly worn from generations of wind and waves. Hilary did her best to scramble up them without jostling the gargoyle too unpleasantly.

"Welcome to our beloved pile of rubble," said Nicholas when they'd all reached the top of the cliff and gathered around the front door of Feathering Keep. A golden door knocker in the shape of a bear's head stared out at them, but it was the only part of the keep that looked less than a thousand years old. "You'll want to step lightly going through the entranceway so you don't dislodge any bits of wall or ceiling. They're mostly held up by magic, but every now and then we lose a chimney or a chunk of parapet."

Claire stared at him. "Why in the world don't you repair the place?"

"According to our parents," said Nicholas, "a home isn't truly grand and noble unless it's coming apart at the seams. It's led to some rather adventurous dinner parties. They say the queen herself was nearly crushed by a plummeting turret."

"I definitely prefer Jasper's bungalow," Charlie whispered to Hilary as they passed through the great stone entranceway. "It may not be grand or noble, but at least it stays upright most of the time."

The only member of their party who truly seemed to appreciate Feathering Keep was the gargoyle. "These stones are even older than I am," he said, bowing to an imposing slab of rock that stood guard along the entranceway. "It's an honor to meet you, sir. My sympathies about the moss."

They wound through the keep's cavernous halls and emerged at last into a high-ceilinged room that looked vast enough to accommodate Miss Greyson's entire floating bookshop. The walls, however, were lined not with books but with oil paintings of old-fashioned men and women; Hilary guessed from the abundance of frilled and ruffled clothes in the portraits that these must be previous generations of Featherings. Clouds scudded over the holes in the roof as Nicholas walked to the drafty hearth and picked up a long golden poker that had been resting against the wall. "We'd like a cozy fire, please," he said, holding the poker with both hands. "In the fireplace, if you don't mind. Nothing too dangerous." In an instant, flames sprang up around the logs in the fireplace, and Nicholas wiped his brow with his handkerchief.

"That was an impressive bit of magic," Hilary said. "You must have been very well trained."

"It helps," said Nicholas, "to have a chunk of magic as large as that poker. And for that you can thank Great-Great-Grandfather Feathering, who was the stingiest man in Augusta." He pointed to one of the oil paintings, where a cruel-looking gentleman glared down at everyone who dared to pass beneath his frame. "He didn't use magic much, from what I've heard, but he was extremely fond of hoarding it." Nicholas shrugged. "Magic," he said to the poker, "could you bring us a few warm blankets for our guests as well? It's the least we can do to make up for swamping them."

Hilary raised her eyebrows as a towering stack of blankets appeared in front of Nicholas. He didn't even seem terribly tired. "Don't mind him," Alice said to Hilary, handing her an exquisitely soft blue blanket. "He can't help showing off for every visitor who passes through." She wrapped a fluffy pink rug around the gargoyle. "But why *are* you passing through? Are you off on a swashbuckling adventure? Have you found another treasure trove?"

"Actually," said Hilary, "we're searching for someone. The Enchantress of the Northlands, to be precise."

Nicholas settled himself next to the gargoyle in front of the fire. "That's awfully kind of you," he said. "I wasn't aware pirates usually did that sort of thing."

"Er, they usually don't," said Hilary. "I suppose you

might call this a special mission."

"I'm afraid the Enchantress isn't here," said Alice, flopping down on the pile of blankets. "And it's lucky for her that she's not. Mother and Father don't think much of her, and if she came for a visit, they'd probably try to squash her under an unsteady bit of the keep."

"Alice!" said Nicholas.

"Well, it's *true*." Alice kicked off her pirate boots.

"All right," said Nicholas, "perhaps it is. Mother and Father say it's awfully distracting to have an Enchantress looking over your shoulder whenever you use a bit of magic." He shrugged. "Personally, I think it's a good deal more distracting to live in a house that might tumble down on you at any moment."

"I agree," said Charlie, eyeing a crumbling chunk of roof with suspicion.

Hilary studied Nicholas as he tucked the fluffy pink rug around the gargoyle's wings. It seemed terribly unlikely that he was truly going to marry a girl like Philomena; she must have made up the entire tale to distract the pirates from her villainy. And, most annoyingly, her plan had succeeded, for they'd wasted nearly a week fixing up the *Squeaker* and sailing to Feathering Keep. "Blast that Philomena," Hilary muttered into her blanket.

Nicholas looked up. "What did you say?"

"Oh!" said Hilary. "It's nothing. But"—she supposed it wouldn't do any harm to ask—"Nicholas, by any chance, do you know a young lady named Philomena Tilbury?"

Nicholas was suddenly overtaken by a fit of coughs.

"Miss Tilbury!" Alice crowed. "Nicholas is *very* fond of Miss Tilbury. I'm not, though," she added. "She reminds me of a jellyfish—the sort that stings. She's disgustingly sweet whenever she's with Nicholas, but as soon as he leaves, her tentacles come out." Alice wiggled her fingers. "And soon enough I'll be stuck with a jellyfish for a sister."

"Alice!" The most eligible gentleman in Augusta suddenly looked very bashful indeed. "It's not funny!" he said as Alice dissolved in giggles. He sat up a bit straighter and poked at the fire. "As a matter of fact," he said to Hilary, "I do have the pleasure of knowing Miss Tilbury. As my sister so rudely revealed, we're planning to marry."

Charlie wrinkled his brow. "And you *like* her?"

Nicholas smiled and rested his chin on his hand, as though thinking about Philomena was an activity he truly enjoyed. "Tremendously," he said. "I suppose she can be a bit prickly, Alice, but if you'd been raised in a family as stern as hers, you'd be prickly too. In fact, I admire her resilience."

"But mostly," said Alice, "he admires her hair."

Nicholas nodded. "Her hair is very golden, isn't it?"

The gargoyle snorted into his rug. "I'm sorry," he said. "I must have choked on a spider."

"Do you know Philomena then, Pirate Westfield?" Nicholas asked. "Or . . ." He frowned. "This doesn't have anything to do with the Enchantress business, does it?"

"I'm afraid it does," said Hilary. She was rather shaken by the rapturous look that passed across Nicholas's face whenever he said Philomena's name, but she couldn't let herself be distracted by such horrors; she had to press on. "We think Philomena may be mixed up in Miss Pimm's disappearance, and we were hoping you could tell us where she was last Friday evening."

"But she was with me!" cried Nicholas at once. "We dined together that very day! I remember particularly, because Philomena's hair is especially golden on Fridays—though Tuesdays suit her nearly as well."

Alice nodded. "I remember it too," she said, "because *someone* made me sail him all the way to Pemberton to see Miss Tilbury, and then he didn't even bother to invite me to dinner."

A log in the fireplace crumbled to embers, and Hilary felt as though her hopes of finding Miss Pimm were crumbling right along with it. If Philomena and Nicholas had truly been dining together all evening, Philomena couldn't have slipped away to kidnap Miss Pimm—and if she hadn't, then who had? "So much for Philomena's villainy, then," she said, drawing her blanket more tightly around her shoulders. "I suppose we're back to where we began."

Claire sighed dramatically. "Which is to say, nowhere at all."

"But you're not!" cried Alice. "You haven't asked me

yet if I know anything about the Enchantress's disappearance, have you?"

Hilary stared at her. "Do you know something, then?"

"She doesn't— Ow!" Nicholas broke off as Alice jabbed him with her elbow.

"Actually," she said, "I do. And thank you very much for asking, Terror. No one else has, you know—and Nicholas says I'm not allowed to tell the queen's inspectors what I saw."

"That's because I don't want you to bother them with your silly tales," Nicholas said, rubbing his side in the spot where it had met Alice's elbow. "I'm sorry, Pirate Westfield. Alice has a particular knack for imagining things."

"But I'm not imagining things!" said Alice. "I'm sure Hilary will believe me, even if you don't." She leaned forward and grasped Hilary's hands.

"Miss Pimm," she said in a whisper, "was captured by the ghost ship."

Hilary sighed. No wonder Nicholas hadn't let Alice take her story to the inspectors. Everyone knew that ghosts resided only in the pages of chilling gothic tales. Alice looked so earnest, however, that Hilary couldn't bear to disappoint her. "That sounds . . . rather unusual," she said at last, "but a good pirate must consider every possibility. Perhaps you'd better tell me what you saw."

"As long as it's not too scary," the gargoyle added.

Alice gave Nicholas a triumphant smile. "I'll start from

the beginning, then," she said. "It all happened last Friday, around six o'clock in the evening. My darling brother had just abandoned me after I'd spent ages sailing him all the way to Pemberton in the *Calamity* because he's too stingy to take the train. I was floating about near Pemberton Bay, bored to tears, and I thought I'd do a bit of exploring."

"You mean you got lost," said Nicholas.

Alice's eyes narrowed. "Pirates never get lost," she said, "and it wasn't my fault that my navigator had gone off to stare at a young lady's hair all evening. Anyway, I was *exploring*, when the *Calamity* passed into a cove I'd never seen before. There were leaves and vines hanging all around it, a bit like a curtain, so it was hard to spot. But as I sailed through the curtain, a terrible chill came over me"—she paused to look around the room—"and I realized I wasn't alone."

The gargoyle wriggled out of his rug and hopped into Hilary's lap.

"Who else was there?" Claire asked in a whisper.

"Why, the ghost ship, of course!" said Alice. "It was hidden away behind the leaves and vines, you see, and it was black and gray, like an enormous shadow. It made a terrible creaking noise in the wind, and its torches were all aglow—but there was nobody on board."

A twig snapped in the fireplace, and everyone jumped.

"It's a good thing I'm a pirate," said Alice, "or I would have been terrified. I sailed the *Calamity* back to Pemberton Bay as quickly as I could, and the ghost ship was thoughtful enough not to follow me. When Nicholas had finally finished his dinner, I sailed the *Calamity* back to the little cove so I could show him the ship. But it was gone."

Claire drew in her breath, and even Hilary shivered despite herself.

Charlie looked up from sharpening the creases in his pirate hat. "Are you sure it was a *ghost* ship?" he asked Alice.

"Of course," she said. "Only ghosts would sail about in such a spine-tingling way. I did think at first that I might have imagined the whole thing, but we heard the next day that the Enchantress had gone missing from Pemberton, and I knew at once that the ghost ship must have gotten her. It's the only possible explanation."

"You didn't see the Enchantress board the ship, though?" Hilary asked.

"Well—no." Alice stuck out her lower lip. "I suppose I didn't. But don't you think it's odd that a ghost ship appeared on the very night she vanished?"

"It *is* odd," Hilary said, doing her best to be kind. Her visit to the Featherings was turning out to be entirely disappointing, and she had less of an idea than ever about who the Mutineers might be, but there was no need to disappoint Alice as well. "Thank you," she said, "for telling us your story. Perhaps it will do us some good."

Nicholas patted the gargoyle's wings. "I think we could all do with a more cheerful tale," he said. "Pirate Westfield, would you tell us how you found the Enchantress's treasure? That must have been a thrilling adventure."

"Oh, it was!" said the gargoyle happily. "Go ahead, Hilary. Tell them how I saved the kingdom."

Just then, however, a bear's ferocious growl echoed through Feathering Keep, and Nicholas leaped to his feet. "That's the door knocker," he explained on his way out of the room. "Grandmother Feathering enchanted it on a whim one day. It's amusing enough, but it does tend to discourage guests."

A few moments later, Nicholas returned to the great hall, looking concerned. "I'm sorry, Pirate Westfield," he said, "but there's someone here to see you, and he seems rather grumpy about it. He says his name is Twigget."

"Twigget?" Hilary pushed herself to her feet and tucked the gargoyle back into her bag. "Oh, blast it all, that's Captain Blacktooth's mate. I can't imagine what he wants with me now."

"We'll just have to tell him to go away," said Charlie, standing up and following Hilary out of the hall.

"That's right," Claire said as she hurried along behind them. "If he wants to see you, he must go about it properly and send you a note requesting the pleasure of your company."

"I'm afraid pirates aren't terribly concerned with propriety," said Hilary. She tugged open the creaky front door to reveal Mr. Twigget in his tattered striped shirt, staring up at the towers of Feathering Keep as though he feared they would come tumbling down around him at any moment. Hilary rather wished they would.

"Hello, Mr. Twigget," she said, doing her best to sound bold and daring. "I heard you wanted to see me."

Mr. Twigget cleared his throat. "Aye, Miss Westfield. It's taken me a good bit o' time to find you. 'Tis a lucky thing I spotted your ship tied up down below. The captain won't be pleased if we're late."

"I don't know what you might be late for," said Hilary, "but I'm quite sure I haven't been invited to it. Now, if you'll excuse me—"

But Mr. Twigget put a calloused hand on Hilary's shoulder. "Sorry, miss," he said in a low voice, "but Captain Blacktooth's waitin' for you down at the Salty Biscuit, and the longer I take bringin' you there, the darker his mood will get. It's a good hour's walk as it is, so if you want to keep your pirate credentials, you'd better come with me."

Charlie drew his sword. "I don't care for anyone dragging my captain away," he said, "no matter whom they work for. Should I run this washed-up pirate through, Hilary?"

Mr. Twigget's bony fingers dug ever so slightly into Hilary's shoulder. He didn't seem inclined to hurt her, but she had no doubt at all that he *could*. Captain Blacktooth employed only the most fearsome pirates in the kingdom, after all. "No," Hilary said, "I don't think it would be wise to run anyone through. The Featherings have been such kind hosts; it would be a shame to make a mess on their front path."

At this, Mr. Twigget's fingers relaxed significantly.

"Then we'll come with you!" said Claire. "I should like to give that Captain Blacktooth my most devastating stare."

"And I'll give him a bit more than that," said Charlie, patting his sword.

But Mr. Twigget shook his head. "The young miss is to go alone," he said.

Truthfully, Hilary felt rather relieved about this. It would have been much nicer to have her crewmates by her side as she faced Captain Blacktooth, of course, but she couldn't let Charlie smudge his reputation if he wanted to be the Scourge of the Northlands, and it was perfectly clear that Blacktooth already cared very little for Claire. "If you two could sail the *Squeaker* to Queensport Harbor," Hilary said to them, "the gargoyle and I will meet you there as soon as we can. And please give my apologies to the Featherings."

The sleeves of Claire's cardigan had unraveled so far that they barely covered her elbows. "Oh, Hilary," she said, "are you sure you'll be all right?"

"Quite sure." Hilary shot her the bravest smile she could summon. "Now, if you'll unhand me, Mr. Twigget, you'll find there's no need to drag me into Queensport like a prisoner. I believe Captain Blacktooth and I have a lot to talk about."

THE VERY NEARLY HONORABLE LEAGUE OF PIRATES
Servin' the High Seas for 153 Years

THE RENEGADE
CABIN OF THE PRESIDENT

✠ ✠ ✠ ✠ ✠

NOTICE OF UNPIRATICAL BEHAVIOR

Pirate Westfield:

I have received your response to my letter, and I am gravely concerned. We must speak at once.

As Mr. Twigget has doubtlessly told you before handing you this note, I have arranged for us to meet at my favorite Queensport groggery, the Salty Biscuit. Come without delay, and come alone. Mr. Twigget will know the way.

I suppose I should mention that this is your

[ ] first warning [ ] second warning [x] third warning

Arr!
Captain Rupert Blacktooth
President, VNHLP

CHAPTER NINE

MR. TWIGGET LED Hilary through the thin, shadowy streets surrounding Queensport Harbor where neither Admiral Westfield nor Miss Greyson had ever permitted Hilary to go. As she squashed past sailors and fishmongers in the narrow lanes, hurrying around corners to keep from losing sight of Mr. Twigget, she felt rather as though she were being digested by a sea monster. She was starting to believe, however, that being caught up in a sea monster's jaws would be a more pleasant pastime than meeting Captain Blacktooth. Matching Twigget's pace was proving to be uncomfortable enough in its own right, and when he slowed to a stop at last, Hilary leaned over to catch her breath.

"We've got no time for lazin' about," said Mr. Twigget. "The captain's due back on Gunpowder Island soon, and he's eager to start loadin' the ship, so you'd better stand at attention." He rapped his knuckles against a heavy wooden door set into the stone wall beside them. Over the door hung an iron sign shaped like a square of hardtack.

The door opened, and a pirate in a fancily embroidered coat stepped out. "You are most welcome, dear mateys, at the Salty Biscuit," he said, bowing low and swirling his hand in the air. Then he stood up rather suddenly and gave Hilary a haughty look. "Who's this?"

"'Tis a little girl with whom the captain wants to have a word," said Mr. Twigget.

"Oh, be quiet," said Hilary, causing Mr. Twigget to look remarkably abashed. "I'm a pirate, of course," she told the fellow in the fancy coat. "Pirate Hilary Westfield, Terror of the Southlands. Perhaps you've heard of me."

The fancy pirate smoothed his sleeves. "Perhaps," he allowed. "In any case, do come in, both of you. You'll find Captain Blacktooth at his usual table."

Although it was just past midday, the groggery was as dark as a ship's hold. Thick glass lanterns flickered along the walls, illuminating the scarred and weatherworn faces of the pirates who sat chortling around wooden tables. The Salty Biscuit was clearly a sophisticated sort of groggery— a whole crew of fancily dressed buccaneers circulated from table to table with flagons of grog and plates piled high with fresh bread and cheese—but it smelled quite distinctly of pirate all the same, and Hilary couldn't help noticing the cutlass gashes in the walls.

Without a word, Mr. Twigget led Hilary to a long table in the farthest, darkest corner of the groggery, where Captain Blacktooth and his mates were playing at cards. Then Mr. Twigget cleared his throat. "Hilary Westfield to see you, sir," he said, tugging Hilary in front of him.

Captain Blacktooth set down his playing cards and skewered them with a dagger. "Thank you, Twigget," he said. "Please have a seat, Pirate Westfield."

Hilary sat. She settled her canvas bag on her lap, resting her hands on the gargoyle's head to keep him from climbing out. She kicked her heels against the chair legs and hoped Captain Blacktooth couldn't hear how loudly her heart was pounding. For a long, unbearable moment, he was silent. Then he took a sip from his flagon and dabbed the grog from his whiskers.

"I don't suppose," Blacktooth said at last, "that you've got the head of a sea monster in that bag of yours? Or perhaps a white flag of surrender from a pirate king?"

Hilary looked down at the tabletop, which was scarred and scratched from hundreds of buccaneers' hooks. "You know perfectly well that I don't."

"Then you've failed once again to follow my orders," said Blacktooth. "But, of course, you already explained as much in your correspondence." He pulled out a damp and wrinkled paper filled with Hilary's own handwriting and smoothed it out on the table in front of him. "I must say that I admire your bravery. Most scallywags wouldn't dare to instruct the president of the pirate league on the true nature of piracy."

Hilary met his gaze. "Well, sir," she said, "you did tell me to be bold and daring."

Captain Blacktooth laughed, but the sound was hardly comforting. "I also told you to impress me," he said, "not to challenge me at every turn. It is not up to you to determine what is piratical and what is not." He took another sip of grog. "However, Pirate Westfield, I am not a tyrant. I see now that if I forbid you to do something, you'll only become more eager to do it, so I am willing to consider your argument. In your particular circumstances, rescuing the Enchantress might indeed be piratical."

"It might?" Hilary leaned forward. "Oh, thank you, sir—"

"I'm not finished, pirate. While saving the Enchantress in a suitably swashbuckling manner might earn you the respect of a handful of rogues, *failing* to save the Enchantress is not piratical in the slightest. I can't imagine your reputation could survive such a blow—nor, of course, could your membership in the League. Are you absolutely certain you can take that risk?"

"Of course!" said Hilary. If she sounded confident enough, perhaps Captain Blacktooth wouldn't question her further. "In fact, my mates and I are already well on our way to finding Miss Pimm."

"Really!" Captain Blacktooth crossed his arms. "You're certain of her whereabouts?"

"Well, no," said Hilary, "but—"

"Ah. Then perhaps you know who's captured her? You're confident you can defeat them?"

The skulls printed on the backs of Captain Blacktooth's playing cards leered up at Hilary, and she didn't care one bit for their mocking expressions. "The villains are called the Mutineers, sir," she said. "Once I track them down, it should be no trouble at all to locate the Enchantress."

"But you don't know who these Mutineers might be."

Hilary stared at him, but she couldn't say a word.

"Precisely," said Captain Blacktooth. "You've been looking for the Enchantress for quite a while now, and it seems to me that you haven't turned up a single bit of useful information."

"Then I'll just have to keep looking," said Hilary. "If the League is so eager to assist me, perhaps I can ask your mates if they've heard of a group of villains—"

But Captain Blacktooth held up his hand. "I'm afraid we can be of no help to you there," he said. "The Enchantress disappeared on the very night of our Midsummer's Eve picnic on Gunpowder Island, and the entire League had its attention turned in that direction. We were all quite caught up in the excitement of the swimming relay."

He gave Hilary a meaningful look. "But you would know that, of course, if you had attended."

Hilary sighed. "I wasn't aware that attending a picnic was a particularly bold or daring thing to do."

Captain Blacktooth ignored this. "I've given you three warnings already, Pirate Westfield, and that's all you'll get. But there is still time to reconsider. If you abandon your quest and set out on a League-approved mission, every scallywag in the kingdom will cheer your name. The finest treasures in Augusta will be yours for the plundering. And I," he said, "will not look like a fool for trusting you. If you insist on pursuing the Enchantress, however, I feel quite sure you will fail. I can't imagine how you'll ever hold your head up on the High Seas again—assuming, of course, that you're not lying at the bottom of them."

Hilary pushed her chair back from the table and stood up. "Perhaps you're forgetting that I'm the Terror of the Southlands," she said. "I don't abandon my quests, and I don't abandon my friends."

"It seems to me," said Captain Blacktooth, "that if she wants to keep her title, the Terror of the Southlands should be wise enough to know when she doesn't have a hope of succeeding."

Hilary picked up Blacktooth's flagon and slammed it down on the table, sloshing grog all over the playing cards. "If I didn't know better," she said more loudly than she'd intended, "I'd think you didn't want me to find the Enchantress at all."

For a moment, the Salty Biscuit fell silent. All the pirates turned to look at Hilary. Then a hiss ran through the groggery as each and every pirate unsheathed his sword. The spilled grog dripped stickily onto Hilary's boots, and she realized that the swords were all pointed at her.

"Captain Blacktooth," one pirate called, "who's this rapscallion who's speakin' mutinous words against ye?"

"Shall we defend yer honor?" asked another.

"Aye!" cried several more pirates in chorus.

"Steady now, mates! That won't be necessary," Captain Blacktooth said, but several of the nearest pirates were already advancing toward Hilary, and the captain's words were lost in the hubbub. She reached for her cutlass and was horrified to discover that her legs were trembling as though she were a landlubber on her first day at sea. Charlie had taught her as much swordplay as he could, but she didn't believe that even he would be able to take on a groggery full of angry pirates and emerge with a full set of limbs.

The gargoyle pulled himself partway out of the canvas bag and studied the advancing pirates. "Um, Hilary," he said, "I might be wrong, but I think those scallywags want to run us through."

"Yes," said Hilary, "I believe you're right."

The gargoyle gave her a nervous sort of look. "You don't need to use me, do you? For protection, I mean?" He hesitated. "It might not hurt me *too* badly."

"I'm sure it won't come to that," Hilary said, "and I don't break my promises to my friends as easily as Captain Blacktooth would like me to." She raised her cutlass as a pirate with a parrot on his shoulder stepped in front of her. Neither the pirate nor the parrot looked particularly pleased to make her acquaintance. "If you touch me," Hilary said to the pirate, "I'll fly your breeches from the flagpole in front of the queen's palace, and the same goes for your friend's tail feathers." She pointed her blade toward the parrot. "Now, back away at once!"

But the pirate didn't back away. Instead he swung his sword toward Hilary, clipping the end of her braid and knocking her cutlass to the floor, where it landed in a puddle of grog. "Ye don't scare me, ye small scallywag," he said. "If ye weren't still a member of the League, I'd have sliced ye to pieces already."

Then the Salty Biscuit's heavy door banged open, and an explosion of piratical noises rose up from the men closest to the entrance.

"Move aside, please," said a very proper voice, "and don't wave that dagger at me, young man. You'll take your own eye out if you're not careful—ah, and I see you haven't been."

The pirate with the parrot on his shoulder wheeled

around to watch the commotion, and Captain Blacktooth furrowed his brow. "Who in the world could that be?" he murmured.

Hilary let out the breath she'd been holding for the better part of a minute. "A friend," she said as she retrieved her cutlass from the floor, "though I'm afraid it's one of whom you don't approve."

The sea of pirates began to part, and Miss Greyson walked briskly through the middle of it. "There's no need to 'Arr!' at me, dear fellow," she said to a short and stout pirate. "I assure you I've met schoolgirls more fearsome than that."

The short and stout pirate sank back and stared at Miss Greyson. So did everyone else. She was dressed in her best traveling clothes and holding her magic crochet hook—for protection against the pirates, Hilary supposed, although she certainly didn't seem to need it. A few steps behind her were Charlie and Claire; Charlie had drawn his sword, and Claire was waving a hairpin at any pirate who dared to lift a weapon in her direction. At the end of the procession was the fancy pirate who'd answered the door, looking half as haughty as before and twice as spineless. Hilary wondered exactly what Miss Greyson had said to him.

"Excuse me," said Miss Greyson, pushing past the pirate with the parrot on his shoulder. Then she caught sight of Hilary and swept her up in a tight embrace. "Are you all right?" Miss Greyson asked. "And the gargoyle, is he all right as well?"

Hilary couldn't decide whether to be relieved or mortified. Soon enough, all the scourges and scallywags on the High Seas would be laughing about how the Terror of the Southlands had been rescued by her governess. It was a wonder Captain Blacktooth didn't expel her from the League on the spot. "We're perfectly fine," said Hilary into the folds of Miss Greyson's traveling jacket, "but would you mind letting me go? I believe you're crushing my fearsomeness."

"Of course. My apologies." Miss Greyson drew back. "And this, I presume, is Captain Blacktooth." She looked the captain up and down. "You don't look much like a sea cucumber to me."

Before Captain Blacktooth could respond, however, Miss Greyson had taken Hilary by the hand and guided her toward the doorway, where Charlie and Claire were waiting. "It's been a pleasure to meet you all," she said to the assembled pirates, "but I'm afraid the Terror and I must leave at once. We have a great deal to catch up on."

"And I," said Hilary, "have an Enchantress to rescue." She nodded to Captain Blacktooth, but he simply stared after her as Miss Greyson bustled her out of the Salty Biscuit and into the street.

"Well," said Miss Greyson, dusting off her white kid gloves, "I can't say I care for that establishment. That fellow who answered the door was dressed quite nicely, but he didn't have the manners to match."

Hilary stared at her. "Please don't tell me you traveled

all the way to Queensport to complain about pirate etiquette," she said. "Whatever are you doing here? And why aren't you on the *Pigeon*?"

Miss Greyson pressed her lips together. She was usually starched and spotless, but today, in the crisp afternoon light, she looked entirely disheveled: the collar of her jacket was stained, she'd neglected to iron her dress, and when she took a step forward, Hilary could see that one of her bootlaces had come loose.

"We must talk," said Miss Greyson at last, "but I won't do it here with those questionable persons standing nearby." She looked over at the Salty Biscuit, where a small group of rough-shaven pirates was gathering by the entrance.

"Our ship's docked in Queensport Harbor," Charlie offered. "We could go there."

Miss Greyson nodded rather more emphatically than usual. "Yes," she said, "I believe that would suffice." Then, without another word of explanation, she gathered up her skirts and began to hurry toward the harbor. Her bootlace trailed behind her, and Hilary had no choice but to follow.

MISS GREYSON NAVIGATED the winding streets so briskly that the others had trouble keeping up with her. "How did you find her?" Hilary asked Charlie as they made their way over the cobblestones.

"Blind luck," he said. "Claire and I sailed the *Squeaker*

into Queensport Harbor, just like you asked, and we set about searching for a place called the Salty Biscuit, since that Twigget fellow said that's where you'd be. But we couldn't find it, and we ended up outside the train station in the center of town."

"We were hoping to ask someone for directions," Claire cut in, "but then a train pulled in, and the first person to step out of the carriage was Miss Greyson! We ran up to greet her, of course. She seemed terribly surprised to see us."

"When we told her you'd gone off to meet with Captain Blacktooth," Charlie said, "she got all stern and governess-like and said she needed to speak with you at once. Then she pulled out that crochet hook of hers and had it take her to the Salty Biscuit—it was lucky the place was close by."

"Something must be terribly wrong," Hilary whispered. "I've never seen her so distraught—not even when I put a tadpole in her teacup during a history lesson."

They rounded a corner and emerged into the harbor, where Miss Greyson was waiting for them with her arms crossed. Charlie guided them to the place where he'd moored the *Squeaker*, and they all clambered onto the deck. With Miss Greyson on board and the gargoyle refusing to leave Hilary's side for the comfort of his Nest, it was rather a cramped fit.

Hilary dug a bottle of ginger beer from the *Squeaker*'s

hatch and poured a bit into the chipped yellow teacup she'd borrowed from Jasper's bungalow. "Now," she said, handing the cup to Miss Greyson, "please tell us what's happened."

Miss Greyson closed her hands around her teacup. "It's Jasper," she said at last. "I believe he's in very grave danger."

"But he's at his freelance pirates' convention!" said Hilary. "Isn't he?"

Miss Greyson took a hesitant sip of ginger beer. "I don't have the slightest idea where he is. He promised to write me a letter as soon as he arrived at the convention, but I never heard from him. At first I thought he'd forgotten, or that the postal courier had lost the letter, so I wrote him several notes to make sure he'd had a safe journey." Miss Greyson set down her teacup. "I thought it was the prudent thing to do."

"But you didn't get a response?" Hilary asked.

"Actually," said Miss Greyson, "I did—but it wasn't from Jasper. I suppose I'd better show you the wretched thing." From her carpetbag she retrieved an envelope addressed in a familiar, elegant hand, stamped with a cracked blue seal.

A great rush of strength left Hilary's body, and the gargoyle went heavy in her arms. "The Mutineers," she said.

Miss Greyson passed the letter to Hilary. "They say they've got Jasper in their grasp, and if I try to write to him or search for him, they'll"—she hesitated—"well, I can't bear to think about it, but they'll treat him in a most improper fashion."

Hilary tried to focus on the Mutineers' letter, but the words swam before her eyes like small and vicious fish. It hardly mattered, though, for she could imagine their threats all too well.

"What about the other freelance pirates?" Charlie asked. His voice wobbled a bit, and he cleared his throat. "Have they been captured too?"

"There are no other pirates," Miss Greyson said briskly. "Jasper's old crewmates have been assisting me on the *Pigeon*, and they contacted all the freelance pirates of their acquaintance. Not a single one of them knew anything about any sort of convention." She polished off the rest of her ginger beer. "I'm afraid the entire event was nothing more than a trap."

Claire shivered. "How awful!"

"I quite agree," said Miss Greyson. "Thanks to your letter, Hilary, I knew that these particular villains were the same ones who'd run off with Miss Pimm, so we sailed the *Pigeon* to Pemberton at once. I'd hoped to ask for help from the queen's inspectors, and I brought the letter along as evidence. But a horrid little man named Hastings told me that he'd never heard of any Mutineers, and he couldn't waste his men's time on such frivolous matters as searching for pirates."

"Hilary spilled tea on him," the gargoyle told Miss

Greyson, "and I'm glad."

"I'd do it again if I could," said Hilary fiercely. "He truly wouldn't raise a finger to help Jasper?"

"He wouldn't even permit me to stay in his office long enough to scold him," said Miss Greyson. "I was furious, of course. I asked Jasper's mates to watch over the *Pigeon*, and I traveled here to Queensport to see if I could convince Mr. Hastings's superiors to take my case—but now that I've found you all, perhaps that won't be necessary."

"It won't be," Charlie assured her. "I don't believe those inspectors could find salt water if they fell into the sea."

Hilary's mouth felt dry, as though she'd eaten nothing but hardtack for months on end. "I suppose this is my fault," she said. "The Mutineers told me that if I kept searching for Miss Pimm, they'd do something horrid to my friends—and now it seems they've actually done it."

"Of course it's not your fault." Claire put her arm around Hilary's shoulders. "The Mutineers took Jasper days ago, before you'd even started looking for Miss Pimm. You mustn't feel responsible."

"But I *am* responsible," said Hilary. "I'm the Terror of the Southlands. If I can't keep my mates safe, the least I can do is rescue them when they've been captured." She glared across the water. "Even if Captain Blacktooth doesn't think I can manage it."

Miss Greyson nodded. "You're quite right, Hilary. We must do whatever we can to find Jasper—and Miss Pimm, of course." She sat up a bit straighter. "Now, for their sake, let us be practical. What have you discovered about the Mutineers?"

Charlie sighed. "Not much. We know that they're villainous, and we know they've got fancy handwriting."

"We thought Philomena Tilbury might be one of them," Claire added, "but it seems she's been too busy dining with High Society gentlemen to steal an Enchantress."

"I'm sorry to hear it," said Miss Greyson. "Then I'm afraid I'm at a loss. If we don't know who these villains are or what they're planning, whatever can we do?"

Everyone looked at Hilary.

This, Hilary knew, was the moment when the pirate captain was supposed to step in with a brilliant solution to their troubles. If Jasper had been there, he would have cleared his throat on cue and announced a clever plan. But Jasper was leagues away, kidnapped by Mutineers, and Hilary had no clever plan to announce. A thick silence hung over the ship.

"There is one thing we haven't tried," Hilary admitted. It was the last thing in the world she wanted to do, and it might not be any help at all, but with Miss Pimm and Jasper both in peril, did she really have much of a choice? The Mutineers were clearly the worst sorts of scoundrels, and Hilary knew of only one person villainous enough to be involved with such a group. She looked around at the tense faces of her crew and scraped up just enough boldness and daring to announce her plan. "Tomorrow morning," she said, "I'm going to the Royal Dungeons, and I'm going to speak to my father."

an extract *From*

The Gargoyle: History of a Hero
BY THE GARGOYLE
AS TOLD TO H. WESTFIELD

The life of a gargoyle is not always as glamorous as you might think. During the centuries I served as the resident gargoyle of Westfield House, generations of Westfields poked me, pulled faces at me, and forgot to dust behind my ears. Hardly any of them ever asked me to do anything useful, though Cecily Westfield did once use my magic to protect the house from a fire that burned down half the neighborhood. She was one of the nicer ones.

But then there was Reginald Westfield, who forced me to protect him from the cook every time he was caught stealing sweets from the pantry. His fingers left sticky bits of toffee on my snout, but did he apologize? Never! And I don't much enjoy the memory of Lady Agatha Westfield, who balanced potted marigolds on my head for nearly thirty years. Most of the others simply ignored me, never offering to read me a thrilling novel or bring me a snack, but never bothering me with ridiculous magical requests, either—until James Westfield came along.

James didn't ignore me, and at first I thought he might not be too bad as far as Westfields go. When he was very young, he asked me to protect him from the boys who bullied him at school, and I did my best. But as James grew older, he started to ask me to do other sorts of magic—to make him the greatest sailor on the High Seas, or to make other boys follow his orders. When I told him I couldn't do those things, he called me a useless beast and told me that if I wouldn't help him, he'd simply find a better magic piece—one that wasn't so chatty and dull. He had his hand on my snout just then, dear reader, and I wish I had bitten it.

Not long after that, James left Westfield House to join the Royal Navy. He came back home years later, bringing his wife and baby with him, but he never visited my doorway again. Now he resides in the Royal Dungeons, and if my assistant doesn't mind me saying so, I hope he'll stay there for at least the next few centuries.

KINGDOM OF AUGUSTA
OFFICE OF THE ROYAL RECORDS KEEPER

FORM 40D: INTENTION TO VISIT
THE ROYAL DUNGEONS

INSTRUCTIONS: Please write legibly in ink. Present this form to the Dungeons clerk at the beginning of your visit. Remember that no picklocks, weapons, magic pieces, or bribes are permitted within the Royal Dungeons.

NAME OF VISITOR: *Pirate Hilary Westfield*
NAME OF PRISONER: *Admiral James Westfield*
PRISONER'S CRIME: *Attempted theft of magic, plotting to overthrow the queen*
VISITOR'S RELATIONSHIP TO PRISONER: *Quite damaged at the moment, I'm afraid*

THIS WILL BE A (please check one):
[x] BUSINESS MEETING ☐ SOCIAL CALL
☐ CHARITABLE VISIT ☐ SCOLDING
☐ CONSPIRACY

ARE YOU A (please check all that apply):
☐ SCOUNDREL   ☐ VILLAIN
☐ FUGITIVE   ☒ PIRATE

If a box is checked in the row above, will you be
TURNING YOURSELF IN at the conclusion of your
visit to the Royal Dungeons? *I sincerely doubt it.*

Will you attempt to SET YOUR PRISONER FREE
during your visit? *Absolutely not.*

You may use the space below to compose a brief
PLEA FOR YOUR PRISONER'S RELEASE. Please be
as eloquent as possible.
*As far as I'm concerned, the prisoner may stay
right where he is.*

Thank you for complying with the rules and
regulations of the Kingdom of Augusta,
and enjoy your visit to the Royal Dungeons!

CHAPTER TEN

LTHOUGH HILARY HAD insisted that she could visit the Dungeons perfectly well by herself, no one had paid her any attention. Now Miss Greyson, Charlie, and Claire followed Hilary through the streets of Queensport, and she had to admit that having her crew with her made her feel much more like the Terror of the Southlands. "After all," she said to the gargoyle, who swung alongside her in her bag, "we're brave buccaneers on our way to interrogate the villain we've captured. What's so scary about that?"

"The darkness," said the gargoyle, "and the dampness. The mice and the mildew." He shuddered. "Not to mention your father."

Hilary had expected the Royal Dungeons to be gray, gloomy, and foreboding—rather like Miss Pimm's finishing school, but with more villains and fewer governesses. When she turned into the drive, however, she saw that the Dungeons were built of the same pale yellow bricks that formed the walls of the queen's palace, and that someone had gone to quite a lot of effort to make the front gardens presentable. Like many of the houses in Queensport, the Dungeons had hallways lined with stained-glass windows, although these particular windows were reinforced with iron bars. Each window depicted a different type of villain or scoundrel: in one pane, a poisoner was pouring a vial of something green into a goblet, and a cutpurse from the next window over was attempting to pick the poisoner's pocket.

"It's lovely, isn't it?" said Claire as they walked up the stepping-stone pathway and knocked on the door. "A bit too lovely to be real."

"Never fear," said Miss Greyson; "it's significantly less pleasant when one is underground." Not so long ago, Miss Greyson herself had been mistaken for a criminal and sent to the Dungeons, and she assured them that the cells were hardly luxurious. "They don't keep the prisoners upstairs, you see; it would ruin the atmosphere."

They were greeted by the Dungeons clerk, a small woman with round spectacles balanced on her nose. "Welcome to the Royal Dungeons," she said. "Weapons and magic pieces in the box, please." Hilary and Charlie balanced their swords atop the crate the woman held out, Hilary clinked in her magic piece, Claire contributed the bag with the remainder of the coins from Cannonball Jack, and Miss Greyson removed her crochet hook from her hair with a reluctant sigh. The clerk looked slightly alarmed by the contents of the box and even more alarmed by the presence of Miss Greyson. "You look terribly familiar," she said. "Might you be a fugitive, by any chance?"

"I am a governess, a bookshop keeper, and a pirate," said Miss Greyson primly, "and although I was once a convict, I am now reformed, thank you very much."

The clerk cleared her throat. "Very well, then," she said. "Have you got your visitors' forms?"

They all handed the clerk the papers Miss Greyson had given them to fill out the night before, and the clerk rifled through them. She clicked her tongue four times in a row. Then she returned to her desk, ran her finger down an extraordinarily long piece of parchment, peered through her round spectacles, and clicked her tongue once more. "I'm afraid," she said, "that I can't allow you all to enter. This prisoner is only allowed two visitors each day, and he's already received one this morning."

"It must have been Mother," said Hilary. "I thought she only visited every fourth Tuesday." She looked at Miss Greyson on her left, then at Charlie and Claire on her right. "Are you quite sure only one of us can enter?"

The clerk looked at Hilary over her spectacles. "Those

are the rules, Miss . . . er . . ." She consulted Hilary's form. "Miss Pirate."

Charlie stepped forward and leaned over the clerk's desk. "It's lucky, then," he said, "that we pirates don't care much for rules. We're Hilary's crew, and we've got to go with her."

"For support," Miss Greyson added.

"And to glare at Admiral Westfield," said Claire. "I've been looking forward to that part all morning."

But the clerk refused to budge. "Only Miss Pirate may enter, and that's that. I shall keep a very sharp eye on the rest of you to make sure no one scuttles away."

"Sorry, Terror." Charlie squeezed her shoulder. "You'll be just fine, you know."

"Thank you, Pirate Dove," said Hilary, hoping he was right.

The clerk pointed down the hall at an iron door labeled DUNGEONS. "You'll find Admiral Westfield that way, Miss Pirate. You haven't got any weapons in your bag, have you? Or any additional magic?"

Hilary put her hand inside the bag and pressed the gargoyle down toward its bottom seams. "Certainly not," she said. "I don't have any magical items at all in this bag. Not a one."

"Hey!" said the gargoyle. "Aren't you forgetting—"

Hilary gave the gargoyle a firm poke in the side and coughed ferociously to drown out his protests. Claire began to cough as well, and Hilary shot her a grateful look. Miss Greyson narrowed her eyes but said nothing. Before the clerk could inquire further, Hilary slipped behind her and walked as bravely as she could manage toward the door marked DUNGEONS.

BEHIND THE DOOR was a damp and dark spiral staircase that grew even damper and darker as it twisted down into the earth. By the time Hilary reached the bottom of it, she could hardly see the walls around her. She could feel them, though; the stones were slick under her fingers, except where they were mossy, and the air smelled as foul as a ship's bilge. Hilary had never enjoyed climbing belowdecks on the *Pigeon*, but at least no villains lurked in its heavy darkness. "I don't like this at all," she whispered to the gargoyle. "Do you think we're making an awful mistake?"

She heard the gargoyle rustle in his bag. "There's light up ahead," he said. "At least, I think there is. Gargoyles have excellent vision."

Hilary took a few careful steps forward, and soon she could see a row of glowing lanterns hanging from hooks on the wall. A sign above them read:

◆ COMPLIMENTARY LANTERNS ◆
COURTESY OF THE ROYAL DUNGEONS
One per visitor, please

◆ ◆ ◆

Hilary lifted the nearest lantern off its hook, and the dreary landscape of the Dungeons flickered into view around her. Only one path led forward, so Hilary took it, casting her lantern light on each prisoner's cell as she passed by. Most of the cells sat empty, but every so often a villainous face would grin at her from behind the bars. They were cutthroats and pickpockets, blackmailers and burglars, and a few of them even looked like pirates, but none of them looked like her father. Each time her light struck an unfamiliar face, Hilary wobbled back and forth between terror and relief.

She skirted the villains' grins and reached into her bag, where the gargoyle wound his tail around her hand for comfort. "A pirate is never scared, right?" the gargoyle asked.

"That's right," said Hilary, though she didn't much care for the way her voice trembled when she said it.

"Then a pirate must never have been to the Royal Dungeons," said the gargoyle. "This place gives me the creeps."

The only other visitor to the Dungeons was a tall woman dressed in peacock blue who bustled toward Hilary and then brushed directly past her without sparing her a glance. A feather plume bounced atop the woman's fashionable hat, and she wore an exasperated expression that Hilary nearly recognized but couldn't quite place. Perhaps she was one of Mrs. Westfield's many friends, or perhaps they had met at one of those interminable High

Society balls at Westfield House, but the woman's lantern light had already disappeared around a corner, and Hilary had no desire to linger in the damp passageway making polite conversation with friends of her mother. She dusted off her pirate coat where the woman had brushed against it and resumed her search for Admiral Westfield.

She found him around the next corner. He was strolling back and forth in his cell as though it were the deck of his fastest ship, the *Augusta Belle*. As he strolled, he hummed a sea chantey that Hilary recognized as the tune he always sang when he was preparing for an ocean voyage. He was dressed in his naval uniform, just as he had been the last time Hilary had seen him, and her lantern light flashed against his orderly rows of brass buttons. Then the admiral stopped humming and stared at Hilary.

He looked older than Hilary remembered, but no less intimidating, and he squinted into the light as though he couldn't quite tell who she was. When he recognized her—*if* he recognized her—he would yell at her; Hilary was quite certain of that. She had heard him dismiss dozens of naval officers for polishing his brown boots instead of his black ones, or for dropping his second-best compass into the sea. The humiliated officers had never escaped without a scolding even sharper than Admiral Westfield's sword, and none of them had done anything nearly as treacherous as capturing the admiral and thwarting his villainous plans. Hilary squeezed the gargoyle's tail and prepared for the worst.

Then Admiral Westfield chuckled, low and rumbling like a wave breaking on the shore, and Hilary nearly wished he had yelled after all. "What's this?" he said. "Has my devoted daughter come to see me at last? Hilary, my dear, I can hardly recall the last time I spoke to you."

Hilary sincerely doubted that was the case, but then again, there had been more than a few occasions when her father hadn't been able to recall her name. "The last time we spoke," she said, "I believe you were ordering me to hand over Miss Pimm's treasure. Or perhaps you were using magic to harm my friends, or cursing my name as the constable dragged you away."

"Ah, yes, I believe you're right." Admiral Westfield nodded. "I see you're still a pirate, bringing shame to the family and so on. Truly, my dear, I don't know what's gotten into you. Are you still sailing about with that wretched Fletcher fellow? And that impertinent governess?"

"Jasper and Miss Greyson aren't wretched or impertinent, Father. Hilary tried to keep her voice low in case any of the other villains in the Dungeons were eavesdroppers. "But if you must know, I'm the Terror of the Southlands now. I have my own ship, and my own pirate crew as well." There was no need to give Admiral Westfield the details of the *Squeaker*.

"Really?" he said. "And you haven't been blasted by the Royal Navy yet? I swear those men have lost their discipline since I've been away."

"Perhaps," said Hilary, "they're afraid of me."

Admiral Westfield frowned. "No, no, that certainly can't be it."

"You villain!" cried the gargoyle. "You scoundrel! You slimy little—"

"So you still have that tiresome creature with you," said Admiral Westfield. "You should be more cautious with it. It bites, you know."

"I certainly do," the gargoyle said. "Would you care for a demonstration?"

"Not now, gargoyle," said Hilary. She held her bag well away from the admiral's reach; the last time he had managed to grab the gargoyle, he'd tried to use the gargoyle's magic, and Hilary couldn't let such a horrid thing happen again. "Father, I didn't come here to chat."

"Good. I detest chatting. It's terribly frivolous." Admiral Westfield leaned against the bars of his cell. "If you've got something to say, then you'd better say it. I haven't got all day, my dear."

It seemed to Hilary that Admiral Westfield *did* have all day, but it was hardly worth an argument. "Miss Pimm has gone missing," she said, "and Jasper's gone, too. I demand to know what's happened to them."

"You demand it, do you?" Admiral Westfield chuckled

more heartily than ever. "I'd heard about That Meddling Old Biddy running off, and I can't say I'm surprised that Fletcher's missing as well. That fellow couldn't sail his way out of a grog bottle."

The gargoyle trembled, and Hilary gripped the iron bars to steady herself. It was probably a good thing that she'd had to leave her cutlass behind, for she wasn't sure she'd be able to resist pointing it in her father's direction. "Jasper," she said fiercely, "is a far better sailor than you'll ever be, and you know it. Now tell me what you've done."

Admiral Westfield stepped backward and raised his hands. "What *I've* done?" he asked. "My dear girl, you give me far too much credit. I've been locked behind bars ever since my treacherous daughter dragged my name through the mud, so I'm afraid I haven't had time to run about after Enchantresses and pirates."

"You know who's taken Miss Pimm and Jasper, though; I'm sure of it. Who are the Mutineers? Are they friends of yours?"

"The Mutineers." Admiral Westfield smiled. "It's a good name, isn't it?"

"Oh, it's terribly villainous," said Hilary. "Tell me who they are."

With one calloused hand, Admiral Westfield reached out and unfolded Hilary's fingers from the bars. "I imagine," he said, "that they prefer to remain anonymous."

"And I'd prefer to send them to the bottom of the sea."

"That seems rather uncalled for," said Admiral Westfield. "After all, they've been kind enough to refrain from doing the same to you. Don't scowl so ferociously, my dear, or you'll never be asked to dance at a High Society ball."

"Then I shall practice my scowling more often from now on," Hilary snapped. "Do you know who the Mutineers are?"

"Of course," said Admiral Westfield.

"And will you tell me a single thing about them? Where they are, or what they want with Miss Pimm and Jasper?"

Admiral Westfield looked confused. "Why in the world should I do that?"

"I know it's not in your nature to be charitable or kind," said Hilary, "but if you help me find the Enchantress, the queen is sure to be grateful. Perhaps you won't have to spend the rest of your days sitting in this cell, watching the moss grow. If you don't help me, though, I'll see to it that the queen keeps you locked up for good—and I'll tell Mother to stop wasting her time with her visits."

For a moment, Admiral Westfield was silent. "My dear," he said at last, "I'd gladly tell you everything I know, but I'm afraid I don't share information with the Terror of the Southlands."

Hilary clenched her teeth. She'd been utterly foolish to think she could wring even a drop of information from her father; they might as well have been captains of enemy ships facing off across a vast stretch of sea. "I suppose that means you won't tell me what you've done with the rest of that magic you stole, either."

"You suppose correctly," said Admiral Westfield. "Really, if those silly inspectors haven't found it by now, I don't think they deserve it, do you?"

Hilary tried to imagine what Inspector Hastings might do with a wagonload of magic pieces. He'd probably wish for a new set of dusting brushes, which was sure to be preferable to anything Admiral Westfield or his friends might be planning. "It's a shame you won't tell me what you know, Father," she said, "but I hope you don't think that will stop me from finding your friends and sending them to join you in the Dungeons. It will be ever so nice for you to have a bit of company down here."

"Oh, I'm sure you'll try your best," said Admiral Westfield. "But you can't sincerely believe that you'll stop the Mutineers from"—he coughed—"er, from doing whatever it is they plan to do."

Hilary glared at him. "I stopped you, didn't I?"

"A mere bit of luck," said Admiral Westfield with a shrug. "You may have fooled Jasper Fletcher, but even underneath that pirate finery you can't fool me. You are my daughter, after all—a Westfield, and a High Society girl!" He smiled approvingly at the notion. "But you're certainly not a Terror."

Hilary stepped back from the cell. "You're wrong," she said.

"Actually," said the admiral, "I rather think I'm right. I can't imagine that a truly terrifying pirate would bother to visit her father in the Dungeons—and yet here you are." Admiral Westfield raised his eyebrows, as though an intriguing thought had just occurred to him. "Is it possible, my dear, that you regret locking me away?"

For a moment, the Dungeons were as still and silent as the air after a cannonball blast. In his bag, the gargoyle tensed. So did Hilary. Then she turned on her heel to leave, snatched up her lantern, and swung it so ferociously that before she knew quite what had happened, the lantern had slipped free from her grasp and shattered against the wall. Shards of glass skittered underfoot, and the candle fell to the floor, where it blazed for a moment before snuffing itself out in the dirt. Hilary blinked into the darkness. Perhaps the smoke from the candle had stung her eyes, for they began to dampen at the corners.

Then lights flickered in the passageway, footsteps crunched through the glass, and two royal guards took Hilary by the elbows. "There's no damage to the queen's property allowed, miss," one of them said. "You'll have to leave now—unless you'd prefer a cell of your own, of course."

"That's perfectly all right," said Hilary. "I don't believe I can tolerate the Dungeons for another moment." She turned to look over her shoulder at Admiral Westfield's cell. "Good-bye, Father," she said with as much dignity as she could scrape up. "I won't be visiting again."

"No, I suppose you won't," said Admiral Westfield. "Run along, then," he called as the guards escorted Hilary away, "and be a good little girl."

BEING MARCHED UP a staircase and down a hall by a pair of guards in unflattering mustard-colored trousers was, Hilary decided, a rather mortifying experience. The tongue click of disapproval that the clerk issued as Hilary passed her desk was more mortifying still, but worst of all was the gasp that Miss Greyson let out when the guards deposited Hilary at the Dungeons' front entrance. "Here's your pirate, ma'am," said one of the guards to Miss Greyson, tipping his hat. "She's not to come back to the Dungeons until she apologizes for the damage she's done."

"Damage?" said Miss Greyson. "Oh dear, whatever happened down there?"

"Father happened," said Hilary. Perhaps if she took long enough slipping her cutlass back onto her belt, she wouldn't have to meet Miss Greyson's eyes. "And I suppose I may have broken a lantern. But I'd prefer not to discuss it, if you don't mind."

Miss Greyson gave the guards a curt nod and guided Hilary out to the drive, where Charlie and Claire were waiting. "You needn't discuss a thing," she murmured to Hilary. "I happen to know for a fact that the Royal Dungeons rarely do much to improve one's character."

As they walked back toward the *Squeaker*, Hilary told the others everything that Admiral Westfield had said—or very nearly everything. "He knows who the Mutineers are," she said, "but he wouldn't tell me a thing about them, except to say we've got no hope of stopping them."

"And," said the gargoyle, "he called me a tiresome creature."

"But he's wrong," said Hilary. "Of course we'll stop the Mutineers." She was quite sure that if they didn't, Admiral Westfield would sit in his cell and chuckle, and the thought of it was too infuriating to bear. "Perhaps I don't know who the villains are, or where to find them, or what they've done with our friends. And perhaps I don't have the slightest idea what they're planning." Hilary shoved her hands into her coat pockets and looked out at Queensport Harbor, where blue-and-gold flags flew from every mast in the Royal Navy's fleet. "But I simply won't give Father the satisfaction of being right."

CHARLIE HAD TIED up the *Squeaker* far from the other ships in the harbor, but when they returned to it, they found it had been joined by a gleaming white pirate ship with the name *Calamity* painted on its hull and Alice Feathering balanced on its bowsprit. She was dressed in a cloud of lavender frills, and her hair flew in all directions underneath her pirate hat. The sight of her cheered Hilary immensely.

"Ahoy!" Alice cried, giving the pirates a vigorous wave.

"I request an audience with the Terror of the Southlands and her mates!"

Miss Greyson raised an eyebrow. "Who's this?"

"A High Society girl," Hilary explained, "and a very fearsome pirate."

"Ah," said Miss Greyson. "That explains the frills, then."

Alice jumped down onto the dock and ran to meet them. "I've been waiting for hours!" she said. "I saw your ship tied up here, and I hoped you'd hurry back. I worried you'd be too late." She glanced over her shoulder and paused to catch her breath. "But you've gotten here just in time!"

Claire knelt down and put her hands on Alice's shoulders. "In time for what?" she asked.

"Well," said Alice, "there's a bit of a story to it. I was sailing about in the *Calamity* this morning, only there's not much to *do* out by Feathering Keep, so I decided to sail toward the city. And as I came into the harbor, I saw the most amazing thing." She pointed out at the sea. "Do you see that ship with black sails that's just going around the point? You'd better look quickly, or you'll miss it."

Hilary squinted at the ship, which was hardly more than a dark smudge on the horizon. Then she pulled out her spyglass to get a better view of its sleek black hull and flaming torches. "That's Captain Blacktooth's galleon," she said. "That's the *Renegade*."

Alice beamed up at her. "That," she said, "is the ghost ship."

Hilary nearly dropped her spyglass. "The ghost ship? Do you mean it's the ship you saw on the night Miss Pimm disappeared?" She passed the spyglass to Charlie. "That *is* the *Renegade*, isn't it?"

He studied the ship for a few moments and frowned. "That's Blacktooth's ship, all right." He lowered the spyglass and looked down at Alice. "Are you absolutely sure that's the same ship you saw in Pemberton Bay?"

"I'd recognize it anywhere," said Alice. "Hardly anyone on the High Seas sails about with so many torches. It had people on board today, though. I thought of chasing them and asking them if they'd taken Miss Pimm, but I'm not an official pirate yet, of course, so I thought I'd better tell the Terror of the Southlands at once, because you'd know what to do." She smoothed the front of her dress and curtsied. "I hope I did the right thing."

"You certainly did." Hilary stared after the *Renegade* as it rounded the eastern point of the harbor. "But it's rather curious. Captain Blacktooth told me just yesterday that he and his crew were on Gunpowder Island on Midsummer's Eve. What was his ship doing in Pemberton?"

"Perhaps someone stole it," Claire offered, but Hilary shook her head. Not even the bravest of villains would dare to steal a galleon belonging to the president of the VNHLP—and in any case, the ship had clearly been returned to Captain Blacktooth's possession.

The harbor was bustling with naval officers and High Society pleasure boaters, but Hilary spotted a small band of pirates passing by in a dinghy and waved to get their attention. "Ahoy!" she called. "Scallywags!"

The pirates looked in her direction, and one of them saluted her with his hook. "Arr!" he said. "Be ye needin' a hand, matey? I'm afraid I've only got the one."

"Actually," said Hilary, "I've got a question. Were you at the VNHLP picnic on Midsummer's Eve?"

The hook-handed pirate gave Hilary a yellowed grin. "Why, of course we were, matey. All pirates worth their breeches make sure to attend the League picnic."

"Of course they do." Hilary sighed. "And did you happen to catch sight of Captain Rupert Blacktooth at the picnic? Or his mates?"

The pirate scratched his chin perilously with his hook. "'Twas strange, now that ye mention it," he said. "We were expectin' the crew of the *Renegade* to wallop us in the swimmin' relay, but they never showed up."

"I heard they all came down with nasty colds," another pirate in the dinghy added.

"Aye," said the hook-handed pirate. "Ye be lookin' at the first-place swimmers from the dread ship *Matilda*, and ye can thank Captain Blacktooth's absence for that."

When the first-place swimmers from the dread ship *Matilda* had bobbed away in their dinghy, Hilary turned back to her mates. "I suppose that settles it," she said. "Captain Blacktooth wasn't on Gunpowder Island that night at all." She knew perfectly well that pirates lied, but still, she was rather distressed that Captain Blacktooth had lied to *her*.

"And I'll bet," said Charlie, "that he didn't have a nasty cold, either."

Claire tugged at her cardigan. "Do you think Captain Blacktooth is a Mutineer, then?"

Hilary crossed her arms. The idea seemed preposterous; whatever would Captain Blacktooth want with Miss Pimm and Jasper? His handwriting looked nothing like the elegant script in the Mutineers' letters, and she couldn't imagine that the president of the VNHLP would have anything at all to do with someone who hated pirates as ferociously as Admiral Westfield did. Still, Captain Blacktooth had been quite persistent about halting Hilary's search for Miss Pimm, and his ship had been hidden very near the place where Miss Pimm had disappeared. The more Hilary thought about it, the more suspicious it all seemed. "I've got no idea what Blacktooth is up to," she said, "but if we follow his ship, perhaps we'll find out."

THE QUEEN'S INSPECTORS
Kingdom of Augusta
DILIGENCE, LOGIC, DISCRETION

Report to H.R.H. Queen Adelaide regarding
THE DISAPPEARANCE OF MISS EUGENIA PIMM

Report No. 3
FIELD INSPECTOR: *John Hastings*
LOCATION: *Pemberton, Augusta*
CASE STATUS: *Truly Perplexing*

Inspector's Comments: *Your Highness, you have no doubt noticed that Miss Eugenia Pimm has still not reappeared. We regret the delay and offer our heartfelt apologies. In addition, we hope it will be some consolation to you to learn that we have made progress in our line of investigation regarding pirates.*

I have corresponded with Captain Rupert Blacktooth, the president of the Very Nearly Honorable League of Pirates, and his insights have proven to be most helpful. I described to Captain Blacktooth the eye patch that was found at the scene of the crime, and he identified it as belonging to Cannonball Jack—the very pirate who had arranged to dine with the Enchantress on the evening of her disappearance. Captain Blacktooth tells me that Cannonball Jack is an unpredictable buccaneer who may very well be responsible for all manner of villainous acts throughout the kingdom. My inspectors have tried to approach Cannonball Jack's houseboat on the High Seas, but the pirate has an extraordinary number of cannons, and my men are armed only with their magnifying glasses. Would the Royal Armory be willing to provide my inspectors with weapons so that they might investigate this case without fearing for their lives?

In my correspondence with Captain Blacktooth, I also made inquiries regarding the pirate who calls herself the Terror of the Southlands. Her name is Hilary Westfield, and Captain Blacktooth reports that she is not a pirate in good standing. Indeed, she is only inches away from being expelled from the League. The girl's father, Admiral James Westfield, is a confirmed criminal mastermind, and I am confident that she has taken up his villainous ways. In fact, my men in Queensport tell me that Pirate Westfield was recently observed visiting the admiral in the Royal Dungeons, where the two were surely planning their next coldhearted scheme. My fellow inspectors are reluctant to apprehend the girl without firm proof that she is involved in the Enchantress's disappearance, but I should very much like to see her locked up alongside her father. She has vexed me for quite some time, Your Highness, and she is doubtlessly guilty of some crime or another. The next time I lay eyes on her, I shall arrest her myself.

Signed
John Hastings
Captain, Queen's Inspectors

Dear Hilary,

I hope this note finds you safe and sound, but I fear it does not, for I read in the *Gazette* that you have embarked on a quest to find the Enchantress. While I quite approve of your urge to do something kind for dear Miss Pimm, I wonder whether your plan is entirely wise? It sounds rather dangerous. But then, I have become much acquainted with danger myself in the past few days, for (as you may have read) a thoroughly cruel turkey stalks the halls of Westfield House, and my cook has not yet managed to roast the villain.

I know that you are busy with your piratical notions, Hilary, but as your mother, I must request that you accompany me to the event that will surely be the highlight of the social season. I have just received a lovely invitation from Mrs. Georgiana Tilbury, who is holding a grand ball at Tilbury Park for her daughter Philomena's debut. Your name is not specifically included on the invitation, but I am certain that this was an oversight on Mrs. Tilbury's part, for I believe Philomena is one of your darling companions from finishing school. Wouldn't you enjoy watching her enter High Society? Mrs. Tilbury hints that a grand announcement will be made that evening as well, and I'm sure all of Augusta will be buzzing about it for days. Do let me know if you'll come.

Your loving
Mother

CHAPTER ELEVEN

B Y THE TIME Hilary and her mates had said good-bye to Alice and sailed out of Queensport Harbor, Captain Blacktooth and his ship were completely out of sight. Even Miss Greyson's crochet hook couldn't shove the *Squeaker* along quickly enough to overtake the *Renegade*. "It's awfully hard to follow Blacktooth," the gargoyle observed, "when we can't even see him."

Such a small inconvenience was hardly enough to stop the Terror of the Southlands in her tracks, however. "On the way to the Salty Biscuit," Hilary called from the helm, "Mr. Twigget told me that Captain Blacktooth was due back on Gunpowder Island any day now. If that's truly where he's headed, then that's where we must go as well."

Miss Greyson, who was resting after her most recent magical attempt to spur the *Squeaker* forward, nodded approvingly. "That's quite a practical plan," she said. "Perhaps my lessons have had some useful effect after all."

"Do you think Blacktooth's got Miss Pimm and Jasper locked up in the bowels of the *Renegade*?" Charlie asked. "Or could he have squirreled them away at League headquarters?"

"*If* Captain Blacktooth is a Mutineer," said Miss Greyson, "there's no telling what he might have done. And if we remain on board this vessel, we shall never find out, for we'll be months behind him. If I might make a suggestion, Hilary, I believe we should remove ourselves to a ship that requires a bit less encouragement."

As much as Hilary appreciated the *Squeaker*'s service, she had to admit that it wasn't quite up to a lengthy High Seas voyage. "Perhaps you're right," she said. "Do you have a particular ship in mind?"

"Of course," said Miss Greyson. "The *Pigeon* should do nicely."

"But it's filled with treasure!"

"I suppose bringing half the kingdom's magic along with us isn't entirely wise," Miss Greyson admitted, "but I don't believe there's anything else to be done with it. We haven't got the time to pile it all into treasure chests and bury it for safekeeping."

Losing Jasper to the Mutineers seemed to have made Miss Greyson a good deal more reckless than usual. "All right, then," said Hilary, "we'll take the *Pigeon*. Pirate Dove, set a course for Little Herring Cove."

At Jasper's bungalow, they were met by the pirates whom Miss Greyson had asked to watch over the ship and its treasure in her absence. There were three of them, and all were sturdy and bearded, though one wore a white coat, one wore a red coat, and one wore a black coat. They all bowed to Hilary and kissed Miss Greyson's hand. "It's a pleasure to see you again, Eloise," said the pirate in the black coat, "and to meet the Terror and her crew. Jasper speaks very highly of you, Terror. I am Mr. Stanley, and these are my colleagues, Mr. Marrow"—he gestured to the white-coated pirate—"and Mr. Slaughter. Perhaps you saw us at Jasper's wedding?"

"I'm sure I did," said Hilary, though there had been a great many pirates packed onto the Westfield House lawn. "You're friends of Jasper's, then?"

"Aye," said Mr. Stanley, who seemed to be the group's spokesman. "We were all crewmates once—we four and Nat Dove, who I hear was this good lad's father." He clapped Charlie on the shoulder, and Charlie looked stubbornly down at his boots. "But we're retired these days, as much as old buccaneers can be. Perhaps you'd like our card." He fished a stiff square of paper out of his pocket and passed it to Hilary. "In case you ever require our services."

The card was engraved with a few words in jet-black ink:

MARROW, SLAUGHTER & STANLEY
PROTECTION • PIRACY • CATERING

"We focus mostly on the catering," said Mr. Slaughter.

Hilary smiled and tucked the card in her pocket. "As a matter of fact," she said, "I believe I do have a job for you. We think we've identified one of the villains who's kidnapped Jasper, but we've got to sail the *Pigeon* to Gunpowder Island to find out what he's up to. We could use a few extra hands on deck—as well as some help guarding the treasure, of course."

Marrow, Slaughter, and Stanley frowned in unison. "Gunpowder Island," said Mr. Stanley. "It's a pirate you're after, then?"

"It's the president of the VNHLP, actually," said Hilary. "I hope that won't make things awkward for you."

Mr. Marrow and Mr. Slaughter grinned. "Not at all," said Mr. Stanley. "We've had nothing to do with the League since our retirement. If someone's got it in for Jasper, we'd be pleased to give that someone a bit of trouble, no matter who he may be." Mr. Stanley bowed to Hilary again, more deeply this time. "Terror, my colleagues and I are at your service."

With the three hired pirates on board, the *Pigeon* fairly flew toward Gunpowder Island. The quarters were slightly cramped—Charlie, Slaughter, and Stanley all shared a small cabin, and Marrow slept in the bookshop—but having a surfeit of pirates made it easier for Hilary to divide the ship's duties. In addition to the usual knot tying, deck swabbing, and watch keeping, Slaughter baked pies that rivaled Miss Greyson's, and Marrow read aloud to the gargoyle when Hilary was busy at the helm. Stanley's particular talent seemed to be for magic. He and Miss Greyson took turns using their magic pieces to summon up favorable winds, and both of them could work for hours before the magic drained them. Claire had settled in with a pair of Miss Greyson's knitting needles and was busy repairing the sleeves of her cardigan, but Hilary noticed her studying Mr. Stanley and Miss Greyson over the tips of her needles: whenever they worked an enchantment, Claire's brow went tight with concentration, her lips moved along with theirs, and she dropped dozens of stitches in her knitting.

On the third day at sea, Claire abandoned her cardigan and disappeared into the cabin she shared with Hilary. When she emerged again a few moments later, she was wearing Jasper's gardening glove on one hand and clutching Cannonball Jack's dwindling supply of magic coins in the other. "I'm sure I've figured out the trick of it now," she said to Hilary; "I've been watching for hours, and I can't imagine I'll blow anything up again."

"Are you sure?" said Hilary. "I don't want to be discouraging, but I can imagine it awfully well."

Claire patted her gloved hand. "I see what you mean," she said, "but I shall do exactly what Miss Greyson does, and everything shall be fine; you'll see."

Charlie climbed down from the rigging, took one look at Claire's gardening glove, and froze. "I don't think you should be using magic here," he said. "What if you blast a hole in the *Pigeon*?"

Claire frowned. "I never blasted a hole in the *Squeaker*, did I?"

"That was lucky for all of us," said Charlie. "I don't know about you, but I'm not the least bit interested in sinking to the bottom of the sea." He turned away and headed toward the Gargoyle's Nest. "Perhaps you High Society girls think being shipwrecked is thrilling and romantic," he said as he went, "but I promise you it's not."

Claire looked after him and sighed. "I'm sorry to worry Charlie," she said, "but now that we're off after the Mutineers, I've simply *got* to learn how to use this stuff. How can I possibly help you all fight the villains otherwise? I can't use a sword, I don't know the first thing about battles, and Captain Blacktooth could most likely squash me flat under his boots in half a minute."

Hilary didn't care one bit for the thought of her friends being squashed under Blacktooth's boots—or anyone else's boots, for that matter. "I suppose a pirate's assistant *should* be able to defend herself in battle," she said at last.

"Exactly!" said Claire, plucking a magic coin from the bag. "Now, what did Miss Greyson say? Oh yes." She cleared her throat. "I wish we might have a fair wind in our sails to speed our ship toward Gunpowder Island, please."

A promising breeze brushed against Hilary's ear, but she was fairly sure it had nothing to do with magic, for the coin was already starting to glow white-hot in Claire's hand. Hilary sighed and ducked behind the helm for safety.

"Oh, crumbs!" Claire said as the coin exploded.

Miss Greyson and the three hired pirates jumped at the sound. Charlie groaned and buried his face in his hat.

"What was that noise?" Miss Greyson said. "Has someone opened fire on our ship? Don't tell me it's the Royal Navy; I'm simply not in the mood for a battle."

"It's not the Royal Navy," the gargoyle called from his Nest. "It's only Claire. She's blowing up magic pieces again."

"Blowing up magic pieces?" Miss Greyson crossed the deck and examined Claire's smoking gardening glove. "But that's not possible."

"It's not?" Claire looked worried.

"Well, if you've done it, I suppose it *is* possible, but I've never seen anything like it before," said Miss Greyson. She turned to Stanley. "Have you?"

"Not in all my years at sea," Stanley said. "How extremely curious."

"Do you mean beginners don't explode their magic pieces all the time?" Claire's lower lip wobbled. "Do you mean it might never get better, and I shall be stuck exploding things for the rest of my life?"

"I'm sure that's not what they mean," said Hilary, but both Stanley and Miss Greyson were nodding.

"I'm hardly an expert when it comes to magic," Miss Greyson said, "but I shouldn't try to use any more of it if I were you."

"That's a relief," Charlie muttered.

Claire flushed, pulled off her gardening glove, and thrust it into Hilary's hand. "If you'll excuse me, Hilary, I believe I've got to go back to our cabin and—um—attend to things." Then, before Hilary could do a thing to stop her, Claire hurried back to the cabin and let the door slam shut behind her.

FOR SEVERAL DAYS afterward, Claire was much quieter than usual, and Hilary worried that the latest magical blast had nearly blown her spirit to bits as well. But the rest of the journey to the Northlands was happily free of explosions, and by the time the *Pigeon* arrived in Gunpowder Bay, the Terror of the Southlands and her crew had grown considerably more cheerful.

"Avast," cried the gargoyle as they entered the bay, "and arr! That's the *Renegade* ahead!"

The black galleon was anchored near the island's west gate, and Hilary was relieved to see it: at least Mr. Twigget had not been villainous enough to lie to her about his captain's destination. Against the gray sky and sea, with its deck empty of pirates and its hull creaking on the waves, the *Renegade* really did look rather ghostly. Even though she had once climbed all the way to its crow's nest, Hilary had to remind herself sternly that this ship and its captain were entirely real.

"There's no one on the deck," said Charlie, setting down the spyglass. "At least, no one that I can see. Shall we go aboard?"

Hilary scanned the Gunpowder Island coast, where pirates bustled back and forth through the west gate, chatting and chortling and swinging their swords with wild abandon. "We're sure to be seen," she said, "and even if those aren't Captain Blacktooth's men, I can't imagine they'll be pleased if they notice us climbing aboard his ship." She pulled her magic coin from her coat pocket and stepped away from the helm. "Pirate Dove, would you mind sailing us a bit closer to the *Renegade*?"

Charlie took the wheel, and Hilary made her way to the bow of the *Pigeon*. "Are we going to sink Blacktooth's ship?" the gargoyle asked. "Can I shout 'fire away'?"

Hilary laughed. "You may shout whatever you like, but I'm going to try to find out if Miss Pimm is on board. We should be close enough for the magic to guide us to her if she's there." She held her magic coin with two fingers and steadied herself against the Gargoyle's Nest. "Magic," she said, "could you please guide us to Miss Pimm, if she's nearby?" She paused for a moment. "Or to Jasper Fletcher?"

Hilary's heart beat faster as the coin began to twitch. It leaned to the left and then to the right. It tilted forward and back. Then, with an air of disappointment, it slid into Hilary's palm and didn't move again.

Hilary took a deep breath. "They're not trapped in the *Renegade*, then. I suppose that's a relief."

Miss Greyson summoned up a thin smile, but Hilary was quite sure she was thinking about Jasper. "Very well, then," Miss Greyson said, as though she were merely proceeding to the next order of business in the day's lessons. "Where shall we search next? Or would you prefer to confront Captain Blacktooth directly? I believe I could get some answers out of him."

Hilary was sorely tempted to watch Captain Blacktooth sweat under Miss Greyson's unwavering gaze, but the pirates on board the *Pigeon* were hardly a match for Blacktooth and all his mates. Instead Hilary ordered her crew to lower the anchor and gather around her, just as

Jasper always did when he was about to make a bold and daring suggestion. She hoped she could manage to be half as convincing as he was.

When her crew stood at attention in front of her—except for the gargoyle, who stood as attentively as he could in his Nest—she put her hands behind her back, lifted her chin, and began to pace back and forth across the deck. Then she glanced down the row of pirates and was pleasantly surprised to see that they all stood up a little straighter as her eyes passed over them. Perhaps this was why Jasper paced back and forth so often. "We've got to do two things while we're here," she said. "We've got to find our missing friends—or at least learn more about where the Mutineers might have taken them—and we've got to protect our cargo. I'm sure I don't need to remind any of you that we've just sailed the largest treasure in the kingdom directly into a pirate stronghold, and pirates aren't known for their scruples when it comes to treasure."

Mr. Slaughter gave a knowing sort of nod, and Claire bit her lip.

"I'd like Mr. Marrow, Mr. Slaughter, and Mr. Stanley to stay on board the *Pigeon* and guard our treasure," Hilary continued. "They've been doing a fine job of it so far, and I'm sure they'll be able to fend off any curious scallywags who might pass by."

"Aye," said Mr. Stanley. "That should be no trouble at all."

"Good. I'd like the rest of you to come with me. But first, could two of the pirates who are staying aboard please loan their coats and hats to Claire and Miss Greyson?"

Miss Greyson patted her hair bun. "I'm sure that's not necessary. My attire is perfectly practical for adventuring."

"But perhaps it's not appropriate for the occasion," Claire pointed out. "Gunpowder Island is swarming with pirates, isn't it? I suppose they've got a very different idea of what's fashionable."

"That's true." Miss Greyson shook her head. "Pirates are a hopeless case." She tugged on the white pirate coat Mr. Marrow offered to her, and Claire wrapped Mr. Stanley's black coat around her like a dressing gown. When they had settled the pirates' hats over their hair, they didn't exactly look fearsome, but they wouldn't be likely to draw unnecessary attention on Gunpowder Island. "Now," said Miss Greyson, "may I ask where we're going in this finery?"

"Certainly." Hilary crossed her arms and smiled at her crew. "We are going to VNHLP headquarters, and we're going to search Captain Blacktooth's rooms. And," she said, "we shall be very well dressed while we're doing it."

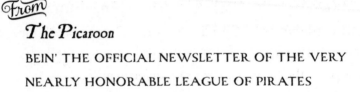

TIME FOR A NEW TERROR? In the pirate community, rumors are swirling that Pirate Hilary Westfield may not be bold and daring enough to keep her grasp on the title of Terror of the Southlands. Not only has Pirate Westfield embarked on a controversial quest to locate the missing Enchantress, but she was recently rescued from a groggery brawl by a governess, and she may soon be expelled from the League for unpiratical behavior. Who do you think should be the next Terror of the Southlands? Write to the Picaroon to share your view!

◎◎

QUEEN'S INSPECTORS SUNK BY SCALLYWAG. In a dramatic showdown on the High Seas yesterday, two queen's inspectors were drenched and humiliated when their boat was fired upon by the pirate Cannonball Jack. The gentlemen had been attempting to question Cannonball Jack after discovering his eye patch near the scene of the Enchantress's disappearance, but the pirate refused to cooperate, although he did toss each inspector a packet of shortbread as they swam back to shore. Both inspectors have returned safely to the mainland, though Cannonball Jack's current location is unknown. The shortbread has regrettably been lost beneath the waves.

◎◎

HELP WANTED. VNHLP president Rupert Blacktooth is seeking pirates to assist the crew of the *Renegade* during a short-term assignment in the Northlands. Candidates must be loyal to the League, must not indulge in gossip, and must be willing to dance if necessary. First-rate dueling skills are required. Pirates will be compensated generously from the president's personal treasure chest. Please write to Captain Blacktooth directly for more information.

❊❊❊❊❊❊❊❊❊❊❊❊❊❊❊❊❊❊❊❊❊❊❊❊❊❊❊

Dear Hilary,

We have noticed that you and your unusual friends have set a northern course for your voyage. Please stop it at once. May we recommend traveling south, east, or west instead? They are far lovelier directions, and we hear they are a good deal less perilous. If you continue to sail northward, you may find yourself in very rough waters indeed.

What a shame that your dear friend Jasper has not been able to join you on your journey. Wherever could he be?

Threateningly yours,
The Mutineers

❊❊❊❊❊❊❊❊❊❊❊❊❊❊❊❊❊❊❊❊❊❊❊❊❊❊❊

CHAPTER TWELVE

ON THE HIGHEST point of Gunpowder Island, at the end of a steep cobblestone lane, the Very Nearly Honorable League of Pirates had built its headquarters. The whitewashed front porch was lined with rocking chairs and flaming torches, and above the porch was a pleasant balcony complete with spyglasses for looking out across the bay. Skull-and-crossbones flags flew from all four corners of the roof, and a real skull stood guard over two crossed cutlasses above the front door. A few pirates were wandering the grounds, swinging in the rope hammocks, and chatting by the rows of cannons that surrounded the building. It was a lovely headquarters, Hilary thought.

She rather regretted having to break into it.

Because Charlie had trained as a pirate apprentice, he'd been to League headquarters dozens of times, and Hilary had sent him to look through Captain Blacktooth's windows. Now he strolled around the corner toward Hilary, whistling both cheerfully and loudly. Hilary narrowed her eyes. "What's the whistling for?" she whispered.

"You said not to act suspicious," Charlie said, "and suspicious people never whistle."

Hilary supposed that was true, for none of the wandering pirates had given Charlie a second glance. "Were you able to see anything?"

"Not much," said Charlie, "but I don't think Blacktooth's in his office. He's got his curtains drawn, and I couldn't hear a thing when I put my ear to the window."

"I've put my crochet hook to good use," Miss Greyson said, coming up behind them. "Neither Jasper nor Miss Pimm seems to be anywhere nearby. Frankly, I doubt they're even on the island."

Hilary stamped her boots against the cobblestones. "Drat," she said. "I suppose it wasn't likely, but I hoped . . ."

"I know," said Miss Greyson. "I hoped, too."

"Well," said Hilary after a few moments, "if Blacktooth isn't in his office, I suppose we can search through his things. Perhaps we'll find something useful."

They had decided on the *Pigeon* that climbing through Captain Blacktooth's window would look terribly suspicious and couldn't be risked, so Hilary had settled on a plan that seemed almost too simple to work. "Are you ready?" she asked Miss Greyson and Claire.

Both of them nodded, and Claire's pirate hat slipped down over her eyes. "Are you sure there won't be any guards?" she asked.

"There's no need for guards when everyone in the building has at least one sword," said Charlie. "As long as you look piratical and say 'Arr!' every so often, you shouldn't run into trouble."

"All right." Claire squeezed Hilary's hand. "We'll see you soon," she whispered, "or at least I hope we will. And please don't get caught."

Truthfully, Hilary was more nervous for Claire and Miss Greyson than she was for herself. She was a pirate and a League member—for the moment, at least—and so was Charlie; it would be perfectly natural for them to visit headquarters in the course of their voyages around the kingdom. But if Miss Greyson's pirate hat flew off her head, or if Claire's vast pirate coat puddled around her boots, every scallywag in the building would know they were up to no good, and most pirates did not take kindly to finishing-school girls or governesses.

After Claire and Miss Greyson passed through the front door, Hilary and Charlie counted to five hundred before following them. The gargoyle had objected to this part of the plan: although he had tried many times, he had never successfully counted higher than seventy-three. Now he slumped down in Hilary's bag and made himself useful by calling out occasional numbers at random. "Thirty-eight!" he said. "Eleven! Two! Is it time yet?"

At last it was time, and Hilary stepped up onto the porch. She studied the skull over the door for a moment, trying not to wonder who it might have been in a previous life—a poor buccaneer who'd been punished for unpiratical behavior, perhaps, or a pirate who'd been caught snooping in the president's private rooms. Then she squared her shoulders, pushed open the squeaky-hinged door, and stepped inside.

The narrow passageway in front of them was lit with torches, and the walls were adorned with artifacts commemorating previous VNHLP presidents: the hat feather of Blackjaw Hawkins, the eye patch of Squinty O'Hara, the peg leg of Pretty Jack Winter, and (Hilary shuddered) the knucklebones of someone named Captain Deadheart. Smaller passageways branched out now and then on either side, with carved wooden arrows pointing the way TO THE ARMORY or TO THE SWIMMIN' POOL. Pirates strode past them carrying important-looking leather books under their arms, and the air was remarkably full of parrots. Something crunched slightly under Hilary's boots; she hoped it was birdseed rather than knucklebones.

At last the passageway opened into a high-ceilinged hall, where a wooden arrow pointing straight ahead said

TO THE PRESIDENT'S QUARTERS. Hilary grinned as she saw that Miss Greyson and Claire were already hard at work distracting Captain Blacktooth's secretary, a pirate sitting behind a desk several times larger than he was.

"My charge is decidin' whether to join the League," Miss Greyson told the secretary in a thick pirate accent, "an' she'd like to learn more about it. Can ye give us some information, Mr. Gull?"

"Do you have pamphlets?" Claire asked, leaning so far over the desk that Mr. Gull shrank down in his chair. "I absolutely love pamphlets. Is the headquarters very old? How many pirates are in the League? Have you ever been in a sword fight? Which do you think is more fearsome, a hook or a peg leg?" She glanced over her shoulder and caught Hilary's eye. "Why, look over there!" she cried, pointing toward a window on the opposite side of the hall. "I believe the queen herself has come for a visit!"

Mr. Gull leaped up and hurried to the window, and Hilary and Charlie slipped past his desk while his back was turned. "Perhaps that's not the queen after all," Hilary heard Claire say as they rounded the corner. "I did think she looked terribly odd with an eye patch and a beard."

"This is it," Charlie whispered. The plaque on the door in front of them bore Captain Blacktooth's name, and Charlie jiggled the doorknob. "Locked, of course," he said.

"That's nothing a pirate can't handle," said Hilary.

She held her magic coin in one hand and rested her other hand on the doorknob. "Magic," she said, "please unlock this door."

Hilary's arm tingled, there was a soft click, and the doorknob turned in her hand. "Thank you, magic," Hilary whispered to the coin as she and Charlie crept into Captain Blacktooth's quarters.

The door closed behind them, and Hilary turned the lock. "Just in case Blacktooth comes back," she explained. "We've got to leave everything just as we found it." The room was remarkably tidy and mostly empty; Hilary supposed Captain Blacktooth kept most of his belongings on the *Renegade*. A battered leather chair sat in front of a fireplace, and books and papers were stacked on a table nearby. In one corner stood a large, sea-weathered trunk nearly identical to the one Captain Blacktooth had delivered to Hilary when he'd welcomed her to the VNHLP, and Hilary's heart sank at the memory. "Perhaps Blacktooth's not a Mutineer after all," she said. She opened the trunk and found nothing but cobwebs. "It's difficult to believe he'd be so villainous."

Charlie was rummaging through the spare pirate coats that hung on a tall wooden rack. "Well, he hasn't got anyone locked away in his office, so that's a point in his favor. And he keeps his pockets empty."

The gargoyle's snout appeared over the edge of Hilary's

bag. "But he didn't defend us at the Salty Biscuit," he said. "He was going to let those scallywags run us through. Remember?"

"How could I forget?" said Hilary. "Perhaps he hoped we could defend ourselves—and we could have, you know." She sat down in the captain's chair and studied the spines of his books, which had titles like *The Pirate's Guide to Plundering* and *Five Weeks to a Better Beard*. All around the books were piles of papers and folders labeled in Captain Blacktooth's spindly hand, though to Hilary's disappointment, none of the folders was labeled VILLAINY.

For ten minutes they sorted through catalogs for seafaring supplies, notes scribbled on VNHLP stationery, and the personal records of half a dozen pirates, but they couldn't find a single scrap of information that mentioned the Mutineers. Hilary hated the thought of giving up the search, but perhaps it was the only thing to do. She sighed and leaned back in Captain Blacktooth's chair.

"Hold on a moment," said Charlie. "What's this?" He pulled a thick white envelope out from the pages of *The Pirate's Guide to Plundering*, where it had been serving as a bookmark. Hilary straightened up at once: the envelope was addressed to Captain Blacktooth in an elegant hand, and its blue wax seal was broken in half.

"So the Mutineers *have* written to Blacktooth," she said, taking the envelope from Charlie's hand. "I wonder what they've got to say."

The gargoyle hopped up and down inside the bag. "Oh, Hilary, open it! You know gargoyles can't stand suspense!"

"Pirates aren't much good at it either," Hilary said, and she pulled a sheet of paper from the envelope. It was covered in the Mutineers' elegant script, but for a long moment it made no sense at all:

Mrs. Georgiana Tilbury

REQUESTS THE PLEASURE OF THE COMPANY OF

Captain Rupert Blacktooth

AT A GRAND BALL TO CELEBRATE THE
HIGH SOCIETY DEBUT OF HER DAUGHTER,

Philomena.

SATURDAY AT EIGHT O'CLOCK
TILBURY PARK, NORDHOLM, THE NORTHLANDS.

AN ANSWER WILL OBLIGE.

Charlie studied the note over Hilary's shoulder. "An invitation to a ball?" he said. "Perhaps it's a threat."

"An invitation to *Philomena's* ball," Hilary corrected, "written by her mother."

"I don't understand," said the gargoyle. "Why does Philomena's mother write like a Mutineer?"

"Because she *is* a Mutineer." Hilary waved the invitation under the gargoyle's snout. "Mrs. Georgiana Tilbury must be the one who's been writing those horrid notes to us, and to Cannonball Jack. Oh, I just *knew* Philomena was involved somehow! Her mother must be even more villainous than she is."

"And the Tilburys are friends with Captain Blacktooth, I suppose," said Charlie, "although I can't imagine Philomena inviting a pirate to her ball. Perhaps she's turned over a new leaf."

"Or perhaps they're all working together." Hilary grinned. "I'd bet my hat that Captain Blacktooth and Mrs. Tilbury are both Mutineers."

"I hope you're right," the gargoyle said. "It would be very sad if you lost your hat."

At that moment, Claire's voice rang out through the building. "MY GOODNESS!" she shouted loud enough for Hilary to hear. "IS THAT CAPTAIN BLACKTOOTH, THE PRESIDENT OF THE PIRATE LEAGUE, ON HIS WAY TO HIS QUARTERS?"

"Oh, curses!" Hilary shoved the invitation back into its envelope and looked around for a place to hide. There wasn't any time to make a dash for the exit, but crouching behind the chair wouldn't do her an ounce of good. "Why doesn't Blacktooth have more furniture?" Charlie squeezed himself into Captain Blacktooth's trunk, and Hilary threw herself and the gargoyle behind the coat rack just as a key scraped in the lock.

"What a strange little pirate girl that was," someone said as the door opened. The voice didn't sound at all like Captain Blacktooth's—it was much too elegant, and several octaves too high. Carefully, Hilary pushed aside the sleeve of one of the captain's many coats and peered through the gap she'd made in the folds of fabric.

Captain Blacktooth had entered his office, but he hadn't come alone. His guest was a tall woman dressed in peacock blue. She removed her fashionable hat and smoothed her graying hair, looking nearly as exasperated as she had when Hilary had passed her in the Royal Dungeons earlier that week. Now, however, in the clear midday light, Hilary knew precisely why the woman looked so familiar: she was an older, sterner version of Philomena.

"She seemed to have thoroughly terrified your poor secretary," Mrs. Tilbury continued. "If someone doesn't keep an eye on her, she'll grow to be as much of a nuisance as James Westfield's daughter."

Hilary prickled. She was not a nuisance, she was a Terror, but perhaps Mrs. Tilbury was too foolish to understand the difference.

"Truthfully," said Captain Blacktooth, "I much prefer James's daughter to James himself. I wouldn't mind sending the dratted fellow off the plank once all this nonsense is finished." He took off his hat and rubbed the bald spot on his head. "I would have done it months ago if you hadn't dragged me into his affairs."

Mrs. Tilbury clicked her tongue. "Now, Rupert, that's very unkind. James can be rather stubborn, I admit; perhaps that's where the girl gets it. Honestly, is there nothing that will frighten her away?"

"They do call her the Terror of the Southlands," Captain Blacktooth pointed out, and Hilary couldn't help smiling into the coats.

"That may be," said Mrs. Tilbury, "but I don't understand why you won't ask a few of your men to abandon her somewhere miserable for a month or two."

"She's a member of the League, Georgiana. I won't have my own scallywags kidnapped. I've already done my best to warn her off." Captain Blacktooth sat down in his chair and began to shuffle through the stacks of books and papers. "I'm not terribly worried, though. I questioned Pirate Westfield in Queensport, and she doesn't know anything at all."

"What about that shabby orphan boy she sails about with?" Mrs. Tilbury asked. "Is he likely to give us any trouble?"

"He's somewhat handy with a sword, but he's not a serious pirate. I've even heard he refuses to use magic!" Captain Blacktooth shook his head. "He's certainly not worth worrying about."

Hilary cringed and looked over at the trunk where Charlie was hidden, willing him not to climb out and challenge Blacktooth to a duel.

"And the queen's inspectors?" Mrs. Tilbury asked.

"Still perfectly befuddled, as usual," said Captain Blacktooth, "but I've advertised for more pirates to stand guard in case that Hastings fellow stumbles across any smart ideas."

"More pirates!" Mrs. Tilbury sighed. "The house shall be overrun with them. They had better not poke about in the china cabinet or tread mud on my good carpets."

"I'll be sure to tell them so," said Captain Blacktooth cheerfully. "Ah, here are the notes I needed." He stood up and replaced his hat. "Shall we discuss them over lunch?"

"At one of those horrid little groggeries?" Mrs. Tilbury wrinkled her nose, reminding Hilary strongly of Philomena. "Can't we go somewhere more civilized?"

"Not on Gunpowder Island," Captain Blacktooth said, "and the crowd at the Sword and Seahorse raises such a ruckus that we won't be overheard." He turned, and to Hilary's horror, he stared directly at the coat rack. "Should I change into the crimson coat, I wonder? I've been wearing this blue one for days."

Hilary stood as still as a sail without a breeze. She wanted to reach for the gargoyle for comfort, but she didn't dare to move her hand; she hardly dared to breathe. If Captain Blacktooth caught her now, he wouldn't just expel her from the League; he'd run her through on the spot—and if he wavered, Mrs. Tilbury would surely do it instead. *Don't change your coat,* she thought fiercely. *Oh, please don't change your coat.*

Captain Blacktooth took a step toward the coat rack.

"Don't be absurd, Rupert," Mrs. Tilbury said. "Crimson is a color for winter, and it's the height of the summer. Simply everyone is wearing blue this season." She flourished her own peacock-colored hat. "Now, let's depart, if you please. You know I can't abide waiting."

When Captain Blacktooth had closed the door behind him and turned his key in the lock, Hilary shoved the coat rack aside and hurried over to the trunk. "Did you hear that?" she whispered as she pushed back the lid to let Charlie out.

"Every word." Charlie coughed and tried to brush the cobwebs from his coat. "Especially the part about how I'm not a serious pirate."

Hilary held out her hands and pulled him out of the trunk. "Never mind what Captain Blacktooth thinks. He's a Mutineer, after all, and I'm sure it's quite piratical to be disliked by villains."

Charlie shrugged. "We don't have to talk about it."

"Are you sure?" Hilary asked.

"Quite," said Charlie flatly. He pulled a spider from his shoulder and put it in Hilary's bag for the gargoyle to munch on. "Who was that woman with Blacktooth? I couldn't see anything through the keyhole."

"That," said Hilary, "was Philomena's delightful mother.

From what Blacktooth said about sending pirates to guard her house, it sounds like they're keeping Miss Pimm at Tilbury Park. Perhaps they've got Jasper there, too."

"And now we can rescue them!" the gargoyle cried.

"I hope so." Hilary looked out the grimy window, where Captain Blacktooth and Mrs. Tilbury had just begun to stroll down the hill. "Come along; let's fetch Claire and Miss Greyson."

"Good idea," said Charlie. "I don't think I can stand to stay in this place another moment."

Hilary marched into the hall, put one hand on Claire's shoulder and the other on Miss Greyson's, and looked down at the secretary's head. "Arr!" she said. "Have these pirates been bothering you, Mr. Gull?"

The secretary quivered.

"Don't worry. I shall take them away at once. But before I go, I'd like to ask you a question, if I may."

Mr. Gull nodded. "Of course, pirate," he said in a tremulous voice. "How can I assist you?"

"I'd like to know why that elegant woman in peacock blue was roaming these halls with Captain Blacktooth," Hilary said. "Surely High Society ladies are not allowed at League headquarters?"

"N-no," said Mr. Gull, "they're not. But we always make an exception for Mrs. Tilbury."

"And why is that?"

Mr. Gull sat up a little straighter. "Because," he said as

though nothing could be more obvious, "Mrs. Tilbury is Captain Blacktooth's sister."

"I WAS TERRIBLY worried!" Claire said as they hurried through the cobblestone streets toward Gunpowder Bay. "I was sure Captain Blacktooth would recognize us, but Miss Greyson had the good sense to step behind a potted plant, and I don't think the captain has ever bothered to give me a second look. So we were all right, but then I saw him going into his office with that horrid tall woman, and I knew you'd be caught!" She paused for a breath. "So I shouted."

"And it's a good thing you did," said Hilary, "or we'd all be skewered on Captain Blacktooth's sword by now, or locked up in Mrs. Tilbury's mansion." The very thought was enough to turn her stomach. "That woman makes Philomena look like a rosebud."

"A rosebud with plenty of thorns," said Charlie, "who captures Enchantresses for sport."

Miss Greyson pushed her pirate hat out of her eyes. "To be perfectly fair, we don't know that Philomena was involved. Perhaps her mother and Captain Blacktooth worked alone."

"I doubt it," said Hilary. "Villainy seems to run in their family. But perhaps we'll learn more when we get to Tilbury Park."

"And fight our way past dozens of Blacktooth's hired

scallywags," said Charlie, "and rescue Miss Pimm, and find Jasper, and escape without getting ourselves run through." He kicked at a loose cobblestone. "It's an awfully difficult job for a shabby orphan boy."

"Then it's fortunate," said Hilary, "that you're nothing of the sort." She turned to Claire. "Don't you think it's rather strange that Philomena has a pirate for an uncle? I wonder if she's as rude to him as she is to us."

Claire considered this. "I suspect," she said at last, "that Philomena is rude to everyone. Except, of course, for Nicholas Feathering." She sighed. "I hope he won't be too distraught when he finds he's betrothed to a villain."

When they climbed aboard the *Pigeon* at last, they found Marrow, Slaughter, and Stanley standing guard with swords outstretched. "Did anyone give you trouble?" Hilary asked them.

"Not particularly," said Mr. Marrow. "We sold a few books, though."

"Oh, good," said Miss Greyson.

"And we think we saw some queen's inspectors poking about," Mr. Stanley said. "They're the gentlemen in red jackets, aren't they? They sailed over from the mainland, and they seemed quite interested in the *Pigeon*, but they didn't stay long when they caught sight of our spyglasses."

"And our swords," Mr. Slaughter added.

"How peculiar." Hilary set down her bag and placed the gargoyle back in his Nest. "But I'm afraid we don't have any time to worry about inspectors. Please set a course for Nordholm."

Mr. Stanley raised his eyebrows. "And what shall we do there, Terror?"

"We shall find our friends," said Hilary, "and we shall trounce the Mutineers."

From

The Augusta Scuttlebutt

WHERE HIGH SOCIETY TURNS FOR SCANDAL

Are you a young High Society lady? Have you always wanted to be an Enchantress? If so, dear reader, your dream may soon come true! Sources close to Queen Adelaide tell the Scuttlebutt in strictest confidence that the queen is prepared to appoint a new Enchantress if Miss Eugenia Pimm, Enchantress of the Northlands, does not return to her post within the next few days. The queen's inspectors have had their hands full with reports of stolen magic pieces and enchantments gone wrong, and royal advisers worry that the magical chaos will only get worse unless a new Enchantress takes charge.

Before her mysterious disappearance, Miss Pimm herself had begun to search for a successor, but the Scuttlebutt hears she couldn't find a candidate who was talented enough for the job. Will Queen Adelaide have better luck? We at the Scuttlebutt are simply dying to learn who the fortunate young lady will be.

WE ASKED, YOU ANSWERED:
Do you think the queen should appoint a new Enchantress?

"In the weeks since Miss Pimm disappeared, a pickpocket stole my magic coins, the mayor of our village accidentally turned himself a rather vivid shade of purple, and the local farmer used his magic piece to teach his pigs to sing opera arias. Finding a new Enchantress may be the only way to get those dreadful creatures to be quiet."
—H. THORNE, WIMBLY-ON-THE-MARSH

"I suppose a new Enchantress would be a useful sort of thing to have about, as long as she's not so awfully fond of rhymes."
—P. SCATTERGOOD, OTTERPOOL

"I don't care for Enchantresses as a matter of principle, but anyone would be an improvement over That Meddling Old Biddy. Thank goodness she's gone at last." —J. WESTFIELD, QUEENSPORT

"Be ye kiddin'? 'Twould be the height of foolishness to go appointin' a new Enchantress. The Terror of the Southlands will bring Eugenia back, ye mark me words." —C. JACK, THE HIGH SEAS

CHAPTER THIRTEEN

HILARY HAD NEVER seen anything like the city of Nord-holm. It was bright and stark and very old, carved up by rivers and polished by waves until it was nearly more water than land. As the *Pigeon* wound around islands and slipped past drawbridges, Charlie pointed out the rocky shore where he'd lived with his mam and pa before their ship had sunk and he'd gone to stay with Jasper. "It was a good place to be a pirate," Charlie said. "There were always plenty of ships to watch through the window, and Mam built me a raft to paddle around on. I tried to sail it through the city once, but I didn't even make it past the bend in the river before I went overboard."

"You're a much better pirate now," said Hilary. "I'm sure your mam would be impressed."

"She was impressed any time I didn't come home dripping wet," said Charlie, "which wasn't very often."

Claire had found Tilbury Park on one of the water-stained maps Jasper kept on board the *Pigeon*. "It's on the edge of the city," she reported, "close to the forest, and it looks nearly large enough to be its own village. Perhaps the map is mistaken."

But the mansion at Tilbury Park was just as grand and terrifying as the map had suggested. It stood high above the water, sheltered by trees, with columns and porticos and great glass windows that stared out at the sea. A low stone wall traced the boundary of the land, doing its best to keep the fields and gardens from sliding into the waves.

The gargoyle started to call "Land ho!" but Hilary hushed him, for she didn't want the residents of Tilbury Park to have any idea that the Terror of the Southlands had come for a visit. Instead she sailed the *Pigeon* into a cove half a mile away and asked Marrow, Slaughter, and Stanley to keep watch while she rowed the dinghy ashore to take a closer look at the mansion. The gargoyle cleared his throat pointedly until Hilary agreed to take him with her, and Claire, Charlie, and Miss Greyson piled into the dinghy without being asked. "If you think we're all going to stay on the *Pigeon* reading romances while you rescue Miss Pimm," the gargoyle said, "you're crazy."

Once they'd reached the shore, Hilary hid the dinghy behind a convenient bush, and the pirates tramped up the hill toward Tilbury Park. As they walked, Miss Greyson removed her crochet hook from her bun and held it straight up in the air. "Please direct me," she said, "toward Miss Eugenia Pimm."

For a moment, the crochet hook stood entirely still. Then, slowly but unmistakably, it tilted in the direction of the Tilburys' mansion.

Hilary grinned, and Claire clapped her hands. "How wonderful!" she cried.

"Quite," said Miss Greyson, looking rather pleased with herself. Then she turned her attention back to the crochet hook. "And would you be so kind as to point me toward Jasper Fletcher?"

The crochet hook wobbled from side to side, seemed to think better of the whole endeavor, and slipped out of Miss Greyson's hand onto the hillside.

Miss Greyson's smile collapsed. "He's not here," she said briskly as she retrieved her crochet hook. "I don't like it one bit."

Hilary squeezed her hand. "At least we've found Miss Pimm," she said. "I'm sure we'll find Jasper as well."

As they drew closer to Tilbury Park, the gargoyle began to squirm in his bag. "Sorry," he said, "it's my ears. They're tingling almost as much as they do on the *Pigeon*. I think someone up there must have lots of magic."

"Oh dear," said Claire, "really? I hope it's not Philomena. She'll enchant me into something dreadful—a centipede, perhaps, or a fungus—and it's likely to ruin the whole afternoon."

When they reached the edge of Tilbury Park, Hilary knelt down behind the low stone wall and pulled out her spyglass. "Blast," she said. "The place is positively crawling with guards." Dozens of men in peacock-blue uniforms stood in straight lines at the front of the mansion. Most of them held sharp-looking swords at their waists, and Hilary thought she spotted at least one cannon. "Those must be the men Captain Blacktooth sent to guard Miss Pimm—and I suppose he'll be sending even more. We'll never be able to fight them off alone."

Charlie took the spyglass and studied Tilbury Park for himself. "You're right," he said at last; "there are too many of them for us to handle, and I bet they've got magic pieces as well." He paused and adjusted the spyglass's focus. "And if that's not enough, it looks like someone's coming up the drive."

The pirates ducked behind the wall and squinted through the cracks in the stones at the passing carriage. It was entirely black, with no family crest painted on its doors. Four jet-black horses pulled it through the gateposts, and dark curtains covered its windows. As Hilary watched, the driver tugged the horses to a halt, and a footman in peacock-blue livery hurried out of the mansion to open the carriage door for Mrs. Tilbury.

"Hurrah," Hilary whispered. "Our hostess is home."

"Hey!" said the gargoyle. "That's the carriage that almost ran into us on the way to Pemberton! Do you remember, Hilary?"

"I'd nearly forgotten." Hilary thought for a moment. "And Miss Pimm disappeared that very night, didn't she? Do you truly think it's the same carriage?"

"I'd know it anywhere," the gargoyle said. "It almost turned me into pebbles!"

Miss Greyson clicked her tongue. "It's very peculiar. Why would a High Society lady like Mrs. Tilbury travel in an unmarked carriage?"

"That's simple enough," said Charlie. "She doesn't want folks to know who she is when she's off lunching with pirates or kidnapping Enchantresses. Can you imagine the Mutineers spiriting Miss Pimm away in a coach painted all over with the Tilbury crest?"

The gargoyle bared his teeth. "Just wait till I get my hands on those Mutineers," he said. "Figuratively speaking, of course."

Hilary couldn't see, though, how they would ever get past the lines of guards to rescue Miss Pimm. "There's nothing more we can do right now," she said at last. Her pirate hat felt heavy on her head, and the collar of her shirt was starting to itch. "And I'm not sure we'll be fearsome enough to face all those guards even if we bring Mr.

Stanley and his friends with us next time. Perhaps we'd better go back to the *Pigeon*."

The gargoyle looked concerned. "We're not giving up, are we?"

"No," said Hilary, "a pirate never gives up. But sometimes a pirate isn't quite sure what to do next."

They walked back toward the dinghy in silence. Miss Greyson's brow was furrowed in thought, and Claire picked at the loose threads in her newly mended cardigan. "We could blast Tilbury Park to bits," Charlie said at last. "A few cannonballs would get rid of those Mutineers in a hurry."

Hilary thought about it. "It would certainly be satisfying, but Miss Pimm is in there, and I don't want to risk hurting her."

"We could alert the queen's inspectors," Miss Greyson suggested.

"Do you really think they'd be a bit of help in a battle?" Hilary kicked a clod of dirt with the toe of her boot. "Anyway, I refuse to let Inspector Hastings take the credit for rescuing Miss Pimm. We're here at the Mutineers' hideout, and he's probably back in Pemberton sipping tea and ironing his trousers."

Claire took a deep breath. "I know this might sound foolish," she said, "but the *Pigeon* is absolutely full of magic. Perhaps if we each took a handful of coins, we could enchant Miss Pimm out of the house."

But Miss Greyson shook her head. "There simply aren't

enough of us for a task that powerful. Mr. Stanley and I could do part of the work, but"—she looked pointedly at Claire—"I don't think it's wise to encourage an accident."

"I suppose you're right." Claire looked down at her bootlaces. "I do wish I weren't still miles away from being in High Society. If I were grand and elegant, I could call on Mrs. Tilbury, and she'd have no choice but to invite me in."

Charlie had been looking glum all day, and now he frowned more deeply than ever. "Really?" he said to Claire. "You've spent weeks on a pirate ship, and you still want to be a High Society lady?"

"Well, yes," said Claire. "Of course I do!"

"That's a shame."

Claire stopped walking, and her voice was sharp. "What do you mean by that?"

"It's nothing." Charlie shoved his hands in his pockets. "Never mind."

"I believe I do mind." Claire turned to face him. "I know you don't care for High Society girls, but I don't understand why they upset you so much."

"I'd think you of all people *would* understand," said Charlie fiercely. "Haven't you heard what people like Philomena and her mother say about us?"

Claire's cheeks flushed. "Of course I've heard what they say, and I've heard a thousand other nasty comments as well. I know High Society folks mock me; I know they look at me as though they'd like to scrape me off the bottom of their boots. But I *also* know how horrid it is to wrap *fish* every day, and if I'm given the chance to dress up and go to balls and enjoy myself, why shouldn't I take it?"

"Because High Society is dull," Charlie practically shouted, "and it's silly. Because High Society people never lift a finger to do anything kind for people like us. Do you really want to be one of those awful girls, waltzing around with your fine gown and your magic piece?" Charlie raised his eyebrows. "I suppose you'd have to wear that gardening glove as well."

Claire turned nearly as red as Inspector Hastings's jacket. "I wish someone *would* turn you into a centipede after all. I believe the look might suit you."

Miss Greyson began to say something about calming down and being practical, but Claire and Charlie simply shouted over her, and Hilary closed her eyes. She suspected that doing battle against all the Mutineers single-handedly would be a thousand times more pleasant than listening to her friends argue. In fact, she almost wished that Mrs. Tilbury would hurry over and capture them, just to give everyone something else to talk about.

"You may think High Society is dull and silly," Claire was saying, "but I happen to *like* embroidery, and waltzing, and smelling of something other than fish for a change." She glared at Charlie. "And anyway, it's not half as silly as trying to be the Scourge of the Northlands."

"You think that's silly?" Charlie went quiet. "Did you

know I've been working for ages just to get scallywags like Captain Blacktooth to notice me? I trained with Jasper; I trained with the League. I helped find that blasted magic you love so much. And I've been trying to rescue Miss Pimm, who I don't even *like*, because if we find her, maybe someone out there will finally realize that I'm a good pirate!"

Claire crossed her arms. "But you'll never be the Scourge of the Northlands," she said, "because you're scared."

"Don't be absurd," said Charlie. "A pirate is never scared."

"You're frightened of High Society girls, aren't you? And what's more, I believe you're frightened of using magic. You pretend you won't touch it out of loyalty to your parents, but truthfully"—Claire took a breath—"I think you're terrified."

For a moment, Charlie stood entirely still. Then he shook his head. "Any sensible person who comes within fifty miles of your exploding coins *should* be frightened of magic," he said. "I honestly don't know why Hilary invited you along in the first place."

"And I don't know why she invited *you*," Claire shot back, "unless it was to be thoroughly infuriating!"

Hilary couldn't stay silent for another moment. "I invited you *both* along," she snapped, "because you're my dearest friends, and I thought I'd enjoy your company. I suppose I was wrong, though, because I'm not enjoying this ridiculous duel one bit. If you two can't behave like decent pirates, I'll—"

"You'll kick us off the ship?" Charlie asked. His hands went slack at his sides, and he blinked at Hilary. "I suppose you *are* the Terror of the Southlands. You probably don't need any help at all from a second-rate pirate who isn't worth worrying about."

"I didn't say that!" cried Hilary, but Charlie paid her no attention.

"In that case," he said, "I'll be leaving." He removed his hat and gave an exaggerated bow. "My apologies for bothering you all with my presence."

"Charlie, wait!" Hilary grabbed his arm. "You can't just abandon your crew, you know; it's completely unpiratical! What am I supposed to do without a first mate?"

Charlie freed his arm from Hilary's grip and wiped his coat sleeve across his eyes. "You're a serious pirate, aren't you?" he said. "I'm sure you'll figure something out." Then he reached into his pocket, tossed a spider to the gargoyle, and walked away through the fields without looking back once.

"I SHOULD HAVE stopped him," said Hilary. "I should have chased after him, or held him at swordpoint." She lay on her cot on the *Pigeon* and stared up at the wooden beams that crossed the cabin's ceiling. "I'm the Terror of the Southlands! My first mate isn't supposed to abandon me; he's supposed to do as I say!" She looked over at the gargoyle, who had nestled into her pillow. "I'm not fearsome enough, am I?"

The gargoyle thought about it. "I don't think being fearsome is a good way to keep your friends."

Hilary and the gargoyle had waited for hours, hurrying out the cabin door every time they heard a creak or thump, but the sun had set and Charlie still hadn't returned. "I thought he'd be back by now," Hilary said. "I didn't truly think he'd leave for good."

Claire hadn't spoken a word since they returned to the *Pigeon*, but now she sat up and pulled herself to the foot of her cot. "I'm sorry," she said. "I'm sure you're furious with me, but I simply couldn't keep quiet." Her eyes went wide. "I don't believe I've ever shouted like that before, you know. I usually quiver and sniffle and sob into my pillow—but perhaps I'm becoming a pirate after all." She hesitated. "Or perhaps I'm becoming a cruel, awful High Society girl just like Charlie said."

Hilary threw a pillow at her. "You're nothing of the sort," she said. Perhaps Claire had been rather cutting, but Charlie had hardly displayed good manners either, and Hilary felt sure that Miss Greyson was thoroughly disappointed in all three of them. "Besides," she said, "I'm your captain. I'm supposed to keep the crew together, not blast it apart. Charlie's been gloomy since we left Gunpowder Island, but I didn't do a thing about it." She sighed. "If he ever comes back, I won't know whether to apologize or run him through."

"He'll come back," the gargoyle said. "I'm sure he already misses me."

But he didn't come back. Hilary lay awake all night listening for footsteps on the deck, but the only ones she heard belonged first to Mr. Marrow on the late watch, and then to Miss Greyson, who had come to tell Hilary and Claire that it was time for breakfast. "And I won't have any sulking," she warned them as they shuffled across the deck in their nightgowns. "It's entirely useless, and it ruins one's complexion."

Hilary didn't care two bits about the state of her complexion, but she had no desire to disappoint Miss Greyson any further. "I suppose," she said, digging into her grapefruit at the *Pigeon*'s long table, "that we'd better come up with a plan to rescue Miss Pimm from Tilbury Park." It was what she'd set out to do in the first place, after all, and perhaps it would distract her from worrying about Charlie. "Has anyone got an idea?" she asked, looking down the table.

Mr. Marrow, Mr. Slaughter, and Mr. Stanley all gazed thoughtfully into their porridge bowls, as though perhaps a stray idea might be lurking inside.

"Our plan needs to be thrilling," the gargoyle said, "so I can write about it in my memoirs."

"And we'll have to work hard not to be seen," Mr.

Slaughter added. "These waters are busier than I've seen 'em in ages, though I couldn't tell you why."

"Oh, but I could!" said Claire. "It's because of the season—the High Society season, I mean. All the fine families in Augusta are traveling about from one ball to the next." She speared a section of grapefruit. "And Philomena's grand debut is this Saturday, of course, so I suppose everyone will be tromping in from across the kingdom."

Hilary dropped her spoon. "And pouring into Tilbury Park," she said. "Claire, I believe you're a genius!"

Claire looked up from her grapefruit. "I am?"

"Yes, you are. And I hope you've all practiced your dancing steps recently. I certainly haven't, but at least I've got a few days to polish up my waltz."

In all her years as Hilary's governess, Miss Greyson had never looked more startled. "Your waltz?" she said. "Are you planning to attend Philomena's debut?"

"Don't you see?" said Hilary. "It's the perfect way to get into Tilbury Park! There will be hundreds of guests, and we'll simply hide in the crowd. The guards won't suspect us, and with any luck the Mutineers won't notice us. When all the other guests are dancing and batting their eyes at Philomena, we can slip away and rescue Miss Pimm."

Mr. Stanley consulted his porridge bowl. "It's a good plan," he said at last.

"A very good plan," Mr. Marrow agreed.

"But we haven't been invited," Miss Greyson pointed out. "Surely the Tilburys won't allow us in without an invitation."

Claire nodded. "And we haven't got anything to wear—other than pirate clothes, I mean."

"That's true," said Hilary, "but I believe I know some people who can help us." As she polished off the last bit of grapefruit, Hilary felt absolutely sure that she could rescue Miss Pimm—and if she could do that, whatever could stop her from finding Jasper, or from bringing Charlie back, or from crushing the blasted Mutineers? Everyone in Augusta would soon know precisely who was the boldest and most daring pirate on the High Seas.

The gargoyle, however, was sitting very still. "Hilary?" he said. "When we go to the ball, will I have to take off my hat?"

"Don't worry, gargoyle," said Hilary; "you look perfectly dashing just as you are. Now, if you'll all excuse me, I've got to write to my mother—and while I'm at it, I believe I'll send a quick note to Cannonball Jack."

My darling daughter,

I have just received your letter, and it nearly caused me to sing out for joy. Bursting unexpectedly into song is hardly genteel behavior, especially when one lacks instrumental accompaniment, so it is fortunate that I was able to restrain myself. I hope the servants will not be too alarmed, however, if I hum a few bars as I compose this letter.

Dearest Hilary, I would be delighted to escort you and your companions to the ball at Tilbury Park! I knew this day would come, but I must admit I didn't expect it to arrive so soon. Of course you will need the very finest gown. I have asked my maid to bring me the most suitable selections from your wardrobe; they will be last season's styles, I'm afraid, but it is too late to do much more than shake our heads and hope for the best. I do hope you have taken care not to grow terribly much in the past year, Hilary. As I have impressed upon you dozens of times, sudden spurts of growth are most inconvenient for one's dressmakers.

Now I must put down my pen, for I do not feel entirely

well. We dined tonight on the turkey that was once Miss Elsie Carter's headpiece, and I am afraid he tasted more of headpiece than of turkey. I plan to leave for Nordholm at dawn tomorrow, however, and I look forward to seeing you shortly on your quaint little pirate ship.

Your loving
Mother

A HEARTY BLAST
from Cannonball Jack

Dear Terror,
Aye, I'll do as ye ask. An' I'll bring a few o' me friends as well.

Yers,
C. J.

THE QUEEN'S INSPECTORS
Kingdom of Augusta
DILIGENCE, LOGIC, DISCRETION

Report to H.R.H. Queen Adelaide regarding
THE DISAPPEARANCE OF MISS EUGENIA PIMM

Report No. 4
FIELD INSPECTOR: *John Hastings*
LOCATION: *Pemberton, Augusta*
CASE STATUS: *Inexcusably Exhausting*

Inspector's Comments: *Your Highness, an
unusual development has recently occurred in our
investigation of the Enchantress's disappearance.
As I have reported previously, the queen's inspectors
are pursuing two known villains: the pirate Hilary
Westfield and the pirate Cannonball Jack. I am
alarmed to say, Your Highness, that these villains
appear to be coordinating a rendezvous. Hilary
Westfield has dropped anchor near Tilbury Park in
Nordholm, and one of my men has recently spotted
Cannonball Jack sailing toward this part of the
Northlands as well. Tilbury Park is, of course, the*

home of Miss Philomena Tilbury, who happens
to be a witness in our case. I am deeply concerned
for Miss Tilbury's safety, for one does not need a
high-quality magnifying glass to see that something
sinister is afoot!

My men and I leave at once for Tilbury Park.
We will protect our delicate witness, arrest both
pirates, and escort them personally to the Royal
Dungeons.

Signed
John Hastings
Captain, Queen's Inspectors

CHAPTER FOURTEEN

M<small>RS.</small> W<small>ESTFIELD</small> C<small>LAPPED</small> her hands together and beamed. "Oh, Hilary," she said, "you look absolutely marvelous."

"I look," said Hilary, "like a cabbage."

"A very beautiful cabbage," said Claire encouragingly.

Hilary groaned. "The Terror of the Southlands isn't supposed to be beautiful; she's supposed to be fearsome! How can I be fearsome if I can't even see my feet?"

"Seeing one's feet," said Mrs. Westfield, "is quite beside the point, especially when one is wearing sailor's boots under one's gown." She knelt down on the deck of the *Pigeon* to adjust the fluffy green layers of Hilary's skirt. "Oh dear, is that a rip? Have you already trodden on your hem?"

Hilary glared at her.

"Well, never mind. We shall have a wonderful time this evening, and that's all that matters. I'm truly honored that you girls have chosen me to be your guide as you venture away from a life of piracy and toward a life of elegance." Mrs. Westfield kissed Hilary on the cheek and hurried across the deck to admire Miss Greyson, who had embellished one of her everyday dresses with some hurried embroidery and (Hilary suspected) a bit of magic.

"Perhaps she's right," Hilary said to Claire. "Rescuing Miss Pimm from peril sounds like a rather lovely way to pass the evening. I just hope the Tilburys' cook doesn't chop me into a salad."

Claire laughed—but then, she could afford to, for she didn't resemble any sort of vegetable. She was wearing one of Hilary's old gowns, though it looked much finer on her than it ever had on Hilary, and waves of orange-gold silk rustled prettily around her feet whenever she moved. "Perhaps you should look on the bright side," she said. "No one would ever think to search for the Terror of the Southlands inside all that silk. And those fluffs and ruffles hide your cutlass ever so well."

Hilary patted the blade at her hip. "That's true," she said. "I don't think Mother's spotted it yet, and I'm quite sure it's not on her list of acceptable accessories for young ladies." She grinned. "I suppose I should warn the gargoyle that he'll be traveling to the ball in Mother's most spacious beaded purse."

She crossed the deck to the Gargoyle's Nest, where the gargoyle was looking out toward the mouth of the cove, watching colorful High Society barges float past on their way to Tilbury Park. "Well," she said, "what do you think of my gown?"

The gargoyle looked her up and down. He hesitated. "It's very *green*," he said at last.

"Exactly," said Hilary. "I believe you'd look less silly in this dress than I would."

The gargoyle shuddered. "Let's not find out."

Hilary peeled off the long white gloves she'd already managed to stain and scratched the gargoyle behind the ears. "Have you seen anyone interesting sail by?"

"The *Renegade* went past a few hours ago," the gargoyle said, "but I don't think they saw us."

"Good. I'd prefer it if Captain Blacktooth didn't know we were here."

"Oh, and the Featherings arrived in the *Calamity*. Other than that, there have been lots of gentlemen in tailcoats and ladies in lace, but they haven't been very interesting." The gargoyle rested his chin on the rim of the Nest. "Now *that*," he said, "is an interesting boat."

Hilary followed the gargoyle's gaze out to the mouth of the cove, where a small, bedraggled fishing boat floated alongside the elegant barges. It rode low in the waves, as though it was taking on a lot of water, but it wobbled along determinedly toward Tilbury Park. Suddenly, quite without warning, it jerked to one side and sailed into the cove where the *Pigeon* was hiding.

Hilary reached for her cutlass. Then she saw that a makeshift Jolly Roger flew from the fishing boat's mast, a parrot—no, a budgerigar—perched on its bowsprit, and two pirates huddled damply on the deck. The gargoyle began to hop up and down as well as he could in his Nest. "I know those scallywags!" he cried. "It's Jasper and Charlie!"

"Thank goodness," Hilary whispered. She cupped her hands around her mouth. "Ahoy, mateys!" she called. "You're very welcome on the *Pigeon* if you'd like to come aboard."

"Who's there?" Miss Greyson hurried to the bow and gave a little shriek when she spotted the pirates. "For heaven's sake, Jasper Fletcher, you've worried me half to death! Are you all right?"

"I've never been better," said Jasper as the fishing boat sidled up to the *Pigeon*. "Blast it all, Eloise, it's awfully good to see you. And is that the Terror next to you?" He squinted up at Hilary. "I don't want to alarm you, Terror, but I believe you're being attacked by a ball gown."

Hilary tossed a rope down to the fishing boat, and

Jasper began to pull himself aboard. "If I weren't so happy to see you," she said, "I'd send the ball gown after you next. It's terribly vicious, you know."

"I can see that," said Jasper. He swung himself over the railing and wrapped Miss Greyson in an embrace that made Mrs. Westfield gasp behind her evening gloves. Then he hugged Hilary, bowed to Claire and Mrs. Westfield, gave Marrow, Slaughter, and Stanley each a hearty handshake, and bestowed a kiss upon the gargoyle's snout. "It's good to be home," he said, peeling off his seawater-soaked coat, "and even better to be off that dratted boat. I had to use all my spare socks to plug its leaks."

"But how did you escape from the Mutineers?" Miss Greyson reached for Jasper's hands and gasped, for his arms were covered with scrapes and bruises, and the skin around his wrists was raw. "Did those villains do this to you?"

At the mention of villains, Mrs. Westfield put a hand to her forehead and hurried back to Hilary's cabin to calm her nerves.

"It's lucky they didn't do more," Jasper said. "When I reached the island where I'd been told the freelance pirates' convention was taking place, two scallywags greeted me and promised they'd take good care of me. I thought it was odd that the three of us were the only pirates on the island—but it was even odder when they confiscated my sword, bound my wrists and ankles, and tied me to a rather uncomfortable palm tree. Fitzwilliam did his best to peck at the scoundrels, but I'm sorry to say he lost a few tail feathers in the process."

Fitzwilliam, who had settled himself on the gargoyle's head, ruffled his plumage self-consciously.

"The pirates kept me well fed, at least," said Jasper, "though they weren't gracious enough to share their grog. They told me their employer didn't want me nosing about in his plans, so they'd been asked to keep me occupied. Then, a few days ago, they received orders to leave me on the island and report to the Northlands to assist this mysterious employer—so, naturally, I followed them." He touched his wrist gingerly. "Fortunately for me, their knot-tying skills were a bit rusty."

"And the pirates led you here?" Hilary asked.

"Nearly. I must admit I lost sight of them near Nordholm—but that, by a stroke of good fortune, is where I found Charlie." Jasper turned around. "Where *is* Charlie?"

Hilary leaned over the ship's railing and looked down at the fishing boat. Charlie was sitting with his back against the mast, looking both damp and miserable. His coat was torn, and his hat was soaked through. "I said you're very welcome on the *Pigeon*," she called down. "I didn't only mean Jasper."

Charlie looked up at her. "You've got no reason to welcome me."

"Perhaps I don't," said Hilary, "but I'll do it anyway."

She gathered up her fluffy green skirts and climbed down the rope to the fishing boat, which rocked from side to side as she made her way to Charlie. Before he could protest, she sat down next to him, hardly caring that her gown was getting damper by the second. "You gave us a lot of worry," she said. "Wherever have you been?"

Charlie didn't meet her eyes. "At my mam and pa's old place," he said quietly. "The house is long gone, but there's a flattish rock that makes a decent bed. I was going to make a name for myself, sailing the High Seas all alone until I was even more dangerous than my pa ever got a chance to be."

"But you didn't," said Hilary. "Did Jasper stop you?"

"No," said Charlie. "It was my pa. I couldn't shake his voice from my mind. 'A pirate doesn't abandon his mates,' he kept saying, and the more he said it, the worse I felt." He drew his knees up to his chest. "I shouldn't have left; it was stupid of me. I won't blame you if you can't forgive me, but I'll swab the deck, or pump out the bilge, or do anything else you want if it will prove to you that I'm a good pirate."

Hilary considered this. "I ought to punish you," she said. "The League has dozens of ways to deal with runaway crewmates, and none of them is pleasant, unless you enjoy having barnacles in your breeches."

Charlie looked grim. Seawater dripped from his hat brim onto his nose.

"But I'm quite fed up with the League's rules," Hilary

continued, "and I'm willing to forgive you on two conditions. First, you must swear you won't storm off again."

"I swear," Charlie said at once. "What's the second condition?"

"You've got to apologize to Claire." Hilary held out the rope that led back to the ship. "And she's got to apologize to you as well. I can't have my mates being furious with each other."

Charlie's face tightened, but he nodded and took hold of the rope, and they climbed back onto the *Pigeon*.

"See?" said the gargoyle as Charlie pulled himself onto the deck. "I knew he'd miss me."

Claire stood nearby, tugging her evening gloves and looking as though she'd rather be anywhere else in the kingdom. Charlie hesitated, and for a moment, Hilary worried he'd leap back over the side of the ship. But he took a long breath and held out his hand toward Claire.

"I'm sorry for mocking you," he said. "I shouldn't have been so unkind. You did a good job rescuing us from Captain Blacktooth on Gunpowder Island. And, er, your gown looks very nice."

Claire flushed. Then she took his hand and shook it. "I'm sorry, too," she said, "for calling you silly, and for saying you'd never be the Scourge of the Northlands. I didn't mean those things, not really. And I'm pleased that you're back, since it means we've got a good sword fighter to help us rescue Miss Pimm."

"Oh, is that what we're doing?" Jasper asked. "That sounds delightful. Would you mind very much, Hilary, if I joined in?"

Hilary thought for a moment. "Captain Blacktooth will probably scorn me for it," she said, "but I don't believe I care much for his opinion at the moment, and I'd be grateful for your assistance if you'd like to give it." She looked from Jasper to Charlie and back again. "I'm afraid, though, that you'll both have to change your clothes—and I can't guarantee that I'll be able to keep you safe from waltzing."

"I can see," said Jasper, "that I've got a good deal of catching up to do. All right, Pirate Westfield. You'd better tell us what you've got planned, and then Charlie and I shall make ourselves presentable."

AT EIGHT O'CLOCK precisely, the gates to Tilbury Park were opened. A long line of carriages squeaked up the drive, and the elegant ladies and gentlemen who had arrived by sea made their way up the lantern-lit path from the docks to the mansion's front entrance. The buzz of High Society chatter tangled with the strains of a string quartet performing from a balcony, and fireflies dotted the lawn. It was an unusual setting for a bold and daring feat of piracy, Hilary thought, but it would have to do. She tied up the dinghy and looked over her shoulder at the cove where the *Pigeon* was hidden. With any luck, the Mutineers wouldn't discover it—and even if they did, they would discover

Marrow, Slaughter, and Stanley as well. At least that was one part of her plan that wasn't likely to go wrong.

"Blast it all, Jasper," said Charlie as they walked toward the mansion, "you've made my trousers too long again." Jasper had managed to convince Mrs. Westfield that he and Charlie would be attending the ball in order to provide the Tilburys with additional security, and both of them were dressed in the peacock-blue guards' uniforms he'd conjured up that afternoon. "Your magic piece must think I'm at least three inches taller than I actually am."

"At least you don't have to wear a suit," Hilary said, "or a vicious ball gown."

"True," said Charlie, sounding considerably more cheerful. "And guards don't have to dance."

"It's a shame," said Jasper. "I was quite looking forward to the quadrille."

Tilbury Park was still entirely surrounded by guards, but several of them now stood on both sides of the front entrance, examining each guest who passed through the door. Hilary let a few waves of hair fall over her face, feeling almost grateful that her mother had insisted on loosing it from its usual braid, and she rested her hand on the lump the gargoyle made in her purse.

Mrs. Westfield presented her invitation at the door and introduced Hilary, Claire, and Miss Greyson as her guests. "Welcome, ladies, to Tilbury Park," said one of the guards, bowing low and tipping his peacock-blue hat. Then he stood up and frowned at Charlie and Jasper. "Aren't you two supposed to be on duty?"

"We've asked these gentlemen to escort us inside," said Hilary. "They were reluctant to leave their posts, but we simply couldn't bear to walk up the path alone. Just think how dreadful it would be if I tripped in the dark and tore my gown! I'm quite sure these guards are saving me and the Tilburys from a good deal of embarrassment."

"Of course," the guard said kindly. "Well, gentlemen, see that you return to your posts in short order. And remember to keep an eye out for pirates."

Claire gasped. "Pirates? Surely there's no danger of *pirates* attending the ball!"

"We hope not, miss," said the guard, "but Mrs. Tilbury has asked us to watch for a small pirate called the Terror of the Southlands. There's no reason to worry, though." He smiled. "I hear she's truly not much of a Terror at all."

Hilary's silk flounces rustled as she lifted her foot and stomped most deliberately upon the guard's toes. "Oh dear," she said. "You'll have to excuse my clumsiness."

"No matter, miss." The guard winced in pain. "Enjoy the ball."

They passed through the entrance and found themselves on a wide balcony overlooking a grand ballroom. Two sets of polished staircases led down to the ballroom, where gentlemen in tailcoats and ladies in bright dresses swirled and curtsied. Gilt-framed mirrors and tall arched windows lined the walls, and a crystal chandelier nearly as large as the *Squeaker* hung from the ceiling, but most impressive of all was the glass-paneled wooden cabinet, stuffed nearly to bursting with golden cutlery, golden candlesticks, golden pitchers, and golden platters. Hilary took one look at it and drew in her breath.

"Oh my," said Claire, staring down at the cabinet. "Do you think that could all be magic?"

Miss Greyson nodded. "An impressive amount of it," she said, "and not very tastefully arranged, if you ask me. I can't imagine how the Tilburys could have gotten their hands on it all."

"I can imagine it quite well," said Hilary, lowering her voice so her mother wouldn't overhear. "I'd bet you anything that it belongs to Father—or rather, to those High Society folks he stole it from last year. He told me those queen's inspectors still haven't managed to find his plunder"—she squirmed a bit at the memory—"but I'm sure they haven't checked Tilbury Park. Father must be out of his wits if he thinks it's wise to put that much magic anywhere near Philomena."

At one end of the ballroom, Philomena sat resplendent in a gown the color of sunshine, looking nothing at all like a cabbage. She embraced the guests who came to greet her and occasionally whispered something to her mother, who stood as rigid as a naval officer on her right, or to Sir Nicholas Feathering, who nodded politely on her left.

"What if old Philodendron spots us?" Claire asked.

"She won't," said Hilary. "We'll find Miss Pimm as quickly as possible and leave before anyone knows we're here. Miss Greyson, are you ready?"

Miss Greyson nodded and pulled out her crochet hook. "I am indeed. I shall be back in an instant—and don't forget your manners while I'm gone." Then she whispered a few words to her crochet hook and flitted away across the balcony.

Mrs. Westfield excused herself to greet a friend she'd spotted across the ballroom, and Hilary scanned the whirling crowd below her. Alice Feathering sat against the wall looking utterly bored. Captain Blacktooth, dressed in a tailored suit, was dancing a jig with a surprising amount of gusto. Hilary supposed the suit was his idea of a disguise, for with the exception of the sword hanging from his belt, he looked far more like a High Society gentleman than a pirate. "Both Blacktooth and Mrs. Tilbury are distracted," Hilary said quietly, "and it looks as though they've stationed most of their guards outside the house."

"That's pretty much perfect, isn't it?" Charlie asked.

"Too perfect." Hilary frowned. "I'm not sure I like it."

Miss Greyson hurried elegantly back to Hilary's side. "The crochet hook seemed quite certain that the Mutineers are keeping Miss Pimm somewhere down that hall." She nodded to an arched doorway to Hilary's right. "But I'm afraid there are two gentlemen standing guard. I tried to stroll right past them, but they say Mrs. Tilbury has ordered them not to let anyone through."

"Two guards?" Hilary gave her cutlass a thoughtful sort of tap. "Charlie and Jasper should be able to take care of them without any trouble."

"We certainly can," said Jasper, "but don't you think a sword fight might attract attention?"

"Well, you probably shouldn't duel them," said Hilary, "but I thought that perhaps you could distract them."

"Ah," said Jasper. "That *does* sound more reasonable. Consider it done." He strolled toward the arched doorway and signaled for the others to follow.

Hilary hurried along after him, tripping over the hem of her gown only twice, but just outside the doorway, she stopped short and grabbed Claire's hand. "Blast!" she whispered. "It's Mr. Twigget!"

He was wearing a guard's uniform instead of his usual striped shirt, and his blue beret looked quite a bit sillier than his pirate hat had, but the guard who stood at the left-hand side of the archway was none other than Captain Blacktooth's first mate. "There's a chance he might not know Jasper," Hilary whispered, "but he's met Charlie, and he certainly knows *me*. He'll alert the Mutineers for sure." She sighed. "This would all have been quite a bit easier if Philomena had hosted a masked ball."

Charlie must have recognized Mr. Twigget as well, for he had the good sense to stand behind Jasper and pull his hat low over his eyes. Jasper, however, marched directly up to Twigget and cleared his throat. "Mrs. Tilbury's sent the two of us to relieve you and your partner," he said. "Perhaps you'd like to nip downstairs for a glass of lemonade?"

Mr. Twigget looked Jasper up and down. "You look familiar," he said after a moment. "Now, why is that? Are you that pirate who insulted Captain Blacktooth at the League banquet a few years back?"

Miss Greyson drew in her breath, and Hilary reached for her magic piece.

"Me, insult Captain Blacktooth?" cried Jasper. "Never!"

Mr. Twigget frowned. "Are you sure?"

"My dear fellow," said Jasper, "I'm positive. You must be confusing me with my cousin, Jasper Fletcher. He's a thoroughly useless scallywag, and I'm ashamed to be related to him—though they do say he's the most handsome pirate on the High Seas."

Charlie put a hand to his mouth to mask his grin.

"In any case," said Jasper, "I really do recommend the lemonade."

Mr. Twigget and his partner exchanged glances. "No one told me anything about switchin' places," Twigget said, "but I like lemonade well enough." He pointed a finger at Jasper. "You'd better take care not to let anyone through this door while I'm gone, you hear, or the captain will have all our heads."

"I assure you," said Jasper, "your head will be safe with me."

Jasper and Charlie took up their places on either side of the doorway, and Mr. Twigget followed his partner toward the staircase. Hilary looked down at her feet and tried her best to be unremarkable, but the blasted cabbage-colored dress must have caught Mr. Twigget's attention, for his shuffling bootsteps slowed as they approached her, and then they stopped entirely.

"Hmm," said Mr. Twigget. "Excuse me, miss."

Hilary looked up to meet Mr. Twigget's eyes. Then she dropped into a curtsy, as she hoped a High Society girl would do; it was rather crooked, but perhaps Mr. Twigget wouldn't notice. She didn't dare say a word, for not even a hideous ball gown could disguise her voice.

"Is something the matter?" Jasper called from the doorway.

Mr. Twigget scratched his chin. "No," he said, "I were mistaken." Then he looked directly at Hilary. "Remember what I said about not lettin' anyone through."

"We'll remember, sir," Charlie said quickly.

For a long moment, Mr. Twigget said nothing. Then he made a gruff harrumphing noise, nodded to Hilary, and stamped down the staircase after his partner.

Hilary didn't say a word until Twigget was safely out of earshot. "I'm almost sure he recognized me," she whispered. "Do you think he's gone to get Captain Black-tooth?"

"If he has, you'd better hurry," said Miss Greyson. "Have you got your cutlass? And your magic piece?"

"Of course, Miss Greyson."

"And you're quite sure you don't need a chaperone?"

Miss Greyson looked so earnest that Hilary couldn't help smiling. "I know it's quite scandalous to run about rescuing Enchantresses without one's governess," she said, "but I'll be perfectly fine on my own."

"Ahem," said a voice from the beaded purse.

"Well, *nearly* on my own. Besides, I need the rest of you to watch the Mutineers and warn me if they're coming."

"We'll do precisely that." Claire gave Hilary a quick hug. "Now run and snap up Miss Pimm before those guards come back with their lemonade."

THE LONG WHITE hallway was lined with closed doors, and Hilary had no idea which one might be concealing an Enchantress. She found a library, a conservatory, and three washrooms, and she had just reached reluctantly for her magic piece when she turned a corner and found herself facing a dead end and a door fitted with padlocks. Beside the door stood the Tilburys' second-best coachman, Lewis.

Hilary said "Blast!" at the very same moment that Lewis said "Oh dear!" and Hilary clapped her hand over Lewis's mouth to keep him from saying anything more.

"That does it!" said the gargoyle as he pushed his way out of Hilary's purse. "Enough is enough! This bag smells funny, and I'm tired of being quiet, and I want to see what's going on." He smiled at Lewis, showing all his teeth. "Oh, it's you again. I hoped it would be someone more interesting."

Hilary pulled her cutlass from her waistband and pressed the tip into Lewis's shoulder, not hard enough to slice through his livery, but hard enough to show she meant business. "If you say a word," she said, "I'll let my sharp-toothed friend here nibble on your toes, and that's just to start. Do you understand?"

Lewis nodded. Hilary removed her hand from his mouth and wiped her glove on her skirt. "Very well," she said. "You're Philomena's coachman, aren't you?"

Lewis trembled.

"I suppose that's a yes," said Hilary. "And I am the Terror of the Southlands. You might remember me from our meeting in Pemberton."

"She wasn't wearing a ball gown then," the gargoyle said helpfully.

Confronting the Tilburys' second-best coachman hadn't been part of Hilary's plan at all, but she suspected that Lewis was even more nervous than she was, and the thought comforted her a bit. "Now, Lewis," she said, "if you'd be kind enough to assist me, perhaps I won't run you through. Is Miss Pimm behind that door you're guarding?"

Lewis's eyes went wide. Then, very slowly, he nodded.

"Will you open the door for me? And will you stand perfectly still, without shouting for your mistress, until I've taken Miss Pimm far away from here?"

Lewis's nose began to twitch. He looked down at Hilary's cutlass, and he looked quite intently at the gargoyle's teeth. Then he closed his eyes and shook his head.

"No, I supposed not. Well, at least you're honest. That's more than I can say for your fellow Mutineers." Hilary sighed. "I suppose I really *should* run you through, blast it all. I don't want all the scallywags in the pirate community gossiping about how the Terror of the Southlands doesn't carry out her threats." She pressed the point of her cutlass more firmly into Lewis's shoulder, but he squirmed beneath it and her stomach lurched more unpleasantly than it ever had on the High Seas.

"Wait!" the gargoyle cried. "Lift me up!"

"What?" The cutlass felt slick in Hilary's grip, and her hand shook as she pulled it away from Lewis's shoulder.

The gargoyle nodded. "Trust me," he said.

"All right," said Hilary. Then she lifted her purse up above her head, and the gargoyle pulled the most terrifying face she'd ever seen. He leaned toward Lewis, baring his teeth, crossing his eyes, wiggling his ears, and flapping his wings so violently that Hilary worried he would fly right out of Tilbury Park. His snout touched Lewis's nose, and he let out a great breath that filled the hall with the scent of damp stone and spiders.

"Arr!" cried the gargoyle, and Lewis crumpled to the floor.

Hilary stared at the peacock-blue lump of coachman. Then she poked him with her boot. He was still breathing, to her relief, but he didn't seem to be conscious. "I can't believe it," she said. "How did you know he'd faint?"

"He seemed like the sort who scares easily," said the gargoyle with a grin. "And I didn't want you to run him through."

"It was very kind of you," said Hilary. "He doesn't seem all that awful, does he? I suppose it's his bad luck to be employed by the Tilburys." She pulled out her magic coin and wished for the door to come unlocked. It required more effort than she'd expected, but slowly, one by one, the padlocks sprang open.

Hilary looked down at the gargoyle. "My dear matey," she said, "are you ready for a bit more boldness and dar-ing?"

"Always," said the gargoyle, and Hilary opened the door.

Dear Hilary,

I hope Fitzwilliam finds you with this note. Mr. Marrow, Mr. Slaughter, and I have just been approached by a gentleman calling himself Inspector Hastings. He struck me as rather foolish—but then, he managed to locate the Pigeon's hiding place, so perhaps he is not so foolish after all.

In any regard, I fear the inspector and his men are looking for you. Not only do they believe that you have captured Miss Pimm, but they are sure you intend to capture Miss Philomena Tilbury as well. We urged them quite strongly to go away, and Inspector Hastings was most impressed by our cutlass blades. He and his men traveled toward Tilbury Park, however, and I suspect that if they find you, we will all end up in the Dungeons. I suggest, therefore, that you move quickly.

Yours truly,
Mr. Stanley

CHAPTER FIFTEEN

I N THE MIDDLE of a small bedroom, Miss Pimm sat in a most uncomfortable-looking wooden chair. Her wrists and ankles were bound with thick ropes, her eyes were closed, and she was snoring softly. Hilary had always assumed that Miss Pimm was far too prim and proper to snore—or even, really, to sleep—but there was hardly any time to wonder about such things. She hurried over to Miss Pimm and put a hand on her shoulder. "Miss Pimm?" she said softly into the Enchantress's ear. "Can you hear me?"

Miss Pimm stirred, and her eyes flicked open. She stared at Hilary, blinked twice, and stared again. "Is that

Hilary Westfield?" she murmured. "No, it can't be; she's wearing a ball gown."

"It's me, Miss Pimm," Hilary said. "I've come to rescue you."

"And so have I," said the gargoyle. "Hurrah! Sound the trumpets!"

Hilary pulled out her cutlass and set to work cutting through the thick ropes around Miss Pimm's wrists and ankles. A third rope, she noticed, held Miss Pimm firmly to the chair. "I'll do my best not to slice you to bits," she said cheerfully, and Miss Pimm gave her a weak smile. "Do you feel quite all right?"

"I am two hundred and thirty-nine years old," said Miss Pimm, "and right now, I feel every bit of it." Her voice was shakier than Hilary had remembered, and she looked rather pale and thin inside her violet traveling clothes. "But that's what comes of being kept apart from my magic pieces. I haven't been able to restore my health for goodness knows how long." She paused. "How long *have* I been here?"

"It's been weeks," said Hilary. The cutlass sliced through the last rope around Miss Pimm's wrists, and Hilary began to work at the bindings on her ankles. "We came as fast as we could, but it took us ages to track down the Mutineers. They're the ones who kidnapped you—but I suppose you probably know all about it." She looked at the dark circles under Miss Pimm's eyes. "I don't want to exhaust you, but if it's not too much trouble, perhaps you could tell us what you remember."

Miss Pimm closed her eyes again. "I'm afraid I don't remember much," she said. "I'm quite sure, though, that it was Midsummer's Eve. I was on my way to visit a friend."

"Cannonball Jack!" the gargoyle interrupted.

Miss Pimm smiled. "Yes, that's right. The weather was lovely that evening, and I thought I'd walk. I was nearly to Pemberton Bay when an unmarked carriage pulled up alongside me and three people leaped out. They had quite a few large magic pieces with them, and they ordered me to get into the carriage."

"Three people?" Hilary frowned. "One of them must have been Mrs. Tilbury, I suppose."

"Yes, Georgiana was there." Miss Pimm stopped to take a shaky breath. "I'm afraid I didn't get a good look at the other two, but of course I heard their voices. I think one of them was Philomena, and the other was someone I didn't recognize. A man's voice—quite young, really, and pleasant. He seemed rather apologetic about the whole ordeal. If he hadn't been a villain, I'd say he'd been well bred."

The gargoyle frowned. "That doesn't sound like Captain Blacktooth."

"You're right about that," said Hilary. "Captain Blacktooth is hardly a pleasant young man, and he wasn't accompanying Philomena that evening." She snapped through the ropes around Miss Pimm's ankles. "It does, however, sound quite a lot like Sir Nicholas Feathering."

"Oh, drat," said the gargoyle. "But I *liked* him!"

"I didn't," Miss Pimm said firmly. "All three of them were trying to order me about with magic, and they were really quite strong. I'd left my most powerful magic pieces at home, for they're much too heavy to carry, and all I had with me was my golden crochet hook." She sighed. "It was enough to irritate the Tilburys, but then a whole crowd of gentlemen charged out from the trees. They wore silly little hats and smelled of the sea, and they were shouting something." Miss Pimm put a hand to her forehead. "I believe it might have been 'Arr!'"

"Now, *that* sounds like Captain Blacktooth," said the gargoyle.

"I tried to stick them to the ground with my crochet hook," Miss Pimm continued, "and I did stop a few of them, but the others pulled the hook out of my hand. They picked me up, which must have been quite a challenge for them, since I confess I was kicking and scratching in a terribly unladylike way. Then something hit me directly on the head, and I don't remember any more. The next thing I knew, it was daylight, my magic piece was gone, and I was sitting here in this chair, letting some silly maid feed me chicken soup." She scowled. "I detest chicken soup."

"Well, you won't have to eat it ever again once we've gotten you out of this place." The rope around Miss Pimm's waist came free, and Hilary stepped back. "Do you think you can stand?"

Miss Pimm put her hands on the chair's armrests and pushed herself up, but she immediately sat right back down again. "I'm afraid I'm very weak," she said. "The magic has kept me going for quite some time, you see, and the Tilburys wouldn't allow me to get within twenty yards of the stuff."

"Here." Hilary pulled her magic coin from her purse and pressed it into Miss Pimm's hand. "Will this help?"

Miss Pimm murmured a few words to the coin. For a moment, she was entirely still, and then she took a long breath that wasn't nearly so shaky. "I'm certainly not myself," she said, "but perhaps you won't have to carry me back to Pemberton. It would be most undignified for both of us."

"It would be even more undignified," the gargoyle pointed out, "if you had to travel in a fancy handbag."

Hilary helped Miss Pimm out of her chair. "I was hoping you'd be able to blast magic at any Mutineers who try to stop us on our way out of Tilbury Park," she said. "Do you feel well enough to manage that? I've got a few more magic coins if you need them."

But Miss Pimm shook her head. "Blasting," she said, "is out of the question, I'm afraid. I'm not strong enough to attempt anything of the sort, and I doubt a mere handful of coins would be much help against the Tilburys' magic pieces in any case. They've got quite a vast collection."

"I've seen it," said Hilary, "and I don't believe I'd enjoy having it used against me. But there's got to be more than one way to rescue an Enchantress." Hilary looked around the room. "Perhaps we can slip out the window," she said, pointing to a small pane of glass above Miss Pimm's chair.

"Georgiana Tilbury assures me that her best guards are stationed directly outside that window," Miss Pimm replied. "And I'm not sure I'm in any condition to climb out of it."

Hilary's gown was beginning to feel far too warm, and she tugged at its satin flounces. "In that case," she said, "we'll simply have to walk out the front door and hope nobody notices. There's such a crush of party guests that we might be able to manage it without getting ourselves skewered by Mrs. Tilbury's guards."

"That," said the gargoyle, "sounds like a terrible plan."

Privately, Hilary rather agreed with the gargoyle, but she certainly wasn't going to let him know it. "It's a bold and daring plan," she said instead. "The Terror of the Southlands wouldn't sneak away into the night, would she?"

"Maybe not," said the gargoyle, "but a gargoyle would. Gargoyles are very good at sneaking."

Hilary offered Miss Pimm her arm, and together they inched forward down the hall. Miss Pimm pressed down on Hilary's shoulder from above, while the gargoyle in his purse tugged at her shoulder from below. If Hilary had been a High Society girl, she might have had the luxury of complaining about the pain, but a sore shoulder was supposed to be nothing at all to a pirate, so she kept her mouth shut.

The gargoyle, however, seemed to be feeling quite chatty. "Sir Nicholas Feathering, a Mutineer," he said for at least the third time. "I can't believe I let him pat my wings."

Then there was a great fluttering of feathers in the air in front of them, and Fitzwilliam the budgerigar came to rest on Hilary's free shoulder. He squawked, dropped a scrap of paper into Hilary's hand, and nestled himself in the layers of her ball gown as she read the note from Mr. Stanley.

"Curses," Hilary muttered. "If we run into any queen's inspectors, Miss Pimm, could you tell them that I'm not a villain?"

"I can certainly try," said Miss Pimm, "but those gentlemen have a maddening tendency to disregard every word I say. A few years in finishing school would do all of them a world of good."

They had reached the end of the hallway, where Jasper and Charlie were still standing guard. Hilary tapped Charlie on the shoulder, and he turned around and grinned when he saw Miss Pimm. "Well done, Terror," he whispered. "But what are you doing here?"

"There's no other way out. I thought if we left while everyone was dancing, we might not be noticed."

But Jasper shook his head. "You'd better wait, then," he said. "They've just started clinking the champagne glasses, and I think someone's going to give a speech. If we leave now, every soul in the ballroom will notice us." He turned and tipped his hat to Miss Pimm. "By the way, Enchantress, it's a pleasure to see you again."

"Likewise," said Miss Pimm. "I do hope you pirates know what you're doing."

Claire and Miss Greyson hurried over to join them and greet Miss Pimm. "They're all coming up the stairs," Claire hissed. "Philomena, I mean, and her mother, and Nicholas Feathering."

"He's a Mutineer, you know," the gargoyle said.

Claire's mouth fell open. "But he has such lovely manners!"

Then Mrs. Tilbury appeared at the top of the staircase, draped in an imposing midnight-blue gown that seemed to take up half the hall. She was flanked by Philomena and Nicholas, who looked, in Hilary's opinion, more nervous and embarrassed than Mutineers had any right to look. "They're all villains," Hilary whispered, "the whole lot of them, and Captain Blacktooth too. It's a shame we can't send them all directly off the plank."

"What are they doing now, do you think?" Charlie

asked. "Have they got some other mutinous plot up their sleeves?"

"I believe," said Claire, "that they're about to announce the betrothal."

Hilary groaned. "That's just marvelous. We may never get Miss Pimm back to the *Pigeon*, but at least Mother will be pleased that I attended the most thrilling event of the season."

Mrs. Tilbury looked out over the ballroom and waved a silken-gloved hand in the air. In an instant, all of Tilbury Park fell silent. "Thank you, my dear friends," she said, "for joining us today as we celebrate my daughter Philomena's entrance into the grand world of High Society. I know I speak for Philomena when I say that we have been looking forward to this day for quite some time."

Philomena smiled, but not kindly, and Hilary wondered if Philomena had ever tried to stick her own mother to the floor, or turn her into a toadstool. If anyone deserved to be a toadstool, it was Mrs. Tilbury.

"As I'm sure some of you have guessed," Mrs. Tilbury continued, "we are here not only to celebrate Philomena's debut but also to share some delightful news about her future. I am simply thrilled to announce that my daughter is betrothed to Sir Nicholas Feathering, of the Queensport Featherings. They plan to be married next year. Go ahead and curtsy, dear."

Philomena followed her mother's instructions, but

Hilary was nearly certain she rolled her eyes as she did it. In the ballroom below, the throngs of guests clapped and cheered.

"Thank goodness that's over with," Charlie murmured. "Perhaps now we'll be able to leave."

"But wait!" said Mrs. Tilbury, and the guests muffled their cheers. "I have more good news to share. As you are no doubt aware, our beloved Enchantress has been missing for several weeks. Perhaps she wandered off one evening—perhaps she is no longer even in Augusta!—but whatever the case may be, I'm sure we can all agree that Miss Pimm's disappearance is most unfortunate indeed."

The pirates exchanged scathing looks, and the gargoyle ground his teeth. "I certainly agree," Miss Pimm said weakly. "I, for one, have been terribly inconvenienced."

"What has she got planned?" Hilary whispered back, but Miss Pimm simply closed her eyes and leaned against the wall.

"Magic users are running wild throughout the country!" Mrs. Tilbury said. "Thieves and villains abound! The queen's inspectors have not been able to locate Miss Pimm, nor have"—she paused—"other persistent individuals."

"Do you think she means us?" the gargoyle whispered. "Am I a persistent individual?"

"I believe you are," said Hilary.

"Now that magic has returned in full force to Augusta,"

Mrs. Tilbury was saying, "it is clear to all responsible citizens that our kingdom must have an Enchantress, and we cannot waste any more time waiting for the old one to return. I am happy to report, however, that I have corresponded with the queen herself." Mrs. Tilbury smiled. "She has just agreed to appoint my darling Philomena as the next Enchantress!"

"What?" cried Hilary, but her voice was buried under the gasps and exclamations that filled the ballroom. There were several cheers, and a few polite-sounding claps, but quite a lot of murmuring as well. Claire clenched her fists, Jasper uttered a pirate curse under his breath, and the gargoyle spit a few pebbles into the hall.

"Do you suppose that's what the Mutineers have been plotting all along?" Hilary whispered. "Getting Miss Pimm out of the way so they can install their own lovely little Enchantress who'll let them do whatever they please with their magic?"

"But Philomena's not lovely," Charlie said darkly. "Not by a long shot."

"No," said Hilary, "and I don't intend to let her take Miss Pimm's place, no matter how much certain people would prefer it." She glanced over at Miss Pimm, who was in no position to do anything about the Mutineers: her eyes were still closed, and she had turned rather gray. Hilary sighed. "Miss Greyson, do you have anything to write with?"

Miss Greyson raised her eyebrows. "Of course," she said, producing a pencil from her reticule. "What are you doing, Hilary?"

"Sending a letter." On the back of Mr. Stanley's note, Hilary scribbled a few words.

Mr. Stanley,
Come at once. Bring the others.
H.

Then she put the scrap of paper into Fitzwilliam's beak. "Fly back to the *Pigeon*, please," she whispered, "as fast as you can." Fitzwilliam flapped away, and she turned to the others. "I hope you're all ready to fight."

"Fight?" the gargoyle asked, but Hilary had already stepped out into the main hall. She drew her cutlass quickly, before she had any time to think about what she was doing, and she held it in front of her as her feet marched her toward the staircase where the Tilburys stood. Captain Blacktooth had wanted boldness and daring, hadn't he? Well then, boldness and daring he would get, even if Hilary had to dig to the very soles of her pirate boots in order to produce it.

Mrs. Tilbury hadn't noticed Hilary yet; she was still addressing the crowd. "My dearest friends," she was saying, "as Philomena accepts the responsibilities of the kingdom's highest magical post, may I ask you all to lend her your support?"

"No, Mrs. Tilbury," Hilary called, "you can't. You Mutineers won't be getting a smidgen of support from me."

an extract *From*

The Gargoyle: History of a Hero

BY THE GARGOYLE

AS TOLD TO H. WESTFIELD

In dangerous situations, a gargoyle knows exactly what to do: hide in your bag, keep your ears down, and hope your trusty assistant doesn't get you both killed.

CHAPTER SIXTEEN

THE BALL GUESTS gasped, and champagne glasses smashed to the ground as Philomena, Nicholas, and Mrs. Tilbury all turned to stare at Hilary. Philomena's face was tight with fury, and Nicholas looked rather panicked, but Mrs. Tilbury remained calm and composed, and that worried Hilary most of all. "Philomena, dear," said Mrs. Tilbury, "do you have the slightest idea who this young lady might be?"

"That's Hilary Westfield," Philomena said sharply, "and I'm quite sure she wasn't invited."

"Why, so it is!" Mrs. Tilbury smiled. "I nearly didn't recognize her in last season's fashions." Her voice carried across the ballroom, and several of her guests chuckled. "Miss Westfield, whatever is the meaning of this outburst?"

As she looked down at the ballroom, Hilary caught a glimpse of her mother pushing through the crowd, trying to reach the staircase. At least the sight of Hilary holding a cutlass hadn't caused her to swoon on the spot. Captain Blacktooth was also making his way toward the staircase, and several of the peacock-clad guards were heading straight toward her; she didn't have much time to spare. *Oh, Fitzwilliam,* Hilary thought, *please hurry.*

"You know perfectly well what I mean," she called to Mrs. Tilbury. "Philomena can't be the Enchantress."

Mrs. Tilbury sniffed. "And why not?"

"Because," said Hilary, "I'm afraid the position's not vacant. You see, Mrs. Tilbury, I've found Miss Pimm."

She nodded toward the doorway, where Jasper and Miss Greyson were helping Miss Pimm walk forward. As the Enchantress came into view, a new wave of murmurs rose up from the crowd, and a handful of people actually applauded, though Philomena whirled around to glare at them.

Hilary was pleased to see that Mrs. Tilbury looked genuinely startled at last. In a matter of seconds, however, she had donned her most pleasant High Society expression, and she clapped her hands together with something very like delight. "How wonderful!" she cried. "Miss Pimm has finally reappeared! But I must say, Miss Westfield, that she doesn't look at all well. I hardly think she is fit to return to her post."

"Of course she doesn't look well," Hilary said. "You kidnapped her and kept her locked up here for weeks. Or is that how you treat all your houseguests?"

"Kidnapped!" Mrs. Tilbury laughed. "Whyever would I do such a cruel thing to dear Miss Pimm?"

Hilary wasn't entirely sure about this, but she could make a decent guess. "Because Miss Pimm won't let you do whatever you like with your magic," she suggested, "and Miss Pimm thinks people like you shouldn't have all the kingdom's magic for themselves. You thought if you simply removed her, you could pop your daughter into her place easily enough—which I have to admit you very nearly did. And I expect you thought you'd be able to order your darling Philomena about once she became the Enchantress."

Hilary felt quite sure she'd guessed correctly, for Mrs. Tilbury's smile flickered, and Philomena flinched. "What an absurd suggestion, Miss Westfield," Mrs. Tilbury said. "Surely you can't expect anyone to believe it."

"I expect Philomena and Sir Nicholas to believe it. They helped you, after all, and so did your brother." Hilary pointed her sword at Captain Blacktooth. "Do your High Society friends know that you've been plotting with pirates, Mrs. Tilbury? Or that you've been sending threatening notes to me and my friends?"

The murmurs from the crowd grew louder, and some of the guests began to inch toward the doorways, as though they were not sure whether it was entirely polite to leave a ball during the hostess's confrontation with a pirate. Captain Blacktooth had reached the bottom of one staircase, and Mrs. Westfield was scrambling up the other. Hilary waved her cutlass at the guards who hovered behind her, but they refused to step back. Charlie and Jasper had drawn their swords now as well, and Miss Greyson was clutching her magic piece, but they were terribly outnumbered by the Mutineers and the entire crew of the *Renegade*, not to mention the additional pirates Captain Blacktooth had hired especially for this occasion. Hilary tried to take a breath to calm her nerves, but the dratted cabbage-colored dress felt tighter than ever around her waist.

Mrs. Tilbury came close enough that Hilary had to wrinkle her nose against the wilting lavender scent of her perfume. "Your father warned me you might be a nuisance," she said, and she wasn't smiling any longer. "You may have flung him into the Dungeons—"

"I didn't *fling* him anywhere," said Hilary through her teeth.

"—but I believe you'll find the rest of us won't be defeated so easily." Then she turned back to her guests. "I'm afraid," she said, "that this villainous young pirate has disrupted our gathering with her ridiculous tales, but please don't be alarmed. My guards shall keep us safe by escorting Miss Westfield away at once." She nodded to the guards behind Hilary. "You may lock her in the conservatory if she promises not to spoil the good furniture."

Hilary scanned the guards' faces, looking for familiar scallywags, but the only pirates she recognized were the ones who had confronted her at the Salty Biscuit. "Stop!" she shouted as one of them took hold of her elbow. "Are you quite sure you want to attack the Terror of the Southlands?"

"She's the most fearsome pirate on the High Seas," Charlie called from somewhere outside the knot of guards.

"And the rest of us are hardly boiled porridge, either," said Jasper.

"Stay back," the gargoyle cried, "or I'll bite. Would you mind telling me which of you tastes the best?"

The guards hesitated, and the pirate who'd been holding Hilary's elbow let go. "I don't know, ma'am," one of them said to Mrs. Tilbury. "She *is* the Terror of the Southlands. She doesn't look like much, but she might still be dangerous."

"And she's a League member," another guard pointed out. "Are you sure we're allowed to lock her up?"

The others shook their heads and began to back away. "That's very wise of you," Hilary said. "Now my friends and I won't have to blast you all to bits."

"Oh, for goodness' sake," said Mrs. Tilbury. She turned to glare at Captain Blacktooth. "Can't your men do anything right? Or must I do it all myself?"

"That's not fair," said the guard closest to Hilary. "We grabbed that Enchantress for you well enough, didn't we?"

"Quiet!" Mrs. Tilbury snapped. She reached into the folds of her gown and removed a golden shoehorn that glinted in the light of the chandelier. Hilary nearly stepped backward at the sight of it, but there was no point in trying to hurry away; Mrs. Tilbury would probably use the magic piece to stick her to the floor. Besides, the guards were surrounding her friends now, and Miss Pimm did not look very steady on her feet. Hilary rather feared her rescue plan was riddled with holes and likely to capsize.

Mrs. Tilbury peeled off her evening gloves. "Philomena," she said, "and Nicholas, I expect your help."

Philomena put her hands on her hips. "Mama," she said, "you mustn't take that tone with me. I am a High Society lady now, aren't I?"

"Perhaps," Mrs. Tilbury said, "but you'll still do as you're told." She tapped the shoehorn against her palm.

Philomena sighed and produced two golden candlesticks from her reticule.

"Er, Philomena," said Nicholas, taking a few steps toward the door, "I'm not sure I'm entirely comfortable with this. I was told there wouldn't be any more villainy, and Miss Westfield is a very pleasant pirate—"

"Mr. Feathering," Mrs. Tilbury snapped, "our circumstances have changed. If you wish to marry my daughter instead of being left penniless in the Dungeons for the rest of your days, you will assist me at once."

Nicholas froze. Then, looking quite reluctant, he walked back to Philomena's side and pulled a solid-looking ball of magic from his pocket.

"You *slime!*" cried Alice Feathering from somewhere in the crowd below. "Don't you *dare* hurt the Terror! Oh, please let me through so I can kick him!"

"I'm terribly sorry, Pirate Westfield," said Nicholas. "I don't have much of a choice, you see, but I'll certainly miss you when you're gone."

"When I'm *gone?*" Hilary cried. "Do you truly think you can make the Terror of the Southlands disappear?" If only she could keep them talking for a few moments longer, perhaps Fitzwilliam would have enough time . . .

"Setting her adrift in the sea would be appropriate, don't you think?" Mrs. Tilbury said to Philomena. "I'm sure we could manage it between the three of us."

"No!" cried the gargoyle. "I'll sink!"

Then several things happened at once. Mrs. Tilbury, Philomena, and Nicholas all raised their magic pieces in the air. Hilary raised her cutlass. The gargoyle bared his teeth. The floor shook as dozens of queen's inspectors marched into the hall, pursued by dozens of guards in peacock blue. And above it all, the great glass ballroom windows smashed to pieces.

The Tilburys' guests shrieked and dodged falling bits

of windowpane as thick ropes flew through the empty window frames and wrapped around the staircase railings, the balconies, and the chandelier. Then, with a great cheer, a multitude of pirates swung into the ballroom. They were eye-patched and elbow-patched, snaggle-toothed and scraggly; they waved their cutlasses in the air and overturned the punch bowls. Hilary nearly applauded as Mr. Slaughter and Mr. Stanley sailed in, accompanied by Fitzwilliam, who was perched on Mr. Stanley's head and looking rather pleased with himself. A dozen pirates from the far north arrived, dressed all in furs, followed closely by the crew of the dread ship *Matilda*. And last of all came Cannonball Jack.

"Arr!" he cried. "We be here to help the Terror of the Southlands—and to skewer the Mutineers!"

Hilary grinned. "I'd suggest you put down your magic pieces," she said to the Mutineers, "for if you enchant me into the sea, you'll displease quite a few scallywags, and I believe they've just sharpened their swords."

Mrs. Tilbury spun around. "They're heading for the magic!" she cried, pointing to half a dozen pirates who'd caught sight of the glass-paneled cabinet in the ballroom below. "Stop those uncivilized villains at once!" Then she rushed down the staircase into the crowd of party guests and pirates. Nicholas Feathering ran in the other direction—in search of an escape route, Hilary supposed—but Alice had fought her way up the staircase, and she hurried after him with her hair ribbons flying and her fists clenched.

Philomena, however, didn't move right away. "I won't forgive you for this, Hilary Westfield," she said. "You let *pirates* trample all over my *debut*."

"If it's any consolation," said Hilary, "I'm sure High Society will be buzzing about it for weeks."

Philomena turned several interesting colors in a row, beginning with rose and finishing somewhere around mauve. Then, without another word, she turned on her heel and stormed down the staircase after her mother.

Hilary itched to go after the Mutineers and show them the sharpened side of her cutlass, but she couldn't do anything of the sort until she'd gotten Miss Pimm safely back to the *Pigeon*. She began to push her way through the crowd of guards and inspectors that had gathered in the hall, but before she had taken more than a few steps, Mrs. Westfield was at her side, taking very deep breaths and fanning herself to keep from fainting. "Whatever is going on, Hilary?" she asked. "Why has dear Miss Pimm been lodging with the Tilburys? And who are all these gentlemen running about with cutlasses? It's scandalous!"

She began to tip forward, but Hilary caught her arm. "Mother," she said, "there's simply no time to swoon. You're the finest hostess here, so you've got a very important job to do."

Mrs. Westfield stopped fanning herself. "I have?"

"Yes," said Hilary. "Could you gather all the party

guests who aren't Mutineers or pirates and take them somewhere safe?"

"I suppose I *could*!" said Mrs. Westfield. Then she raised her voice. "Attention!" she called. "Would anyone who is not a Mutineer or a pirate please join me on the front lawn immediately? I believe it's a lovely night for stargazing."

Several High Society guests hurried gratefully toward the exits as Hilary made her way over to the crew of the *Pigeon*. Jasper and Charlie were fighting off the guards who'd surrounded them, and Miss Greyson was using her crochet hook to blast several of them off their feet, while Claire jabbed all the guards within reach with two of her very sharp hairpins. Miss Pimm sat on the floor against the wall, still managing to look proper and imposing with her legs straight out in front of her and her violet skirts arranged neatly around her. "I'm sorry about the delay," Hilary said to her, "but I'll take you back to the *Pigeon* now. We've got quite a lot of magic on board, and perhaps it will help you feel better."

Miss Pimm nodded. "Thank you, Hilary. That sounds rather pleasant."

Hilary helped Miss Pimm to her feet and began to lead her toward the door. In front of them, Mrs. Westfield shepherded a gaggle of High Society ladies out to the lawn as pirates and queen's inspectors fended off the Tilburys' guards. To Hilary's great annoyance, some of the inspectors were trying to fight the pirates as well. Swords, magnifying glasses, and little dusting brushes flew through the air, and Hilary caught a glimpse through the crowd of Inspector Hastings kicking a guard in the shin. She guided Miss Pimm as well as she could around the worst of the battle, ducking every few seconds to avoid a magic piece or a cutlass blade. "I'm sorry about all this, Miss Pimm," she said. "I hope we're not sliced to ribbons."

"I can help ye with that, Terror." Cannonball Jack pushed through the crowd. "Here, Eugenia. Rest yer other hand right here on me shoulder. 'Tis a bit soiled with parrot leavin's, but I apologize fer that."

Miss Pimm gave a hint of a smile. "I should apologize to you for missing our last meeting. I'm afraid I was unavoidably delayed."

"Ah," said Cannonball Jack, "but I knew the Terror would find ye, and I were right."

As they pushed toward the doorway, Hilary looked out over the battle that raged in the ballroom. At one end of the room, Mr. Slaughter chased a guard around a shattered punch bowl. At the other, Fitzwilliam was doing his best to build a nest in Philomena's hair. Charlie was making an impressive show of disarming guard after guard, and a small crowd had gathered around him to cheer him on. Nicholas Feathering leaped out of one of the shattered ballroom windows and headed toward the forest, but Alice followed close behind, swinging a sword she must have borrowed from another pirate.

All in all, Hilary thought, it was proving to be quite a satisfactory evening. A fierce battle swirled around her more delightfully than any High Society ball, she was rescuing Miss Pimm, and she'd be away on the *Pigeon* before her mother could discover the sorry state of her ball gown. Its train was being ripped to shreds under the boots of careless inspectors and guards, but Hilary hardly cared, for with every rip, she felt less like a cabbage and more like the Terror of the Southlands.

Then something sharp and cold was pressed against her back. "Turn around slowly, Pirate Westfield," Captain Blacktooth said in her ear. "I'd truly hate to run you through."

HILARY DID AS Captain Blacktooth ordered. He held his sword frighteningly close to her chin, and his expression was so fearsome that she froze with her hand on the hilt of her cutlass. "I can't possibly let you leave with the Enchantress after all the work my men and I did to bring her here," Blacktooth said. "It would be terribly inconvenient."

Cannonball Jack drew his own sword. "Ye scurvy traitor," he thundered. "When I heard they found me eye patch at the scene o' the crime, I guessed ye were behind it all. Ye stole that patch when ye came to visit, didn't ye?

Ye tried to frame me—yer own fellow pirate! An' I gave ye shortbread!"

Captain Blacktooth's sword inched closer to Hilary's neck, and she swallowed. "That's enough, Jack," he said. "Unless you want to harm Pirate Westfield—and I'm quite sure you don't—you'll leave us be. And don't you dare let that Enchantress out of this room, or I'll send you both off the plank."

Cannonball Jack hesitated, but Hilary nodded at him as well as she could without cutting herself on Blacktooth's sword. "It's all right," she said. "You take care of Miss Pimm, and I'll deal with Captain Blacktooth."

"Spoken like a true Terror of the Southlands," Captain Blacktooth observed as Cannonball Jack retreated. "I have to admit I'm impressed."

"You should be," said Hilary. "I told you I'd find Miss Pimm, and now I've done it, so you won't have to send me off the plank." Her heart was beating fast, and the sword at her neck certainly wasn't helping matters. "Do you still think I'm unpiratical, sir? Do you still doubt my talents?"

"You certainly have a talent for making trouble," said Blacktooth. "I wish you'd gone off to slay a sea monster or fight a pirate king, for then we wouldn't be in this unpleasant situation."

"You mean you wish you'd gotten rid of us," the gargoyle said, "the way you got rid of Jasper."

Blacktooth frowned. "That's rather blunt."

"Too bad," said the gargoyle. "Maybe I'd be friendlier if I were a parrot." He grinned up at Blacktooth. "But I doubt it."

"Pirate Westfield," said Blacktooth, "I didn't pull you aside to bicker with you and your pet." He lowered his sword slightly. Then, to Hilary's astonishment, he smiled. "I hoped we could settle this battle captain to captain, in a friendly sort of way."

"I'm sorry, sir, but I don't think we're friends."

"But surely your mates don't intend to fight forever. Pirates battling pirates, delicate High Society ladies being dragged into the melee—it all seems rather unnecessary."

"You're right," Hilary said. "It wouldn't be necessary at all if you hadn't kidnapped Miss Pimm." She brushed her hair out of her face, wishing it were back in its practical pirate braid. "Do you really want Philomena to be the Enchantress, Captain Blacktooth? Do you honestly believe it's a good idea?"

Captain Blacktooth's eyes narrowed. "I am very fond of my niece," he said. "And I can't say I'm very fond of Miss Pimm. She wants to control our treasure—how much of it we can have, and what we can do with it once we've plundered it." He put a hand on Hilary's shoulder. "Surely you understand that I must do what's best for my fellow scallywags, what's best for the League."

Hilary stared at the rows of silver buttons that marched obediently along the front of Captain Blacktooth's tailcoat, not a single one out of place. "I suppose you must," she said at last.

"And so must you," said Captain Blacktooth. "If you'll agree to call off your pirates, we can put this business behind us at last, and I'll ask my secretary to remove those warnings from your VNHLP record. No one on the High Seas will dare to challenge you once I've told them you have the League's full support. After all, Hilary, you are quite piratical—even in that dreadful ball gown." He chuckled and held out his hand. "Do we have a truce?"

Captain Blacktooth's hand was rough and scarred from years of sailing and swashbuckling. Hilary had shaken it when he'd welcomed her into the VNHLP, and she'd shaken it again when she'd promised to do something bold and daring. She had done everything she could to prove herself to him—and to the rest of his dratted scallywags—but truthfully, she was growing rather tired of shaking Captain Blacktooth's hand.

"No," she said. "We don't."

The smile disappeared from Blacktooth's face.

"I won't agree to a truce," Hilary said, more loudly this time. "I swore I'd rescue Miss Pimm, and that's what I'm going to do, even if you and your men don't like it."

"I'm afraid the League won't look kindly—"

"Oh, blast the League!" Hilary cried, and the floor of Tilbury Park seemed to give way below her like a ship's deck during a storm. "If all the scallywags in the

VNHLP support you, Captain Blacktooth, then I can't be a member."

Captain Blacktooth stepped back and stared at her. "What do you mean?" he asked.

The great hall rocked back and forth, or at least it seemed that way to Hilary. "Perhaps I'm not always as bold as I could be," she said, "or as daring. I'm not much good at swordplay, I've never buried a treasure, and I don't even *want* to own a parrot. I feel absolutely horrid that I've put my own father in the Dungeons, and sometimes I don't know if I'm any good at being the Terror of the Southlands." She felt herself sway as the words broke over her. "But I know I'm nothing like you, Captain Blacktooth. You may be bold and daring, but you're not honorable—not even very nearly—and you don't have my respect."

For a moment, Hilary thought the whole mansion might capsize. The floorboards would split, the waves would rush in, and she would sink to the bottom of the High Seas without any hope of rescue. Then, faintly, she heard the gargoyle cheering. She held him close, and Tilbury Park began to right itself around her.

"Very well, then," Captain Blacktooth said at last, though he didn't sound happy about it. "Hilary Westfield, you are no longer a member of the Very Nearly Honorable League of Pirates. Please forfeit the sword that was issued to you by the League."

Hilary was hardly aware of her own hands as they

picked up her cutlass—her beautiful, fearsome pirate cutlass—and passed it to Captain Blacktooth. He took it in his own hands and nodded.

"The League accepts your forfeit," he said solemnly.

Then he looked out over the ballroom. "If this battle is going to continue, I suggest you hurry downstairs and help your friend. She seems to be in trouble, and I warn you: my niece is extremely talented when it comes to magic."

Hilary spun around. "Oh, blast," she whispered, for Philomena had plucked one of the magic pitchers from the glass-paneled cabinet, and she was using it to dangle Claire several feet above everyone else's heads. Pirates, guards, and inspectors alike had paused their sword fighting to stare up at Claire, floating in her orange-gold silk like a stray bit of sunset. She didn't scream, and she didn't cry, but Hilary took one look at her face and knew she was terrified.

"I'll be needing this back," Hilary said, snatching her cutlass out of Captain Blacktooth's hands. "I know it's against the rules, but you told me once that being a pirate requires a certain disregard for good behavior." Then, before Captain Blacktooth could do a single thing about it, Hilary sliced her cutlass through the air in front of her and ran as fast as she could down the staircase, through the crowd, and toward Philomena.

Mrs. Tilbury tried to grab her arm, but Hilary shoved her aside and hurried on. All she could hear was Philomena taunting Claire. "Where did you get such a lovely dress?" Philomena was saying. "Did you steal it, perhaps? Have you been picking up horrid habits from your pirate friends?"

Hilary grabbed Philomena from one side just as Charlie grabbed her from the other. They both held up their swords, and Philomena stopped laughing.

"Let Claire down this instant," said Hilary, "or I shall find a way to send you somewhere that makes the Royal Dungeons look like the finest mansion in Queensport."

"And I'll just run you through," Charlie said. "So you'd better be quick about it."

Philomena looked at each of them, and then she looked down at their swords. "If I let her down," she said, "will you get your grubby pirate hands off of me?"

"Maybe," said Hilary.

"All right, then." Philomena smirked. "Magic pitcher, please release Miss Dupree from the air."

With a yelp of pain, Claire crashed to the floor at Philomena's feet.

"Hey!" the gargoyle cried. "You dropped her on purpose!"

Philomena glared at him. "I won't be scolded by a silly little pebble," she said, "especially not at my debut."

"He's right, though," said Hilary. She struck the flat of her cutlass blade against Philomena's golden pitcher, sending it rolling across the ballroom floor. "And don't you dare call him a pebble. Have you got something cruel to say about each of my friends?"

"Actually—" Philomena broke off, and the room went quiet. Claire had limped over to the cabinet full of magic, and as they watched, she pulled an enormous golden serving tray from the lowest shelf. "For heaven's sake, Miss Dupree," said Philomena, "you've gone and found the largest magic piece in our collection. Surely you can't expect to use it."

"But if I'm holding it," said Claire, "you won't dare to send me into the air again, will you?" She smiled at Philomena. "Just imagine what I could do with it."

"She could explode Tilbury Park," Charlie whispered to Hilary behind Philomena's back, "and blow all the Northlands to rubble. What is she up to?"

"I think she's bluffing," Hilary whispered back. "She's a very good actress."

Philomena hesitated for a moment. Then she laughed. "It would be one thing," she said, "if you were truly a High Society girl. But you can barely curtsy! Can you even use a magic crochet hook?"

Claire flushed and nearly dropped the serving tray.

Philomena gave a dramatic little gasp. "You *can't* use a crochet hook, can you? Well, I certainly can't say I'm surprised."

"Oh," cried Claire, "I am so *sick* of you, Philomena!" She waved the serving tray in the air. "In fact, I'm sick of your whole villainous family! You can't just storm through the kingdom snatching up Enchantresses and forcing us all to do what you say, you know; it's frightfully rude! Of course, I don't believe rudeness bothers any of you one bit. But do you know what I wish?" The serving tray shook in her grip. "I wish all you dratted Mutineers would disappear to some horrid little deserted island and leave me alone!"

"No!" cried Hilary, Charlie, Miss Greyson, and Mr. Stanley at once, but it was too late. Claire stared in horror at the serving tray. "Oh dear," she whispered. "I didn't mean to wish . . ."

And then, with a very loud pop, Philomena vanished.

At first Hilary thought she'd imagined it, but when she looked around the ballroom, she couldn't see Philomena anywhere. In fact, Tilbury Park seemed far less full of people than it had a few moments before. The queen's inspectors were still accounted for, as were all the pirates Cannonball Jack had invited, but the guards in peacock blue had disappeared, and there was no sign of Mrs. Tilbury. Even Captain Blacktooth was gone, and no amount of staring or blinking on Hilary's part would retrieve him.

"Claire?" Hilary said into the echoing space Philomena had left behind. "I think the magic worked."

Claire set down the serving tray, but her hands were still shaking. "No," she said, "it couldn't have worked. It should have exploded." She sat down on the floor right in the middle of the ballroom.

Behind her, Alice Feathering climbed back through

the shattered window. She was nearly out of breath, and she looked as though she really had seen a ghost. "Terror!" she called to Hilary. "Something's happened to Nicholas! I'd just gotten him pinned against a tree when he disappeared from under my blade, and—" Alice looked around the ballroom. "I don't understand," she said. "Where did everyone go?"

"Perhaps I can provide an explanation." Miss Pimm walked unsteadily down the stairs, still leaning on Cannonball Jack's arm and looking very grave. "I believe I know exactly what's happened."

Claire looked like she might cry. "You do?"

"Please don't be angry with Claire, Miss Pimm," Hilary cut in. "It was an accident; she didn't mean to use all that magic, and I'm sure she's very sorry. You won't expel her from school, will you? Or chide her in rhyme? Or—"

"Miss Westfield," said Miss Pimm, "please stop blathering. You are a very good pirate, but right now you're being terribly silly." Then she turned to Claire and smiled. "Whyever would I be angry with the girl who's going to be our next Enchantress?"

TERROR OF THE SOUTHLANDS RESCUES ENCHANTRESS

NORDHOLM, AUGUSTA—Miss Eugenia Pimm, Enchantress of the Northlands, is on her way home to Pemberton at long last, thanks to the brave actions of Pirate Hilary Westfield, Pirate Charlie Dove, Miss Claire Dupree, and their mates. Pirate Westfield, whom the Gazette knows fondly as the Terror of the Southlands, caused quite a splash in High Society yesterday evening when she presented Miss Pimm at Tilbury Park during the debut ball of Miss Philomena Tilbury. "I'm not entirely sure how Pirate Westfield managed to find the Enchantress," said Inspector John Hastings. "I don't believe she owns a magnifying glass or a fingerprint kit." The inspector admitted that he was grateful to Pirate Westfield for her help in solving the case, though he insisted he would have found Miss Pimm himself if only he'd been given a few more minutes to search for her.

Accounts of the ball are rather muddled: some guests claim the Enchantress fell ill while visiting the Tilburys, while others believe the Tilburys personally arranged for Miss Pimm's disappearance. It seems clear, however, that quite a lot of pirates attended last night's event, and that they staunchly refused to mind their manners.

Shortly before Miss Pimm's sudden and surprising return, Queen Adelaide had agreed to appoint Miss Philomena Tilbury as the next Enchantress, but the queen is now reconsidering that agreement. "I am happy to welcome Miss Pimm back to her post," the queen told the Gazette, "and I look forward to having her guidance as we determine who her successor shall be." Miss Pimm is currently traveling to Pemberton on the pirate ship the *Pigeon*, which will resume distributing magic throughout the kingdom within the month.

According to Inspector Hastings, the queen's inspectors are searching for Mrs. Georgiana Tilbury in order to question her further about the Enchantress's disappearance. They are also eager to learn more about the vast quantity of stolen magic that inspectors discovered at Tilbury Park, which seems to be identical to the missing loot hidden by Admiral James Westfield before his arrest last year. It is believed that Mrs. Tilbury and several of her friends and family members are residing temporarily on a horrid little deserted island somewhere on the High Seas.

RESIGNATIONS SHAKE THE LEAGUE. The Picaroon has confirmed rumors from last week's thrilling pirate battle that Pirate Hilary Westfield, the Terror of the Southlands, has withdrawn from the Very Nearly Honorable League of Pirates. The Terror had received three warnings for unpiratical behavior from VNHLP president Rupert Blacktooth, but it is unknown whether these warnings were the cause of her shocking and scandalous departure from the League. Captain Blacktooth welcomed the Terror into the League with open arms only last year, and we at the Picaroon cannot understand why any pirate would be foolhardy enough to turn down membership in our illustrious organization. But the Terror appears to have her admirers, for the pirates Charlie Dove and Cannonball Jack have resigned from the League as well in support of her decision. We firmly remind all three scallywags that freelance pirates must forfeit their subscriptions to the Picaroon and may not attend any League picnics.

∽

RENEGADE CREW LOCATED. After several days of searching, representatives from the VNHLP have found Captain Blacktooth and his crew on a remote, miserable island several leagues south of Augusta. For reasons unknown to this publication, most of the crew members were dressed in unflattering peacock-blue uniforms that had been thoroughly soaked during their week on the island. Captain Blacktooth and his men are reported to be remarkably grumpy, perhaps due to the fact that they were forced to share their island with two High Society ladies and one young man who is reported to be the most eligible gentleman in Augusta. When told that the queen's inspectors were on their way to the island, Captain Blacktooth groaned and buried his face in the sleeves of his rather curious tailcoat.

CHAPTER SEVENTEEN

HILARY STOOD AT the bow of the *Pigeon* and watched as the spires and rooftops of Pemberton rose up along the coastline in front of her. "We're almost there, gargoyle," she said softly. "It's nearly time to say 'Land ho!'"

The gargoyle, who had been napping in his Nest, yawned and stretched his wings. "Land ho!" he murmured sleepily. "Make way for the Terror of the Southlands and her fearsome beast!" He looked up at Hilary. "We won't stay in Pemberton for ages, will we? I was just getting settled back in my Nest."

"We won't be there for long," Hilary assured him. "We've just got to bring Miss Pimm and Claire back to finishing school, and I'd like to buy some new pirate clothes. These were a gift from Blacktooth, and I don't believe I want to keep wearing them now that I know what he's truly like." She adjusted the gargoyle's hat, which had slipped toward his snout as he dozed. "Do you really think I did the right thing?"

"You mean leaving the VNHLP?" The gargoyle thought for a moment. Then he nodded. "Being a pirate," he said, "isn't the same as being a villain, but I don't think Captain Blacktooth knows the difference."

"I believe you're right," said Hilary. "And it's absolutely infuriating that he's still in charge of all those scourges and scallywags. The finest pirate league on the High Seas simply shouldn't be run by a villain!" She slapped her hands against the ship's rail. "Do you think it's possible that losing a battle to the Terror of the Southlands has given Blacktooth a change of heart?"

"If it hasn't," said the gargoyle, "we should make him walk the plank."

Hilary smiled at the thought of it. "I'll have half the scallywags in the kingdom after me if I try something like that," she said. "They're free to blast me to pieces whenever they'd like now that I've left the League."

"Then you'll just have to be an even better pirate than they are," the gargoyle said. "Rescuing Miss Pimm was a very good start."

Miss Pimm had not returned to her usual commanding

state, but a few days on the *Pigeon* seemed to have done her some good. Miss Greyson had plied her with hearty food and small doses of magic until she was strong enough to walk down to the *Pigeon's* storeroom, where she collected a generous handful of golden coins and crochet hooks. Some of these she used to improve her health, but most she gave to Claire, who had spent nearly the entire trip from Nordholm trying to train her knack for magic.

"Those explosions of yours," Miss Pimm had explained, "are quite natural, for you've got a good deal more magical strength than those small coins can contain. When I was a girl, I blew up half my family's collection of magic tooth-picks before I found a golden soup tureen that was large enough to hold my power without exploding to bits." She smiled. "At the time, I believe, I was wishing for something interesting to happen, and the next thing I knew, a sheep burst into the room and began to dance the hornpipe."

Claire and Miss Pimm joined Hilary at the *Pigeon's* bow as Jasper steered the ship into Pemberton Bay. "Is Claire really going to be the Enchantress, then?" the gargoyle asked.

Miss Pimm nodded. "As soon as she's learned to con-trol her talent," she said, "and only if she wants to be. I must admit I am eager to retire, but I certainly won't force another young girl into the job if she can't stand the thought of it."

"I can absolutely stand it," Claire said cheerfully. "And

I believe I'm making progress. I only exploded two crochet hooks today."

"Excellent," said Miss Pimm. "When we return to school, you shall take private lessons with me. Shall we say four days a week, bright and early before breakfast?"

Claire gulped.

"If anyone's going to be the new Enchantress," Hilary said, "I'm very glad it's you. You'll be loads better than Philomena."

Miss Pimm shook her head. "Georgiana Tilbury had been pestering me for ages, you know, insisting that I train Philomena as the next Enchantress. I knew the woman was ruthless, and I suspected her of sending intruders to Pemberton to watch my movements. As a matter of fact, that's why I wrote to Mr. Fletcher. But I never dreamed she'd nearly succeed at shoving me aside." She pursed her lips. "I do hope that Inspector Hastings doesn't set her loose upon Augusta."

Once the *Pigeon* was safely anchored in Pemberton Bay, with Mr. Stanley in place to watch over its treasure, Hilary scooped the gargoyle into her bag and set off for the mainland with the other pirates. Even Charlie didn't seem at all dismayed to be marching back to Miss Pimm's Finishing School for Delicate Ladies. He had impressed several pirates with his sword-fighting skills at Philomena's ball, and a few scallywags had already written him to ask him for dueling advice, which had put him in a remarkably cheerful mood. "If I'd known High Society balls could be so much fun," he'd remarked to Hilary, "I would have attended more of them."

They made quite a grand procession, Hilary thought: Miss Greyson discussing books with Mr. Marrow; Jasper and Charlie swinging their swords in the midday sun; Claire delivering a virtuoso performance on her tin whistle; Mr. Slaughter escorting Miss Pimm; and Hilary at the end of the line with the gargoyle by her side. "Do you know," she said to the gargoyle, "I feel rather bold and daring at the moment."

The gargoyle studied her. "It helps," he said, "that you don't look like a cabbage."

Then the road curved west, they entered the center of Pemberton, and Hilary drew in her breath. She couldn't quite believe it, but the front gate of Miss Pimm's finishing school was blocked by a small but energetic crowd of people who clapped and cheered as the pirates approached. Some of them were finishing-school girls with dancing sheep embroidered on their cardigans, and others were queen's inspectors in tidy red jackets. Then there were several people Hilary didn't recognize at all, though she could see Alice Feathering jumping up and down to get a better view. A banner reading WELCOME HOME, MISS PIMM flapped above the gate, and underneath it, someone had hung another banner that said THANK YOU, PIRATES. Hilary put her arms around Charlie and Claire as they admired the banners, and for a few moments, none of them could do anything but grin.

The gargoyle craned his neck so far that he nearly fell out of his bag. "What's going on?" he asked. "Oh, Hilary, are these my admirers?"

"Yes," she said, "I believe they are."

"And could that be—" The gargoyle paused, and his ears twitched. "Well, what do you know," he said happily as a queen's inspector struck up a fanfare from a window across the street. "They remembered the trumpets."

AFTER HILARY HAD hugged Claire good-bye and given Miss Pimm a hearty handshake, and after she had bought a new pirate wardrobe and a fine new hat that the gargoyle declared to be breathtaking, she trudged back to the *Pigeon* and tossed her brown-paper packages down on the deck. Then she settled the gargoyle back into his Nest and watched the wavelets break against the ship's hull far below them.

Charlie asked if she wanted to practice a new dueling strategy Jasper had described to him, but Hilary shook her head. "It's kind of you to offer," she said, "but I'm not much in the mood for dueling."

"That's all right," said Charlie. "Pirates don't always have to duel. Sometimes they can look out at the waves with their friends."

Hilary smiled. "Is that one of the VNHLP's rules?"

"Absolutely not," said Charlie. "It's my own, and you're welcome to borrow it."

"Thank you," said Hilary. "I believe I will."

They looked out at the waves for quite some time, munching on hardtack and trading fearsome pirate tales until the sky above the horizon was streaked with sunset. Then the gargoyle stirred in his Nest. "Shiver me timbers!" he said. "It's the *Blunderbuss!*"

A cheerful bell rang out from Cannonball Jack's houseboat as it approached the *Pigeon*. "Ahoy, Terror!" Cannonball Jack called out. "I was hopin' I'd find ye here. I've got some scallywags who'd like to talk to ye."

As Hilary watched, a handful of pirates shuffled out onto the *Blunderbuss*'s deck. They all wore bedraggled peacock-blue uniforms, and they all looked utterly exhausted. Hilary nearly swallowed her hardtack whole when she saw that the pirate at the front of the group was Captain Blacktooth's first mate, Mr. Twigget.

"I found 'em floatin' on a little raft a few leagues south o' here," Cannonball Jack explained. "They say they gave ol' Blacktooth the slip, and they want to talk to Pirate Hilary Westfield." He paused and gave Hilary an apologetic sort of smile. "Which is who ye be."

"But they're Mutineers," said Charlie. "Why should we listen to them?"

"Hold on a moment," said Hilary. "I suppose we should hear what they want." She stood up straight and studied the line of pirates who looked up at her from the *Blunder-buss*. "Well, Mr. Twigget? What is it?"

Mr. Twigget cleared his throat and shuffled forward when Cannonball Jack poked him with the tip of his sword. "Ahoy, Pirate Westfield," he said. "We—my mates and I, I mean—we've been thinkin' a bit about our careers, and we were hopin' we might be able to join your crew."

"But you work for Captain Blacktooth." Hilary reached for her cutlass.

"Not anymore," Mr. Twigget said earnestly. "There are a few of us who don't care for his methods—meanin' the kidnappin' and all. It's not very nearly honorable, if you know what I mean."

Hilary nodded. "I know perfectly well."

"Anyway, we're tired of bein' ordered about by that Mrs. Tilbury, and we heard you stood up to Captain Blacktooth. Some scallywags are already talkin' about takin' sides, and we'd rather be on your side than his." Mr. Twigget wrung his hands. "It's all right if you say no. We can find other hobbies. . . . There's more to life than piratin', I suppose. . . ."

The other pirates looked at Mr. Twigget as though they were not at all sure this was true.

Hilary raised her eyebrows at Charlie and the gargoyle. Then she turned back to Mr. Twigget. "I can see we've got a lot to discuss," she said, "so you might as well stay for dinner. You too, Cannonball Jack. Miss Greyson always cooks twice as much food as we need anyway."

Charlie tossed a rope down to the *Blunderbuss,* and the pirates scrambled aboard. Mr. Twigget took Hilary's hand in both of his and shook it up and down until Hilary was sure it would come loose from her arm. "Thank you, Terror," he said. "I promise you won't regret it."

"You're welcome," Hilary said as she freed herself from Mr. Twigget. "Charlie, could you take these scallywags down to the galley and explain things to Miss Greyson?"

When all the pirates had clomped down the deck after Charlie, Hilary sighed and scratched the gargoyle behind the ears. "I suppose a pirate never gets much of a rest from adventure," she said.

The gargoyle agreed. "And it's a good thing, too," he said. "I think I'd get awfully bored otherwise."

"Well, then," said Hilary, "where should we set our course? To the far corners of Augusta, perhaps? To someplace so perilous that not even Captain Blacktooth would dare to follow?"

The gargoyle thought for a moment. He sniffed the air. "To the galley," he said at last. "I think Miss Greyson is baking a pie."

Hilary laughed and scooped the gargoyle from his Nest, and as the sun set over Pemberton Bay, they followed the rest of the pirates down to dinner.

TURN THE PAGE FOR A PEEK AT
HILARY'S NEXT VERY NEARLY
HONORABLE ADVENTURE
(GARGOYLE INCLUDED).

ATTENTION PIRATES!

The VNHLP regrets to report that an unscrupulous band of rebels is traveling the kingdom in an attempt to recruit pirates to their cause. They are led by Pirate Hilary Westfield, who aims to seize control of the League from its rightful president, Captain Rupert Blacktooth. If she dares to approach you, do not allow her to enlist you in her ranks! According to League regulations, Pirate Westfield may not be harmed, but the VNHLP recommends that all scallywags on the High Seas stay as far from her as possible. Do not talk to Pirate Westfield. Do not look her in the eye. Do not be lured into conversation with her gargoyle. Any pirate who is seen communicating with Pirate Westfield or her friends will be interrogated, stripped of his cutlass, and keelhauled by Captain Blacktooth. And remember: each loyal scallywag who chooses to support the president in his battle against Pirate Westfield will receive a purse of magic coins and a new hat feather of his choice.

Acknowledgments

EVERY BOOK RELIES on the talents of a daring and heroic band of scallywags, and this one is no exception. Thanks to my editor, Toni Markiet, whose keen eye makes me a better writer, and whose confidence makes me a braver one. Thanks also to Rachel Abrams, who is a true professional both when editing and when hailing cabs; to Abbe Goldberg, who calmly does more than I can possibly imagine; to Dave Phillips for his beautiful illustrations; and to everyone at HarperCollins and Simon & Schuster UK who has done amazing work on the pirates' behalf, particularly Amy Ryan, Emilie Polster, Mary Ann Zissimos, Gina Rizzo, Karen Sherman, and Alana Whitman.

As always, I owe heaps of gratitude to my agent, Sarah Davies, and to the team at Rights People, who take excellent care of my books.

Thanks to Hannah Moderow, Meg Wiviott, Alison Cherry, Melanie Crowder, and Anna Drury for their smart, spot-on advice, and to all the writers who so generously offered up suggestions and support: Jonathan Auxier, Anna Boll, Brandy Colbert, Corey Ann Haydu, Val Howlett, Kristen Kittscher, Jessica Leader, Helen Pyne, Lindsay Ribar, Tom Sweterlitsch, Liz Whelan, Kathleen Wilson, the L.E.C.S., and the Vermont College of Fine Arts community.

And thanks to my family—Zach Pezzementi and Jane, Chris, and Jonathan Carlson—for their love, their enthusiasm, and their willingness to read many, many drafts.